*A Head Full of Joy*

Ognjen Spahić

# A HEAD FULL OF JOY

Translated from Montenegrin by Will Firth

DALKEY ARCHIVE PRESS

Originally published in Montenegrin by Nova knjiga (Montenegro) as *Puna glava radosti* in 2014.

First Dalkey Archive edition, 2018.

Library of Congress Cataloging-in-Publication Data
Names: Spahić, Ognjen, 1977- author. | Firth, Will, translator.
Title: A head full of joy / Ognjen Spahić ; translated by Will Firth.
Other titles: Puna glava radosti. English
Description: First Dalkey Archive edition. | Victoria, TX : Dalkey Archive Press, 2018.
Identifiers: LCCN 2018026042 | ISBN 9781628972733 (pbk. : acid-free paper)
Classification: LCC PG1420.29.P34 P8613 2018 | DDC 891.8/236--dc23
LC record available at https://lccn.loc.gov/2018026042

 Co-funded by the Creative Europe Programme of the European Union

www.dalkeyarchive.com
McLean, IL / Dublin

The European Commission support for the production of this publication does not constitute an endorsement of the contents which reflects the views only of the author, and the commission cannot be held responsible for any use which may be made of the information contained therein.

Printed on permanent/durable acid-free paper

# Contents

# The Heliocentric Sermons of Dr. Maxim Junkić

THE SUNSET SEEMED to last for hours. The sun was compressed along the vertical axis and distended in length. "But it's only the sun," he said, as if the word *only* was meant to amend all the predicaments they'd run into that afternoon, return the distorted celestial body to its previous form, and make all visible things the way they really are. And they believed they knew the way those things are. The polluted atmosphere is a thick substance and bends the reflections of cosmic light that travels ever so slowly through the universe out there, through blackness and meaningless expanses, however you imagine them, and you can be sure there are many or even an infinite number of different kinds of meaninglessness. That's why the sun warps as it sets, that's just the way it is. Grains of sand return to the sea, and somewhat heavier, black particles of unknown metals roll on the crests of the waves. All these pictures can be seen even better if you use your time rationally, so instead of just sitting on the sand and watching the sun like *that couple*, you roam the rippled, yellow dunes that are most beautiful in the early evening. As I walked past them, minding not to get impolitely close, I heard the young man say: "But it's only the sun," and I took an interest in the possible development of the situation. The young woman didn't reply to that mendacious utterance. I know this because I stopped to get the sand out of my shoes. I untied the laces of the one shoe, shook out the sand, and slowly tied the laces up again, and then did the same with the other shoe in the hope of satisfying my curiosity and hearing what someone, anyone, had to say in reaction to: "But it's only the sun." She should have said: "If it's only the sun, then you're only a man," but she didn't. She left me without material for reflection, but I couldn't seriously blame her, because I didn't know her. If I got to know her, I'd try to bring our conversation back to the topic of the sun and score a few points by using a slightly different sentence, one with the word *woman* instead of *man*, although *man* can be used generically for both sexes. She could take all that as a compliment and blush, which is a characteristic of temperamental people liable to passion. From that moment on, I would easily be able to imagine her naked and, if I was bored, masturbate while rolling her into several different positions. But that didn't interest me now. A black dog came dashing up and sniffed around at my shoes. It annoyed me that it specifically chose my expensive black oxhide shoes when there were so many bare feet around, but it was probably repelled from the naked bodies by all the lotions people use to protect themselves from the things from space that I sometimes think about and they take as a given. If it had been some kind of short-haired, white dog with a vicious jaw that promised to inflict pain, I probably wouldn't have dared to energetically thrust it away with the tip of my shoe, hitting its wet and sensitive nose. It wasn't a kick in the true sense of the word, more of a jerk or jolt—a normal reaction in someone who doesn't like dogs, but it squealed loudly and shrilly in frequency ranges particular to female children and certain animals. It ran around in circles, occasionally sticking its muzzle into the sand, and then it shot off toward the waves and started lapping at the salty water. How could I have known it was their dog? Turned toward each other as they were, cross-legged and engrossed in an argument about the sun, they were the last people in my field of vision who I could have imagined to have anything to do with that animal. The woman ran and shouted: "Max, Rex, Dix," or something like that, and the man was picking up their things and preparing to head after her. While she was still sitting, I got the impression that she had large breasts. A white cotton T-shirt hung loosely on her body and outlined shapes that were clearly in motion now as she ran. The dog gave a start and tensed up, trying to pinpoint the familiar silhouette through its thick brows. Its legs were concealed in the water, making it look like the floating carcass of an unknown sea monster. From twenty yards away *Rex* could clearly be heard, while her companion called out: "Ana, Tijana, Dijana," or something like that from the middle of the beach, but she didn't look back. The man walked slowly, laden with towels and bags, which explained his lack of interest in the problems of the animal and reduced the possibility of a conflict in which I would have been the focus of two adults' ire. Besides, *I* didn't sniff at the dog. *It* sniffed at *me* and my shoes. I protected myself as befits a person who can't stand those animals, and I already regretted the pain I'd caused Rex. From ten yards away I could tell she was no more than thirty-five and that her face was contorted in an expression of anger. The graceful curve of her eyebrows puckered in the middle above her nose, which was covered in a thick layer of sun cream. "Hey, are you crazy? Why did you kick my dog?" she said from just two yards away. The man came closer and I could make out that he called her Ana, but she couldn't or didn't want to hear him, in her blinding rage, which she now articulated in a more refined tone. "I asked you why you kicked him. I saw you kick him!" she said and pointed at my well-polished left shoe, on whose tip a reflection of the small, red sun gleamed. But I'd nudged Rex with my right, not with my left foot. Rex now came cheerfully running up, splashing through the waves and whining lowly; the dog reared up on its hind legs and leaned on its owner's body. "My cutie! My little cutie! Let me have a look!" She clasped its muzzle in her hands and turned it. I moved closer to have a look myself, but she paid no attention. With a sudden movement of its paw, the dog tore off the thin scarf tied loosely around her hips, leaving her in her bikini bottom, which showed below her T-shirt. The small triangle of fabric was covered by a printed blue flower. Her groin was freshly shaven and somewhat redder than the rest of her legs. When she glanced at me again, her eyebrows changed shape and her face looked more relaxed. Then it was time for me to speak and end the encounter with a few polite words of apology, but her red groin suggested they'd only just arrived at the coast and would be spending the next several days here on vacation. My stay was coming to an end on Wednesday. Another morning and an hour in the train, after a handshake with the receptionist and a cordial: "Come and stay again next summer," which the old man pronounces with one tooth less every time. Although we are of similar age, I still get compliments that: "I look great." Which is definitely aided by the flawless porcelain veneers covering my worn-out enamel. I'd stuff my shoes with newspaper, put them in the cardboard box on top of the cupboard, and pay the thirty euros for the cleaning of my apartment. Last year it was twenty-five, but the fat woman stank indescribably and left her greasy marks everywhere. This year it would be the lady from the next block who smells so nice and buys fresh bread and lots of vegetables for her children every morning. Everything was settled over the phone. My next-door neighbor had recommended her, and I called her today from my hotel. She was polite and had a good grasp of basic affirmative phrases that made sense. But I called her once more the same day to change the date, and the Scottish terrier Rex was to blame for it all, which obviously I didn't tell her. Watching Ana as she carefully examined her sweetheart's scalp—while also casting glances behind her at the man of most respectable appearance and manners who didn't wish to enter a dispute about a shoe and a dog—I thought it would be nice to spend a few more evenings by the sea, with some wine and pleasant conversation with the young couple. But the crucial moment that determined the outcome of this intention was the vacuum of those several seconds Ana waited for me to speak and give what amounted to an apology for the incident. When she'd finished her inspection and stood in front of me with her hands planted pugnaciously on her hips, I said: "Rex! Come here, Rex!" but the dog tensed up again as it glanced at me and its owner in turn. "Come on, Rex!" I said a little more softly, and I knelt down on the sand and reached my hands out to the animal. The sun was cut in two by the hill. The dog briskly shook the sea from itself and calmly walked right up between my knees, wagging its tail to show its approval of my gesture. I gave it an energetic rub on the top of its head and back, and it let out a cheerful squeal and pressed itself tremblingly against my body. It smelled of that sour hint of testosterone that every small male dog has, and left invisible layers of grease and bacteria on my hands. But the effect was achieved. Ana turned toward the man, whom she called Pavle, and said: "Look." Pavle smiled and shrugged his shoulders, glancing in my direction. "Look at the sun," I said, and they turned to catch sight of the semicircular, red rim that shrank before our eyes and vanished behind the hills within a few seconds. The sand abruptly changed color: without the direct light of that star, it was showered by bundles of photons that reflected from the earth, air, and water in turn, while keeping the red tint of distant eruptions. The remote silhouettes of isolated walkers swiftly went black, as if the darkness was infused first into souls and bodies, and only then spread all over the landscape and objects. "Sorry for getting loud. It was rude of me. But he's a good dog and I'm sure he only wanted a new friend. Pavle? Isn't that right?" Pavle, his back turned, was watching what remained of the twilight. The wind had carried away the clouds of cigarette smoke above his head. "Give me the leash, Pavle," she said nervously. "There's the chair. Go and get it, and I'll put the leash on this ninny," she said in a voice that suggested a normal conversation again. I assumed there had been some disagreement between them in the hours past that had put them in a bad mood. The man Pavle abruptly dropped all the things that had been hanging from his arms and shoulders. It looked as if he'd switched off a magnetic force field by his own inner volition, and nothing adhered to his body anymore. "Look for it yourself," he snapped, and the dog continued to mill around my legs. She went up to the things and started rummaging furiously in the rucksack. The noise of the waves prevented me from joining her words together into meaningful sentences, but I was able to clearly distinguish: "There's no point," as well as "finally" and "now"—a sufficient hint as to the rhythm of their thoughts and the state of fatigue that in a particular moment can affect the innermost feelings of two people of average intelligence. That was all I could conclude from the short encounter, and of course I knew nothing about the details. She found the leash and grabbed Rex roughly by the collar. The dog growled and tried to return to yours truly, but Ana was forceful in her intention and worked with a trained hand. "I can look after him if you like," I offered and held out my hand. She gave me the black band without hesitation and said: "I'll be right back." She drove her feet angrily into the sand and walked along an imaginary line that joined the spot where she'd been standing to the red deck chair, about a hundred yards away. She stopped halfway, raised her left foot, and then sat down and carefully examined her sole for a few seconds. She rubbed and scratched the spot, patted the sand off her bottom, and went on, hobbling on her left leg. The aluminum deck chair defied logic like a giant insect in rigor mortis: the only object of that kind on the horizon, and when you're *the only one* you look dignified and sad. First Ana sat down next to the chair and inspected her foot. Then with a few nimble moves she changed the shape of the metal and red-canvas construction. Her Pavle finished his cigarette and flicked the butt away with the wind. He looked at me attentively and then came up to me. "What sort of clown are you?" he sneered, eyeing my gray linen suit all the way down to my shoes, the most comfortable ones I'd ever had. I took a pack of cigarettes out of my pocket and offered him another one, but he kept looking at me as if he was searching for a secret identification mark to classify me with, to put me in a box of reality, even if he didn't seem to think I was for real. "Dr. Maxim Junkić, retired urologist, if you want to know," I said, trying to do justice to the situation. I tried to light up several times, and then Pavle took out a Zippo and held it up to me. For a moment our faces were illuminated by the small flame and I could see the deep furrow of a scar below his left eye. He looked toward Ana, who was carrying the chair. He gazed as if he was estimating whether there was time for another question. "So you're Pavle . . . ," he didn't let me finish but completed the sentence with: "Ana's husband." The dog wound the leash around my left leg. "He suits you. The dog. He's forgiven you for the shoe. Stupid mutt. If I'd've kicked him he'd be yelping for two days," he said, revealing the tangled web of relations connecting those three characters. "Spoiled old grump. He reminds me of my father," Pavle said and started to pick up their scattered things. Ana slammed the chair down on the sand, sat on it, and lifted the sole of her foot. "Have a look what it is, Pavle. It hurts. The pigs throw litter everywhere. What is it?" He stood there adorned with all their things and stared down. "It's nothing. Can't see a thing . . . Probably some thorn. Shall we go back? It's getting cold," he said and headed off slowly over the sand. Several large, black letters were printed on his shirt. The top of his head revealed a patch of shiny skin: premature baldness, which gives insecure men morning anxiety. "I'll have a look if you like," I offered and unwound the leash from around my leg. "Go ahead then," Ana said and held her foot a little higher. As I was taking my glasses out of my inner pocket, the dog started to lick her right knee. I took her foot by the heel and pressed the middle of the sole with my thumb. She reacted with a strange, muffled shriek, a sound I didn't expect in her voice. Pavle stopped at the path up from the beach, turned around briefly to look, and then went on. I took a little piece of green glass between my fingernails and turned it to the light. "Here it is . . . A little diamond with blood," I commented, while she lowered her leg and patted the dog. "Thank you," she said with a relieved smile. Rex smelled the fresh erythrocytes and came up to lick the red stain on her foot. I grabbed the leash and pulled the animal toward me. The tide was coming in and the waves were pounding ever closer. Tiny crabs peeked out of the sand in search of food. The little scavengers eat morsels of carrion when night falls. The smell of the sea is always the smell of decay and decomposition. She asked me for a hand when she decided to get up and painstakingly pressed her foot against the now-cool sand. "I feel it throbbing. The cold does it good," she said, leaning on my shoulder. Her perfume made its way through the smell of fresh sun lotion. "Can you walk?" I asked. "What if I can't—will you carry me?" she joked and quickly added, "But I can. Of course I can. Don't worry. Only . . . I'd be grateful if you took the chair, or the dog." I chose the inanimate option. As I was about to take the chair, Rex came running up and released a stream of yellow at the middle of the red canvas. For which he was punished with a jerk on the leash and a curse. From then on we could only walk slowly. The darkness coming from the sea drove people to safer places. Along the miles of sand couples and families were folding up isolated parasols. They left in the hope that the sun would be there again the next day and that the star would warm the water and make it pleasant for swimming—simple expectations that make existence possible. Ana was silent, preoccupied with her sore foot and the hungry dog. When we entered the avenue of pines she said they were staying in the green bungalows and pointed to the nearby stand of poplars and centennial ashes. She told me they enjoyed the peace and quiet, because there weren't many guests yet. I said I'd been coming to the hotel across the road for years because my pension fund partially covered the stay. I mentioned that every room had a reproduction of Van Gogh's *Cypresses* over the bed and that, from my balcony, I could see exactly the part of the beach where we'd been standing a little while ago. The bit about Van Gogh was a lie, and I immediately tried to comprehend my motive for lying, but Ana interrupted my ponderings and said there was some white wine in the fridge, and she thought it would be nice to have a glass or two together. She apologized for the inconvenience and was grateful for my help with the piece of glass and the chair. She'd like to repay me, so to speak. I wasn't trying to devise a plan, but the images simply imposed themselves on me: an interesting friendship in one's later years, an invigoration that would connect me with people again—new conversations, new words and thoughts, where there was no place for hatred. I felt euphoric, imagining myself as an unassuming gentleman who gracefully accepted a glass of chilled wine and attentively listened to opinions that essentially didn't interest him but deserved a polite commentary. I thought I was ready for a change like that. At first Ana seemed to show natural charm and to behave toward me the way a gray-headed gentleman deserves. But later, after a few glasses of chardonnay, she'd start to giggle vulgarly and speak to me like I was some old crony. Anyway, as we were walking beneath the tall trees near the darkened green bungalows, I said that would be lovely and that I enjoyed wine, particularly white. "I'll get changed, and I also have a phone call to make. I hope it won't be too late if I come at around ten?" I asked. We came closer to their bungalow with a generous veranda and a set of big club chairs. "Of course it won't be too late. Whenever you come is fine," she said and waved dismissively to Pavle, who was already sitting on the steps with a bottle of beer between his legs. "Why are you drinking that trash, you idiot?" she scoffed. "I drink what I drink," he snorted and took a long swig, which made him turn red in the face. "Where's Rex?" Ana asked, and he gestured with his cigarette to the base of the veranda and the yellow plastic dish full of black lumps of food. She tied Rex to the railing. "Eat now, piglet," she said, nudging the bowl with her foot. "Can I put the chair down here?" I asked. "Wherever you like . . . here next to the railing's fine." I carefully put the chair down, fearing that an awkward metallic creak could disrupt the fragile equilibrium of the moment. I was superstitious that way, especially in situations where my nerves have been strained to breaking point. I tried to look relaxed and in control of my movements. I breathed deeply, filling my lungs with fresh air down to the last alveoli. Cold sweat ran down my back and soaked the rim of my trousers. My neck began to itch, attacked by swarming clouds of tiny flies. The darkness now crept between the ghastly trees and ugly houses; night came from the sea, filling the air with the smell of putrid plankton and iodine. I'd have to invest extra effort. I didn't want the couple to notice my trembling hands and the rigid smiles that seized control of my face. These were understandable symptoms of aging that turn your body into a disjointed circus performance and rob you of your dignity. Everything would be all right once I'd had a shower, after I'd taken my medication, and spent ten minutes in my darkened room, I thought. It *had* to be all right, I thought, because a strenuous night was in store for me. More conversation, people-contact again, deliberate gestures, and the self-control one expects of a surgeon. I took two careful steps backward and said: "Dear people, I'll be off for now. But I'll see you soon." Pavle didn't understand why we'd be meeting again and cast a compressed into a few images and smells, decades are emptied of meaning and filled with a firm, almost palpable nebula that freezes everything that once seemed important to me in a fog, making it futile and unrecognizable. To fight against such an enemy is pointless. It's best to give in to the forces of existence, to that slow decline, which, if you're lucky, will spare your vital organs any malignant diseases. My prostate functions impeccably. I urinate abundantly and with enjoyment, like a wet dog. I land the tiny key in the lock of room 42 without any difficulty and open the door of my room. The woman in the elevator smelled of sweet, cheap perfume, so the pungency of bathroom disinfectant did me good. I took a deep breath, breathed out again for as long as I could in that plastic darkness, and then I noticed that the light on the answering machine was rhythmically flickering, bathing the room in ruby red for a second at a time. I saw my silhouette and my face cast in a red gleam in the glass of the balcony door, and the next moment my face vanished, clad in darkness. I sat down on the bed, switched on the reading light, and pressed the dirty plastic button to listen to the dirty plastic voice announcing two voice messages. I started relaxedly unbuttoning my shirt in the assumption that they were both run-of-the-mill messages from the reception telling me when I had to vacate the room by and announcing a change of meal times. But first came the insecure voice of my son who, feigning good cheer, asked: "How are things, old boy?" and "All still in one piece?" and went on to say a number of other unnecessary phrases, the sort of trite expressions people use when they don't have the courage to actually say what they want. A trickle of snot ran from his nose—a boyish trait he never grew out of. As he briefly recounted his problems, he snorted and wiped his nose on his sleeve. His ugly wife sat in the armchair opposite. I could sense her presence in my son's voice. She reclined there in her layers of blubber and listened because I was the one who would lend them money: an old grouch with savings he jealously guarded in different accounts. I knew that was their opinion of me. I thought I heard her come up to the phone and whisper something when my simpleminded son announced the figure, and he went on about how much they needed the money and that it would be great if they had it by the end of the week. They were so grateful I was willing to help and they knew they were asking a lot, but I was the only person they felt to be a real friend. I pressed the red button and interrupted my son midsentence. I didn't want to think about him tonight. I'd put on my green shirt with my black blazer. A few tranquilizer tablets would eliminate the possibility of abrupt mood changes that I'm prone to in the evening hours. Combined with moderate doses of alcohol, the tiny red capsules filled with powder make my body lighter and transparent. A large advertising poster hung above the bed under glass in a black frame. It showed two unbearably old and jocund people—a married couple in their eighties sitting on the terrace of a restaurant facing the sea. They were looking into the camera and clinking glasses. Artificial fruit in the colors of the rainbow lay piled on the table. Crystal glasses shone beneath the neon, as did their teeth. All this was to highlight the favorable terms of payment for pensioners' summer vacations. Tiny black letters that were hardly visible notified that, in the event of death at the hotel, the pension fund covered the costs of transferring the body. The walls of the rooms had been bare in previous years. As soon as I arrived, I tried to take that scene down, but the frame was bolted to the wall. That's why I said to Ana that Van Gogh's *Cypresses* hung above my head. If I'd told her the truth, there wouldn't be any wine. She would have thought, here was someone who needed free transport to the cemetery rather than a glass of chardonnay. The first impression is the most important. All the words, gestures, and things you offer by way of associations at that first encounter begin to merge into one, forming a certain code of your personality in the eyes of your counterpart. By mentioning Van Gogh and cypresses, I made Ana connect those beautiful turquoise hues and the unique darkness of Van Gogh's night landscapes, in a way, with my exterior, my voice, and my movements. Once I'd listened to the first message, I went into the bathroom and poured myself a large glass of water in the soothing cool of the marble tiles. The button on the answering machine continued to pulsate red. I now thought it was blinking in a slower rhythm. Or was that my internal clock starting to tick more slowly after the afternoon's excitement? I put two capsules on my tongue and drained the glass with gusto. I felt the refreshing cold slide down and tickle the mucous lining of my esophagus on the way. I looked at my pupils in the mirror and concluded that my face had gotten a slight suntan. My two-hour walks along the shore had nourished my skin. The brown spots on my forehead and nose had merged with a new bronze tone that I really liked, and the salt-saturated air had helped the deep creases around my eyes become less visible. I knew these changes were only brief pauses in the uncheckable process of the body breaking down. I knew that my joints would continue to creak painfully the very next day. But invigorated by a new optimism that burgeoned like a mushroom, and aided by the capsules, I stood in front of the large mirror in the hall and squared my shoulders. From the next room came the racking cough which old people gather their phlegm with. Their porous cells successively die, creating a yellowish pulp in the chest that impedes breathing. I don't have any problems like that yet. Dry curtains of wrinkled skin may droop from my upper arms, but my muscles react flawlessly to all commands. I smoke several cigarettes a day. My lungs wheeze a little when I breathe deeply, but for now they don't show any serious signs of deterioration. Standing in front of the mirror, I felt a pleasant warmth in my hands and neck. The tablets released thousands of tiny molecules that rushed to my nerve endings. I'd skip the hotel dinner and let the wine make its way into my blood faster. I took away the pillow and turned off the lights. The sheet smelled of withered leaves. Ten minutes of meditation in the dark would further prepare me for the events ahead. The only source of light was the button on the answering machine, which I'd press to hear the second message. I touched it with my eyes closed, carefully, as if I was touching the flame of a candle. The recording began with a buzz and sounds of a receiver being put up against the person's cheek. I waited for a voice: a male voice and a few boring sentences about anything at all, but there came only a deep, husky breathing that immediately filled the dark of the room. The little red light wasn't glowing anymore. I looked at the glass of the balcony door and tried to find a trace of light in the distance, but I couldn't see a thing. That thick, black darkness flowed out into space and the world, I thought, and I felt an indefinable fear instilled by that heavy breathing and distant noises in the background. My sense of hearing became acute. I was convinced that my acoustic tormentor was sitting by an open window because occasionally I heard something that resembled the stirring of treetops in the breeze. Without a trace of human voices and actions, without the creak of furniture or the clatter of crockery, one indistinct package of sounds poured from one sea of solitude to another. I lay riveted to the cold mattress and started to reflect on the days and years when my life stood still: the cynical constant of the same hours passing, of the same intentions and the same pain. My lungs contracted in disappointment. It took so little for the fine glass bell to shatter, pitting me against the vast, mighty emptiness I couldn't struggle against anymore. I lay in the darkness of room 42, abandoning the precious little pieces of reality that I collect painstakingly and fondle in my thoughts every day like the greatest of treasures. The man's breathing had gone on for several minutes already and thoroughly drained the strength from my bones, flinging me into the deepest pits of adversity, old age, and loneliness. But then something changed abruptly in the frequency: the receiver seemed to have fallen out of the man's hands, and the breathing stopped. Soon, sharp rhythmical sounds intruded, harsh noises and scratching, and the next moment there came the barking of a dog. The man quickly broke the connection and the message was over. My legs went numb. I felt a heat in my lungs and my heart started to beat hard because the only dog I could think of was the black Scottish terrier, and the only man—that lazy beer-guzzler. I had no proof it was Pavle at the other end of the line or that it was actually a man at all. But I could directly associate that silence devoid of meaning with his appearance and behavior. He knew my name and hotel. He just had to call in the ten minutes it took for me to return from the door of their ugly green house. He didn't do it for fun, nor was it an attempt to intimidate me.

and the sea. That's why I never go for walks along the shore after a southerly. My impaired vision sees a human corpse in every tree trunk, a grave mound in every heap of sand. If tonight's storm reached the shore, the sea would change its color tomorrow and would rage. From where I was sitting on the veranda I couldn't see the southern sky. Facing the blackness of the northwest, poor in stars, I tried to calm my breathing as I stared at the green roofs beset by creepers. My Gauloise slowly burned down, and the thin paper stuck to my lips. I felt bitter crumbs of tobacco on the tip of my tongue. I heard a popping in my sinuses, like a wave rolling pebbles. Now I breathed more easily and my anger of a few minutes earlier seemed far away, like one's memory after a hangover. In moments like that I can't help but reflect on old age and loneliness. Those are facts I just can't get out of my head. I don't want to say that I actually try, but sometimes I just want to forget them. Therefore I can't stand it when strangers remind me of my age. I always refuse assistance at the supermarket or when crossing the street. I sit alone on park benches because I don't want to listen to histories of prostate and urinary-tract illness. But a glass of wine in the company of young bodies: that was an invitation not to be turned down. A few hours at the wellspring of life; with healthy teeth and smiles free of cynicism; with fast thoughts and agile movements—all that would allow me to forget my years for a moment and enjoy the illusion of eternal life. That's why I was prepared to sully my own dignity and wait out on the veranda, sweating like the chilled bottle of chardonnay. The burning end of the cigarette came close to my fingers. My nerve receptors are dying away, so the heat of red-hot tobacco only pleasantly stimulates me. As I took a last draw of the cigarette, there was a stirring in the hall. Rex came running up out of the bushes and waved his tail, expecting the familiar silhouette. Ana was wearing a long black T-shirt that went halfway down her thighs. She peeped cautiously through the half-open door, switched on the light on the veranda and said: "Ah, it's you smoking. I thought it was Pavle. What's the time? Surely it's not eleven already?" She sat down with a yawn and reached for the pack of Gauloises. "May I?" she asked and took a cigarette. When I offered her the lighter she said: "Later, thanks. Pavle isn't with you?" I told her I'd already been sitting and smoking for forty minutes, waiting for someone to turn up, and Ana stared into the darkness between the next houses and the oaks, as if her Pavle might be one of the houses or the trees. "I fell asleep in the armchair. Sorry. This sea air is intoxicating like . . ." She didn't finish the sentence but slapped her left thigh hard and cursed the mosquitoes. "Did you bring the wine, Doctor? How sweet of you," she cooed now and took the bottle. Her saying *doctor* and calling my humble self *sweet* caused new beads of perspiration to pop out on my forehead and made me nervous. Because I never told her I'm a doctor. It was her indolent husband Pavle who told her, meaning that I'd been the subject of conversation, in which I'm sure I played anything but a positive role. I imagined them commenting on my suit, my shoes, and my socks with the blue rhombus pattern; Ana will have apologized for so hastily inviting an unfamiliar old man and said I definitely wouldn't come—people like me simply *don't come* she emphasized—but smart-ass Pavle probably said I was exactly one of the kind who *always come*. Now Ana looked aimlessly at the treetops, trying to think up topics to start a conversation; anything would do. I was her new reality. I sat cross-legged in the comfortable chair, almost reclining, and lit another aromatic cigarette. She expected her Pavle to turn up out of the dark and rescue her from the awkwardness that was festering between us like a sullen, spoiled child. Rex insisted on climbing onto her lap. He licked her knees and his head raised the black T-shirt a little. "Just look at the silly dog, he adores people's skin. Hey, stop it!" she said and pushed him away. He capered around on the spot for a few seconds longer and then ran off to pee by the railing of the veranda. "Shall I bring a corkscrew?" she asked, holding the cold bottle between her knees. "By all means. Or should we wait for your husband?" I suggested. "Pavle is my brother," she said and stared at me seriously. "Ah, I see. Pavle is your brother. I understand. Of course," I replied, reaching for another cigarette. She watched my fingers tremble as I lit up. She sought a reaction and expected a twitch of the lines on my face, and then she started to giggle and pummel her knee. "A bit gullible, aren't you?" she said, trying to muffle her laughter. "You believed for a moment that Pavle was my brother and now you're trying to conceal your disgust. Maybe you're crossing your legs to cover up an erection. You're imagining my brother, my sweaty brother, moving up and down, you're imagining me naked with my brother between my thighs instead of this bottle of chardonnay. Etcetera, etcetera . . . I'm sorry. What rubbish I'm talking. Please forgive me. I don't know what came over me. Or maybe I do? I apologize in any case. I'm ashamed. Well, not a lot . . . but please believe me, I'm embarrassed after this nonsense. I talk, talk, talk . . . sor-ry, sor-ry, sor-ry!" Rex attacked my shoes again. He licked with a passion dogs apply to unfamiliar things. So Pavle was not Ana's brother; Pavle was Ana's husband. Pavle, who was coming up the path illuminated by the pale neon light, carrying some red flowers—that Pavle was Ana's husband. He put his finger to his lips as a sign for me not to say anything as he approached her from behind. He stopped behind the corner of the ugly green house. He peeked out, winked, and signaled with his hand for us to continue our conversation. Ana didn't see him—or pretended not to. I looked in his direction for a few moments and then said something that made them laugh—I let them make fun of me. "Good evening," I went. Ana turned and followed my gaze. Pavle knelt down on the steps and offered her the flowers, and she said, "Good evening," imitating my tone of voice, and both of them burst out laughing. How quaint and old-fashioned it sounded. I ought to have left that instant, together with the bottle of chardonnay. If I'd gone then, the only consequence would probably have been bad insomnia and a few more capsules. In the morning I would have told the hotel reception I was booking out, and that same evening I would have called the lady from the next block back home who smells so nice and buys fresh bread and lots of vegetables for her children every morning; she would have put my apartment in order in the course of the morning, and I would have arrived home around noon to all the familiar smells. On the train I would have thought about my simpleminded son and decided to lend him money after all. He and his wife would have invited me to dinner, and so I would have forgotten Ana, Pavle, Rex, and the chardonnay before midnight and fallen asleep like a baby. Now I made a move to get up. I stuck the cigarettes and lighter into my inner pocket, straightened my lapels, and did up the last button of my shirt, but then Ana began to moan sweetly, "Oh no, please stay. Surely you're not going . . . we're just in high spirits. I'm sorry . . . the corkscrew is coming," and I lowered my scrawny ass back into the chair and lit another cigarette. "Thaaat's the way," Ana said, stood up, and brushed a few specks of dust from my shoulders. "Now for some music!" she exclaimed and glanced at Pavle, who walked leisurely into the house and put a small portable radio on the windowsill. "Come on now . . . ," Pavle pressed the button at the top and a hum started coming from the speaker mixed with the barely audible chords of a classical guitar. "Louder, louder, louder," Ana called, and Pavle kept turning the dial. A deep baritone began the weather forecast and announced *the incursion of a cold air mass from the north of the continent. The time is exactly fifteen minutes past midnight.* But just then the inclement weather was coming from the south. The wind beat and tore at the trees, bringing the sounds and smells of the sea. Gusts of warm air swirled up leaves and blew open the shutters. Pavle changed channels and finally stopped at monotonous electronic rhythms interrupted by the synthetic sound of a saxophone. "Okay?" Ana said. "Of course, of course," I replied and stared at the tattoo on her right shoulder. She pushed up the short sleeve and tucked the folds into her armpit. A stylized letter Z wreathed in barbed wire and beneath it a butterfly with its wings spread. She noticed I was looking and said, "It's from my husband. My former husband." She spoke that *former* in a whisper. She glanced toward the door of the ugly green house where her current husband, Pavle, was shuffling around in search of the corkscrew. We heard the clang of crockery accompanied by grunted swearwords. "Bring some glasses too," Ana called out. She sat down again and crossed her legs. "How's the foot going?" I inquired. "You really are sweet! You're worried about my foot?" she quickly straightened up, turned the sole upward, and moved it close to my face. "Have a look yourself, Doctor. What do you think? Amputation?" She was wearing black panties with a little red ribbon at the top. Everything smelled of body lotion with nuances of citrus. "It would be a shame to send meat like this to the worms. Wouldn't it, Doctor?" she said, imitating sorrow, and leaned back again. "Huh, you don't care, *you old geezers,*" she scoffed, lighting up the Gauloise. I wished I could say something, but at that moment I had a bout of the arrhythmia that shakes my chest whenever my nervous system is shocked by insults, human stupidity, or ugliness. Ana was a very beautiful woman. Although far into her thirties, her breasts stood firm and swelled under her T-shirt whenever she inhaled the smoke of her cigarette. Ana was an intelligent woman, but fickle and mean. When she spoke that funereal You old geezers, all the wavelengths on which I tried to detect some positive aspects of her personality abruptly became blocked and from then on only let through bad signs. And it was unavoidable that I create an image of Ana full of a strange instant hatred, which picked up on tiny, perhaps insignificant details and imputed all the malice and misfortune of the world into her character. I was sitting in front of her neatly dressed and willing to respond to the slightest sign of benevolent emotions with gestures of empathy in order to make our ephemeral acquaintance memorable, or to at least give it a semblance of importance. But my heart pumped my blood faster and my head was awhirl. In saying that steely You old geezers, Ana left no doubt that my disintegrating body, hoarse voice, and bleary eyes represented an unbridgeable gap, a deep black hole that it's interesting to peer into from the edge, but nothing more. Because at the bottom there's only tedium, decay, and death. Still quite some way from their young bodies. I took out the box of capsules and laid it on the table. I didn't want to try and open it straightaway. I felt my fingers trembling and knew I might be stupid and spill the precious contents on that floor alive with the dog's bacteria. Ana would notice that my hands were shaking, and that would further increase my nervousness. I hoped Pavle would come with the corkscrew before Ana asked what was in the box, but the cretin was still banging around in the kitchen, opening and closing all the drawers. "What's in that box of yours?" she asked, her eyes glued to the red piece of plastic at the edge of the table. "This?" I said, hiding my trembling hands under the table. "It's a remedy for old age." I smiled, though I didn't understand what emotions that smile had to force its way through to get to my face. "Pavle!" she yelled that same instant. Her eyes moved back and forth between my face and the box. "Paaa-vle! Come here, you numskull!" she screamed even louder, and I kept staring at her with that vacuous smile, which wasn't typical of my behavior. "The doctor has a remedy for old age," she shouted, stamping her feet on the concrete. That idle, ungainly guy appeared at the door holding the corkscrew and another bottle. He put the wine down on the table and handed me the implement. He waited several seconds, and still I didn't want to show my hands. Then he put the thing down on the table, right next to the plastic box with my pills. "What are you yelling for?" he asked and stood above Ana, who was rocking on the back legs of her chair. "Out of the way, you're blocking my view," she barked. She grabbed him by the upper arm and pulled him to the left. "Our doctor has a remedy for old age," she whispered, "the box," and laughed. Rex came running up out of the dark. He reared up with the help of his front paws and tried to reach my hands with his tongue. Pavle caught him by the collar and jerked him away, which made Ana snap: "You'll kill him, you monster!" and she hugged the dog to her knees. "You're my sweetie, you're my pretty boy, you're good . . . Pavle is dumb, Pavle is ugly, Pavle is rough . . . He thinks we'll drink wine out of bottles. We sent him to get the corkscrew and some glasses, but he only brought the corkscrew," she whispered straight at the dog's muzzle. "But we'll go and get the glasses if that's too hard for the others. Isn't that right, Rex?" She stood up abruptly, and the dog whined endearingly and squirmed about at her feet. The lightbulbs that lit up the paths between the houses now gave off a dirty hue of yellow. Bolts of lightning attacked the powerlines, tapping energy from the thick cables. It started to thunder more violently. The hordes of mosquitoes left the dark treetops, which weren't safe havens anymore. Nature spawned danger.

Brittle, partially withered oak branches banged down on the roofs of the houses. People lay in the darkness under those roofs, and the wind and the unfamiliar sounds banished sleep, bringing on troubled thoughts, and fear gathered in their eyes. They all pretended to be asleep and tried to summon up a good mood that should be a natural ingredient of a summer vacation. But misfortunes come in droves like swarms of mosquitoes. They keep whirring, waiting for something to finish, for something to happen that would reshuffle things and make this life, this hanging around in the fear-filled darkness, tolerable again. When a whopping female tried to hover its way into my left ear, I instinctively slapped it with the flat of my hand. "They bite well," Pavle said and started to twist in the corkscrew. Ana went to get the glasses, while Rex fidgeted around Pavle's chair, trying to cajole a tummy-scratch. My hands calmed down. I spread my fingers and put the tips together without any trouble. The cork came out with a pop. Pavle took a long swig straight out of the bottle and said: "I hope you don't mind," and then wiped his mouth with the back of his hand. "You'll wait for a glass, Doctor, I suppose? Or would you like the bottle? Oh, you're a real gentleman," he sneered and took one more swig. I opened my box, chose a capsule and stuck it deep into my throat. "And now a little wine?" Pavle offered. I shook my head and concentrated so as to best feel the satiny red pod sliding down to my stomach. That was half the effect. "Nourishing your brain, Doctor? Some miracle cure for old age? A bit suspicious, if you ask me," he said and reached for the box. "Very pretty, I love red," he remarked. He took two, gluttonously crammed them into his mouth, and washed them down with wine. "A few for Ana," he said and put three pills out onto the table. Before closing the box, he stuck another under his tongue. "You pig! All the glasses are greasy and stink of beer. Now I have to wash them," Ana screamed in the house. A bird flew from roof to roof, and Rex followed its movements. The plastic shell dissolved in my esophagus and now a sharp, indefinable alkaloid aroma came to my nostrils. While Ana ranted, Pavle made a face and pointed to the front door. "She always puts on a performance in front of guests. She wants to astonish people. She's not so terrible and nervous when we're alone. Sometimes she's apish . . . But all considered . . . it's okay," Pavle said. Ana emerged with the glasses and asked from the door: "Did he drink out of the bottle?!" Pavle nodded, and Ana scolded me: "Doctor, Doctor . . . It's not nice to behave like that when you're a guest. Where are your manners?" She put a glass down in front of me, and Pavle quickly filled it to the brim. "There. Now you can drink like a human being," Ana said. "I didn't drink out of the bottle. You know . . . ," I started to explain in a squeaky little voice that bashfully peeped from my throat, and my hands began to tremble again. I wanted to leave, and at the same time I was restrained by a fine, invisible web woven by those two reprobates who had sunk to the very bottom of their life together. Thunder filled the western sky. The treetops outlined hideous shapes. The saxophone abruptly fell silent and the radio started to emit rhythmic electric distortions. I reached for my glass and drained it in several gulps. Ana filled their glasses and sat down in Pavle's lap. She kissed him on the neck, and then grabbed the tip of her tongue in disgust. "You're all sweaty!" she said and spat away to the side. She drank a sip of wine and picked up the capsules from the table. "So this is your miracle cure, Doctor?" She quickly stuffed all three into her mouth. A few gulps of the cheap chardonnay consigned those red meteors to her gastric juices. Three little explosions occurred down there, releasing millions of sublime molecules that soon, aided by alcohol, rushed to join her bloodstream. She petted the neck of her greasy husband for a few more minutes and then tried to get up. Her knees started to shake, and she fell back into his lap. The wind now bore the musty smell of rotting leaves that collected in the copper rain gutters, at the base of the veranda, and beneath the roofs of the ugly green houses. Or was it the stench of those two people, their sweaty bodies, and the chaos of their emotions? Pavle stared at the palms of his hands. He slowly clenched and spread his fingers, discovering some new feeling at the tips of his nerve endings. His body weight meant that the substance was slower to act. Only when he saw Ana stagger did he realize that his hands were losing their strength and becoming lighter.

"Doctor . . . Doctor . . . Abracadabra, Doctor," he said bemusedly, and Ana began to laugh at his words. Rex sat beneath their chair. I felt both of them were now watching me for the first time with looks that weren't false. Ana clearly emitted revulsion, which mixed with amazement at my presence in the theater of their life. She analyzed my material manifestation, and her eyes passed lightly from the tips of my shoes via my impeccably ironed trouser-legs and sleeves, right up to my ears and the gray locks of my hair. I was convinced she wasn't looking me in the eyes because she felt some kind of banal fear of the fundamentally unknown. Pavle stared much more openly, with an expression that said straightforwardly that I was superfluous there, an object that created an imbalance in the scale of universal stupidity their existence stood on, and that my added dash of stupidity now only ruined things that happened as they'd happened for years and would finish the way they had to finish. The red box lay in the middle of the table. I grabbed the bottle and shared out what was left into all three glasses, and then opened the box. I offered them to help themselves again. Pavle took one first. Then his index finger found its way in between Ana's lips and pushed two capsules under her lax tongue. He tossed his own helping into the air and adeptly caught and swallowed it with his gaping jaws. His wife giggled and rolled her eyes. She tried to take her glass but her hand kept missing it by an inch or two. "Look, Doctor . . . She's zonked . . ." Pavle gently fondled her back. Then he poured some wine into the palm of his hand and rubbed it under her T-shirt. "Chuck him out, Pavle. Tell him to fuck off." she continued with a laugh. She tried again and again to get hold of her glass, which Pavle was shifting left and right. "Get rid of the goof. See how he's watching us. The mean old bastard . . . He hurt our dog. He kicked Rex on the beach. And now he's sitting here . . . Just sitting here as if nothing happened." When Ana finished her monologue she continued with a mumbling that came from deep inside her chest. Pavle looked at me as if he was weighing up her words, as if he really had to make a decision. Then he held her wine up to her face. "Come on, darling . . . Let this be a nightcap." She put her lips to the rim and emptied the glass to the last drop. "Good girl," Pavle said. I enjoyed watching those creatures saturate themselves with wine and alkaloids and gradually lose control. Their bodies, now sluggish and clumsy, slumped in that dirty chair. My own mind and body were almost unaffected. The nervous tension and great expectations, coupled with the daily consumption of those little red devils, enabled me to sit there calm and ready to analyze events. I hoped Ana would vomit the contents of her stomach all over Pavle's neck, which would have given me further satisfaction. But she just curled up coyly on the hairy chest of her husband, who didn't restrain himself from sticking his big hand under Ana's long T-shirt and resting it on her ass. When she said she had to go for a pee, Pavle winked to me and stood Ana on her legs with difficulty. She put her arm around his shoulder and together they tottered off toward the darkness of the front door. I felt unusual because the first thing I thought of when I was sitting alone on the veranda was my son, my simpleminded and boring son, who always talks about not having enough money. I thought of his rotten teeth and offensively bad breath. I opened my bottle of wine with ease and took a good swig, counting the gulps. After eight mouthfuls I put the bottle back on the table. A third was gone. What happened next was the work of my hands. It wasn't me. I'd repeat that a thousand times if necessary, and I say it again: my hands were to blame. The consciousness and conscience of urologist Dr. Maxim Junkić had nothing whatsoever to do with it. Really, deep inside I see things more as a generous gesture, a spontaneous need to satisfy people regardless of how much evil there is in them. I reached for my precious little plastic box, wedged the bottle between my legs, and started to open the remaining capsules and tip their white, diamond-like contents into the acidic wine. After a gentle swirl, the bitterish substance without any detectable taste or smell thoroughly integrated into the beverage. If Ana had known anything about wine, the slight distortion of the aroma would have made her leave that trash rather than guzzle it down as if it was fine champagne. Besides, there was no doubt that our socializing was over. I had to activate the mental mechanisms as soon as possible that would help me forget the fiasco of that little

party and return to my simple routine of resignation and loneliness. After topping up their glasses, I put the bottle down on
the table. I felt a slight pain in the chest from overindulging in
cigarettes, but I decided I needed another. There came the sounds
of someone vomiting in the bathroom, but soon Ana's laughter
was heard, which made Rex go back into the house and start
barking. She appeared on the veranda with her T-shirt covered in
yellowish splotches. She held her belly and laughed, baring her
teeth. "Pavle made a fucking mess of the whole bathroom . . . I'll
leave the swine because of that . . . You think it's just a trifle,
don't you . . . You little old man . . . Slimy old man." She kept
repeating that *Slimy old man* in a tone reminiscent of a theatrical
performance full of insults. She kept repeating those three words
until she'd lowered herself back into the chair and laughed again
because her husband's loud snoring started to come from behind
the bedroom shutters. I didn't offer her the wine. She'd already
had quite a lot to drink and popped four or five capsules on top
of that. I wouldn't have thought of bumping her off, although I
had reason enough to. She grabbed her glass herself and poured
the contents down her throat, and then she took the other glass
and did the same. The wind blew her hair into her face so I
couldn't see the effects. For a moment I thought she was sobbing,
and that sincerely pleased me because I believed emotions would
elicit at least a few coherent words and feelings from that creature.
But no, it was just the backrest of her chair creaking. She rocked
back and forward, and the worn-out wood produced rat-like
squeaks that attracted swarms of mosquitoes. Yes, just then I
believed that high-pitched tone was the reason for the mass of
insects suddenly turning up around my face; they were trying to
get into my nose and ears, hoping to tap some fresh blood from
the capillaries inside my nose. My geriatric face is thick and dry,
so it's impossible for them to pierce the layers of cells tanned
dead by decades of sun. I instinctively got up and waved several
times in front of my face. I don't remember if it was me who
moved the bottle with what was left of the wine closer to Ana,
or if she took it herself. But as I stood in front of her in the semidarkness of the veranda, I saw her tilt the green bottle above her

lips. They didn't touch the glass. The liquid poured into her gorge like a final gift, and then a few turbid whitish drops of crystal sediment oozed through the neck of the bottle, which Ana welcomed and savored with the tip of her tongue. I think I blushed because my member started to rise gently beneath the fine linen of my trousers. I've never managed to understand what it was in that image that excited me, but I'm sure her sharp tongue had nothing at all to do with it. I did up my blazer and took the bottle from her hands. Her fingers were cold. She smelled of her husband's vomit. I helped her to recline the back-rest of the chair and make herself more comfortable. She spread her legs, and I noticed several large bruises on the inside of her thighs. Ana's hair now fell down across the backrest. It was beau-tiful and well-groomed hair. I stroked her forehead and the smoothed-down black tresses. My hand gathered sweetish aro-mas of jasmine with traces of lemon. But all that was mixed with the gruelly, half-dried blotches left by her husband. It stank of banality and a wasted life. Of suffering, havoc, decay, and great delusions. Ana's T-shirt rose up over her hips. Her underwear molded her vulva. I was interested solely in her breasts, but they were concealed by the fouled creases of cotton, between which I tried to make out the marks of her nipples. She looked aslant, through her eyelashes, and when she concluded I was watching her, she lowered her hand and turned back the top of her panties with her thumb to reveal her shaven labia. She opened them with her fingers and said: "Do you want my pussy, Doctor?" At the same moment she began to laugh, but her face no longer reflected those intentions. Her serious expression and heavy eyelids didn't go together with the feigned laughter. Her pale cheeks were loose and sagging, her eyelids red and heavy. The powder dissolved in the wine quickly penetrated even the furthest lagoons of her bloodstream. As I looked down on that body, I decided that I felt well and that nothing hurt. Everything around me radiated a marvelous clarity that I couldn't put down to my capsules alone. My erection lost intensity, so I undid my blazer again because I no longer had to conceal the bulge in my trousers. I carefully took out a Gauloise and put it in my front pocket, and

I left one for Ana as a refreshment after her hangover. When I took a stride toward the steps, her arm tried to bar my way. She loosely grabbed the railing and lifted her eyelids with effort. Only the bloodshot whites could be seen beneath them. I gently took her by the upper arm, held her hand, and checked the pulse. The vein bulged and slackened sluggishly. I sniffed at her cold, sticky fingers and saw traces of fresh menstrual blood. The acrid smell crept deep into my nostrils, overpowering the taste of cheap alcohol and cigarettes. I licked her hand from the middle of the palm, slowly, along the lifeline, and then briefly sucked the tips of her fingers. The metallic taste of erythrocytes lodged itself in my palate. For a moment, Pavle stopped snoring, and then after a few unintelligible words continued even louder than before. I laid Ana's hand on the armrest of the chair. I emptied the ashtray and gave the table a quick wipe with my hand. The little red lamp on the mute portable radio flickered to the rhythm of some secret message. Ana lay peacefully, her head tossed back over the backrest, with her mouth open and a fine thread of dense saliva trickling from it. Her breasts rose slowly. The black T-shirt became taut and her big nipples now stood forth between the yellowish stains of Pavle's vomit. Everything was in place. The wind died down. A choir of crickets stirred in the treetops. The sea changed frequency too. A slow, rhythmical murmur reached up from the shore to coincide with Ana's breathing. I wanted to leave and remember just that order of things, just those images. But I stood in the same place for several more minutes, trying to work out where that strange feeling of triumph came from that unexpectedly led me to the verge of euphoria. I stood on the veranda under the porch of the ugly green house with my head absurdly high, like a victor in tilting at windmills. But I knew that I had ample time ahead of me to analyze the facts. Then I decided it was the right moment to leave the field of battle and return to a familiar cadence. A few more nights like this would have sped things up unnecessarily. I strode down the steps and didn't look back. The eastern sky announced dawn. Rex was barking at my back from the veranda. That malevolent little dog was the spark that caused this fire. I'd been deep in thought as I watched the setting of the great red sun, but he had to come running up and direct his pedigreed, bestial glee at my shoe. I assume indolent, sweaty Pavle's sperm was no good. So the dog was a kind of solution. The little black nugget he turned up with at the door one morning looked at Ana with sad, clear eyes, and she immediately decided to keep it. As I approached the beach, detouring the flowering tamarisk bushes, I had the impression that this black creature, an embodiment of all creatures, was ominously observing me from behind a tree. As if it, of all things, had been given a knowledge of my future and destiny. I felt hungry and thought of breakfast at the hotel. I could see the line of the waves that had pushed their way up to the middle of the beach, supported by the tide. I didn't want to get my shoes wet. I sat down a good way back from the water and made myself comfortable on an overturned fishing boat. I read its name on the bottom of the stern: *Stella*. A mile or two farther, I noticed the tiny silhouettes of the first walkers. The whole family would collect shells that the sea had cast out in the past night. They'd turn those washed-up shells into souvenirs. I fumbled in my inner pocket and was glad when I found the cigarette. I shielded the flame and inhaled with relish. The ruddying east tinged the smoke, and my shoes called for a thorough cleaning. A piece of linen cloth and a little hand cream really make the leather shine. With every puff of the cigarette several more brisk walkers could be seen on the horizon, limbering up and filling their lungs with the salubrious air. But when the rim of the large star emerged from behind the hills in the east, they all stopped and turned their heads. The gleam on the surface of the sea bent with the movements of the leviathan. The hills were cast in black as I looked at them, facing the sun. Several fishing boats slowly approached the shore. Lost island tribes come to the New World, I thought, and felt very hungry again. Well-organized families were already marching through the sand. They didn't want to expose their children to the heat of midday. Swimming is most pleasant early in the morning and in the evening. They knew that. As I walked back toward the hotel, I teased the top of my mouth with my tongue. I could still taste traces of Ana's blood.

Those dying molecules were slowly disappearing and would soon be erased by a cup of hot coffee. I went in through the main gate, hoping it would be a shortcut to the dining room. But the police were already waiting in the courtyard near the tall, bent palm tree, whose clusters of flowers smelled of rotten grapes. Two young men in uniform asked me for my ID and then took me away to the manager's office, where they shooed his secretary with some harsh words. In the inner pocket of my woolen blazer they found the little red plastic box, which was used as evidence. Pavle had called the police shortly after I left, as I found out. Pavle was sitting on a bench in front of the reception desk together with the two officers. Rex's barking had woken him from his heavy slumber. He finally summoned up enough courage and hatred to put an end to that frightful din with one powerful blow. But Ana thwarted that idea—Ana, who lay sprawling in the chair, with the whites of her eyes showing; Ana, whose thighs were smeared with blood, which kept on seeping from her cold vulva; Ana, whose labia were encrusted with congealed clumps. After death, her body went limp and all orifices produced a flow of what had to flow. That sight had nothing to do with my intentions. The autopsy later revealed that she died of an overdose of tranquilizer tablets, and Pavle claimed it wasn't he whose fingers had pushed the little red capsules into her mouth. That liar cried in the courtroom like a child that has crapped its pants. Traces of alkaloids in the wine bottle irrevocably incriminated me. When I said, "I didn't do it—it was my hands," several of those present, including my son, laughed loudly. Fifteen years in prison for premeditated murder. A double cell as a bit of luxury in view of my advanced age. A hard, cold floor with remnants of feces, and food that ruins my stomach. A thin ray makes its way through the wire and bars on summer days. I lean back against the wall and close my eyes, and that beautiful light floods my eyelids for a few minutes, turning the world into a boundless, rosy universe. Then I stand stiff, without thoughts and reminiscences, reconciled with life, devoid of memories, intentions, and pain. I absorb the wonderful rays, knowing, after all, that it's more than *only the sun*.

# Winter Search

HE SAT IN his armchair, twirling a thick loose yarn that hung from his sleeve, and spoke about the bad weather. He was given this green woolen sweater with the six snowflakes in the middle of the chest for his sixtieth birthday. My mother bought the sweater at the market and embroidered the snowflakes on it herself. "One for each decade," she said as he tried to squeeze his head through the narrow neck. "It'll widen in time." My father seemed to be happy with the present and to feel well in it. He didn't take the sweater off until after his birthday dinner. Under the influence of the wine and the surge of good cheer, he gave my mother a pinch on the bum as she was putting the dirty plates and dishes in the sink. She sent him a smile and a surprised glance, then looked at the company at the table and blushed slightly. I, my wife, and her sister were sitting there. My mother died five days later. The massive heart attack left purple marks on her chest and neck. My father was the first to get up that morning. He didn't go straight to the bathroom. Seeing that the light was on, he went on through into the kitchen and put the coffee water on the stove. He turned on the television. The weather forecast announced a northern wind and the possibility of snow even in southern parts. That made him shiver, take the green sweater from on top of the chair, and put it on over his pajamas. The water started to boil. He put one spoonful of sugar and two of coffee into the long-necked pot, and later poured two cups. He took all that into the dining room and waited a bit longer. The bathroom door had a characteristic creak, so he could tell exactly when Marija came out. He'd drunk two glasses of water during the night and another when he got up. His kidneys worked well and so his bladder swelled. He decided to light a cigarette. He'd smoke it to the butt, then stub it out and go and knock because he really needed to piss. But he only lasted halfway through his Winston. He rubbed his bulging belly and hurried toward the bathroom. From halfway along the hall he called to announce the impending invasion, but she didn't reply. He hopped around in place, shouted *Marija* one more time, and then jerked open the door, ready to drop his pants and relieve himself. My mother was still sitting on the toilet seat. He was struck by the sweetish odor of feces intensified by the heat of the radiator on the wall. My mother was leaning with her forehead on the edge of the washing machine. Her arms hung down by her side, and thick pus mixed with blood ran from her mouth. It left a stain on the white tiles in the shape of a fish, my father said, who for days afterward revealed intricate details that in his thoughts made up the wretched mosaic of that morning.

A green wisp stuck out of the sleeve of his birthday sweater, and my father twisted it between his forefinger and thumb. For five years now, he's put on that sweater with the first fall of rain or the first cold air, and then he wears it for as long as he can bear. He only wears it around the house. He washes it properly in lukewarm water and darns it when necessary.

We spent more time together after my mother died. He retired six months after Marija's heart attack and visited the cemetery once a week. On the first anniversary of her death he planted ten cypress saplings around Marija's grave. He explained to me the same evening that the cypress is a typical cemetery tree and that it was the symbol and attribute of Saturn in the ancient Mediterranean world, but also of Aesculapius and Apollo because of its flame-like form. That was the first time he'd mentioned the names of ancient deities, I thought. He watered the cypresses and broke off the low branches. He asked for his name to be engraved below Marija's. They carved his name and in brackets the year of his birth, followed by a short horizontal line, after which the year of death would be engraved. "That line is the whole of life," he said and laughed. I put on a smile and thought: My father has often been speaking in definitions recently. The taciturn man has turned into a talker. I'm frightened of his moods. He talks in whole passages, nineteen to the dozen, and then it's as if he takes a sharp turn along the way, veers off, and continues in an unfamiliar direction; he doesn't speak about my mother . . . he avoids the topic even when I try to enforce it . . . he prefers to speak about the bad weather or the absolute mess the city is in; I can't get to the bottom of what's behind these attitudes and this behavior; and then again, perhaps there's nothing strange about it? The loss of the person he spent so many years of his life with imposed a new context; and with it new thoughts, new expressions, and gestures . . .

I reflected on all this while he was gathering up his gardening tools by Marija's grave, brushing the red soil from his hands, and pressing down the gravel around the seedlings with his heel. Actually, it was more as though I'd felt all this in one brief second, rather than as a clear torrent of thoughts, let alone correct sentences. I wasn't sure what remained of his world after my mother's funeral. For a few moments it looked as if his famous dark mood, a character thing with him, had suddenly changed for the better, because sometimes he was cheerful beyond recognition. He'd read out aphorisms from the daily papers and make fun of the horoscope, which describes the health of the signs of the zodiac with one, or at most two, words: your lungs, your throat, mind your step, avoid drafts . . . He sank ever more often in memories that led back to the time before his marriage, before he got to know Marija, and then it seemed to me as if someone else began to speak inside him, and it wasn't my father, Marija's husband. He'd talk about cities: Zagreb, Vienna, Ljubljana, Vukovar, Vinkovci, and Sarajevo. He described those cities as if there were never any people there: an empty land populated by streets and houses, but without people. I had such pictures in my head because my father simply didn't mention people. The names of cafes, suburbs, and hotels had no connection with this world. They were levitating material facts that eluded any familiar geography, just as my father himself kept slipping away from the image I'd formed of him over the years in my thoughts and feelings.

It was exactly five years since Marija's death. I watched him sitting there in his armchair and unconsciously twisting the greasy yarn of green wool. He hadn't cut his fingernails for a long time, and the motion of his fingers produced a clicking sound. The nail of his right index finger had gone yellow from smoking. He pointed that nail at the window and said he'd seen several snowflakes early that morning. They were large and fell sluggishly, "like big flakes of ash," he told me. He believed "proper" snow would start falling today. "Proper snow will start falling today," he said and rubbed the snowflakes on his chest.

His suit, shirt, and tie were on a coat hanger fastened to the living-room door. Everything was impeccably ironed and clean: his cemetery clothes. He put his low black shoes on a sheet of newspaper next to the stove, hoping to warm them. Yesterday he'd bought five thin candles and a bag of artificial fertilizer that he'd tip next to the cypresses. I waited for him to finish his cigarette and get up, but he lit another and started to talk about the Inter vs. Roma soccer match that ended 1–1. I thought he'd forgotten the reason for our early meeting, but he blew a cloud of smoke toward the ceiling and said that his memories of Marija were fading. He couldn't recall her face, her forehead, or the shape of her ears. That annoyed him. He refused to get out the photographs because that would be an artificial evocation of memories and emotions. He stubbed out the cigarette halfway through, lit another straightaway, and said that his feelings for that woman, that person, no longer existed. He closed his eyes and rapidly twirled the loose end of green wool sticking out of his sleeve. For a moment I thought that greasy yarn was the only thing that connected him to my mother. My eyes filled with tears. When he opened his eyes again, he stared at the glowing tip of his cigarette. I expected him to say more and try to explain. But my father got up and took the small pair of curved scissors from the shelf. He showed me his claw-like nails and then started to attentively cut them. Thick pieces flew about the room. His eyes would follow their fall, and then he'd continue with a pained

can I throw this?" she asked, glancing around. "Just chuck it anywhere," I said. She found a piece of paper, stubbed out the cigarette in the snow, and carefully wrapped up the butt. She gave the wad to her sister, who zealously stuck it into her pocket and twice patted the spot as a sign of work well done: "We look after our g-g . . . graves," she said with a smile. A dark piece of chard or some other green vegetable clung to her front tooth. All of us were standing at different sides of the concrete bunker where my mother was buried; where my father would be buried. The wind blew from the north, so only the facing side of the grave slab was sprinkled with snowflakes. That emphasized the letters and numbers. I tried to brush off the snow with my hand but everything was icy. The cypresses wouldn't survive the winter, I thought. And my father wouldn't survive this day. The year of his birth waited for the year of his death. That line in between was the whole of life, my father said. Were those his words I'd always remember when he was gone, I wondered? The sisters were still standing there rooted to the spot because it was prob- ably me who had to say when was enough. Each of them staring at her own point.

"Shall we go? I don't want you to freeze," I said. They exchanged glances. I rubbed my hands together and took a step backward, hoping that would animate them. They glanced at each other again and then set off for the main path of the cem- etery. My ex-wife had put on weight. Her sister dyed her hair black. Her right leg was rigid at the knee. She dragged it like deadwood. She always wore a long coat to try and conceal the impediment, but she achieved the opposite effect. Watching her from behind made me think of a mechanical dummy. But who would make a dummy that imitated a limp? As we walked along the worn cobblestones, my ex-wife and her sister periodically shrieked and spread their arms to keep their balance. My ex-wife stopped. They both scrambled to the side of the way. I heard a murmur and muffled crying. A coffin showed at the bottom of the path. Four small figures like black caryatids were carrying it on their shoulders. Behind them came about twenty people with heads bowed. The loudest, a short lady, was trying to touch the coffin as it moved along. She kept calling and reaching out her arm to stroke it. A thin boy stopped her time and again, grabbing her by the upper arm, but she tried to pull free and moved to touch the coffin again. The three of us waited at the side. There was no way of bypassing the procession. "There's a side gate—" I started to say, but my ex-wife cut me short. She put her finger to her lips and hissed: "Have some respect." I thought of my father and the smell of burned nails and said: "I'm going."

"You—" my ex-wife said. "You—" her sister repeated. I strode over the hedge that flanked the path. I sprang over withered bouquets of flowers, oleander branches, and marble slabs. Names and faces passed by, black-and-white photographs of the dead wrought into the marble. Two drenched workers sat under a tree next to a half-dug grave. They were holding huge pieces of bread smeared with a red paste. They stopped their chewing as I went by. I said hello, they said nothing.

The side gate was locked. A cat snuck through the bars and dashed to the next tomb. I cursed the locked gate. I had to vault the fence. I brushed the snow from the top with my hand, wedged my shoe into the cavity of a concrete block, and swung up with all my strength. Sitting on top, I looked down at the two worlds, one on each side. I leaped onto the sidewalk and felt a stab of pain in my right knee. A woman pulled away her umbrella. She took several steps backward and then went around me while I straightened up my clothes. On the way to the car, snowballs flew past my head. Children on the other side of the street were flinging them with abandon. I wiped the snow off the windscreen. I'd forgotten to turn off the radio. A male baritone spoke about snowstorms in the north of the country and the *white blanket* that had taken the population of the south unawares. Then they played *The Four Seasons* to establish the weather conditions as the theme of the day. All channels discussed the weather and the situation on the roads. Long delays, traffic jams, snowdrifts. Epic pictures, I thought and started the engine. People here aren't used to driving in the snow.

As I waited at the traffic lights, I imagined I'd arrive back to find an ambulance at the front door. That would mean the worst had happened. One of the neighbors had heard a shot and went to check the situation. My father had gotten out his old Walther pistol hidden under the cushions. He'd held it up to his forehead and pulled the trigger. The wonder-nine bullet made a mess at the back of his head, I thought and put my foot to the floor. I turned off the radio. My eyes filled with tears. I expected I'd remember my childhood and beautiful moments spent with the man. But the image of my dear father's shattered skull was stronger than any reminiscences. If I found him in a pool of blood, my life would be ruined, I thought. My decision not to stay at home but to go to the cemetery among the dead, to stand for ten minutes near their cold, putrid remains—that would be the nightmare that haunted me.

There was nothing unusual down at the front entrance. The wind had died away and the snow fell in silence. *Into silence*, I thought. A few dirty gulls were hanging around on the lampposts. And again, children, frenzied by so much white. My hands began to sweat. I felt the cold in my legs and my belly. Every step I climbed intensified my belief that I wouldn't find him alive. His derangement had reached a crescendo, I thought. The woman from the fourth floor was at the door seeing her children off to school. She straightened the red cap on the girl's head and the blue cap on the boy's. The children said hello in unison as I went past, and their mother laughed. I said nothing. I stopped in front of our door and spoke the name engraved on the brass plaque. My beloved father, I thought, and seized the ice-cold handle. It was unlocked. I made for the living room. His armchair was empty, and the air cold and dank. I stood for several moments and looked at the furniture. The emptiness that had settled in here smelled of old newspapers.

I heard his voice behind my back. He didn't say my name but instead: "My son." He was sitting in the hall on the floor and leaning against the wall concealed by the shelf. His right hand clenched the receiver that he held against his chest. Almost as if he was going to commit suicide with it, I thought. I took the receiver and put it back in the cradle. Still he didn't stand up. Cigarette butts lay scattered around on the shelf. The

December-landscape calendar was marred by their being stubbed out. The man beneath the lamppost showed a big burn where his head should have been. Instead of the headlights of the car there were two black holes. Two dark circles emitting light. I reached him my hand and waited for him to grab on and get to his feet, but he just stared at an imaginary point on the wall opposite. "Would you like a cigarette?" I asked, and he nodded gently. When I came back from the living room with a lit-up Winston, my father was standing and brushing ash from the green sweater with languid movements. He hardly seemed able to stand. His feet weighed heavily on the ground and moved with the grace of two jellyfish on dry land. He walked with his knees slightly bent, as if he was carrying someone on his shoulders. I tried to support him under his arms and guide him to his chair, but he signaled for me not to and went on by himself.

I felt I was watching a ghost, a man who was losing part of his self every second and gradually turning into something nameless and indefinite. He collapsed into his armchair and firmly clenched the armrests. The cigarette drooped from his bottom lip. From time to time he'd grip it in his teeth and take a drag. Beads of perspiration collected on his eyebrows. The smoke crept up his face, wound around his nose and eyelashes, and ended between the wisps of his sparse hair. His head seemed to be steaming, glowing, and wet. Seeing him alive suppressed my urge to react. I stood and watched, without knowing what was going on inside my father's skull and what kind of black hole he was being sucked into.

I emptied the ashtray. He leaned up to it and spat out his cigarette butt. "I'll make coffee," I said, but he didn't answer. "Uh-huh, there's no coffee. I'll make tea then," I said after scouring the kitchen. Still no word from him. There were some flowers of Saint-John's-wort at the bottom of a jar. We'll make tea from the dried flowers, I thought and tipped the contents of the jar into the metal tea strainer.

My father settled down in his armchair and again took the green yarn that protruded from his sleeve. He twisted it again and again with rhythmical movements as if he was painstakingly doing a rosary. The snow kept falling. The kettle whistled. I noticed several small black flies at the bottom of the jar and threw it into the trash can. In the can: hundreds of cigarette butts and a few greasy tins. I lowered the tea strainer into the teapot. A film of dust and particles floated on the surface of the water. I ought to have rinsed out the teapot before using it. No one had made tea in this house for a long time.

The cups were painted with hunting scenes. A German bird-dog carried a pheasant in its jaws. A hunter took aim at a bird flying over the treetops. I washed the cups and poured the tea: a yellowish liquid with no smell. The glass surface of the living-room table reflected my father's silhouette. I put his tea down where his face was reflected. The glass near the searing cup fogged up. Only the humming of the fridge could be heard, mixed with the heavy gasps of his lungs. It was growing dark. I switched on the light. He covered his face with his hands and asked me to turn it off again. "We can't sit in the dark," I said. "Why not?" my father grunted. I turned off the light. He seemed to be finally returning to the world, so I fulfilled all his demands without hesitation. I moved the tea closer to him. He looked at the picture on the cup and said: "Freaks." He wanted a teaspoon and some sugar. I asked where the sugar jar was just to elicit a few more ordinary words from him. "You know where the sugar is," he said.

When I came back with the jar and a teaspoon, he was standing at the window gaping at the dark curtain of snow flecked with light. I sweetened the tea and reached him his cup. He was surprised, as if he'd never seen me before—he looked me in the eyes and took the tea. His hands were perfectly calm. He clasped the cup in his hand. "Take it by the handle. It's very hot," I said, but my father continued to squeeze it with his whole hand. I hoped the pain would sober him, take the edge off his temper, and make him return to some kind of stable lethargy like the one he'd struggled with since Marija's death. He took a swig, sat down in his armchair, and put the cup down on the table. He stared at his bright-red palm and looked from close up as if he was examining the lines and trying to reinterpret them. "I'll bring a wet cloth to cool your hand," I offered. He raised his red-hot palm to his forehead. "There's no need. It doesn't hurt . . . Why a wet cloth, what the heck?" he said and lit a cigarette.

Usually I responded to his whims and impertinences in kind. My father would shoot back a few more times, let some strong words fly, fall silent, and several minutes later try to return us to a normal conversation. But today his calm consistency made me go silent. That state aroused a kind of sorrow that I couldn't find a name and definition for. My iron father was dissolving, crumbling into little pieces, and disappearing before my eyes, and I didn't know how to help him. It wasn't enough to open and close the window, make strawy tea, light cigarettes for him, and gaze at his sweat-beaded face. It wasn't enough to put his moods down to the movements of an aged and worn-out body. All that wasn't enough, I knew. Marija alone could have found a remedy. But she was gone and wouldn't be coming back.

I took tiny sips of the insipid tea and looked at my father's massive hands. I don't remember when I last touched him. Probably the moment he announced my mother had died, I thought, and tried to recall an embrace.

The previous anniversaries of Marija's death had passed without incident. The two of us would sit together until late in the evening. On the first anniversary, about twenty people came to the cemetery: a few forgotten relatives with flowers, Marija's sister, and two of my father's friends. He'd wear his suit and take part in subdued conversations that evoked memories of the deceased. The people dropped away over the years, and their place in the procession was taken by cypresses. Three years later there were more cypresses than people.

I put my hand on my father's. He seemed not to notice. He kept sitting with his eyes half closed and staring at a point. His point. I rubbed the back of his hand and was surprised how rough it had become. Only then did he look at me. I wasn't sure what I read on his face. I wanted to believe it was a gentle smile, but the expression resembled more of a sneer. When I removed my hand his features went back to their normal position. I actually only wanted to touch him to see what that contact would prompt in my own world. But I didn't feel anything except naked fear and confusion. It was as if something dark and powerful had taken shape inside him, as if he realized he couldn't fight it and win. All aid was pointless, and therefore my attention could only be met with a sneer, as proverbial kindness, stupidity, and lack of understanding.

I decided I'd sit on the couch for as long as necessary. Until something changed. Later I'd perhaps serve him some food and beer; pressed by those tiny particles of reality, his mind and body would consent to elementary communication. That was the plan. Primitive and condescending, but the only one I could come up with in my distress.

We were sitting in almost complete darkness. The only point of light was the tiny red lamp on the thermostat of the electric heater. As darkness fell, our eyes accepted that scarlet sfumato. I began to distinguish things bathed in a fine haze of red, the contours of my father's face, and the gleaming beads of perspiration on his forehead. Whenever he lit a cigarette, the steady gasoline flame of the Zippo briefly illuminated the room. His pupils abruptly narrowed, and the objects in the room were joined by elongated, trembling shadows. Those moments passed in regular intervals and were engraved like clear photographs. After the sixth cigarette, the lighter fell silent. The time spent with my father had to be measured by the number of cigarettes he smoked, I thought. The smoke stung my eyes. It pressed in from all sides and gave the red glow a milky softness. I tried to make out what he was doing with his hands, but I didn't dare switch on the light. Just now, I thought, that would have had the dimensions of a cataclysmic change.

But then my father suddenly asked me to turn on the television. I needed several seconds to digest that word and attach meaning to it. I realized that a moment earlier he'd looked at the clock; it was now exactly seven thirty and he wanted to watch the Channel 2 news on national television. "What do you need that infotainment for?" I groaned, thoroughly annoyed by the situation. I felt cheated. The cathode tube would glisten in all the colors of the rainbow, with billions of photons that, like a massive army, would wipe out all subtle nuances of thoughts, traces of matter, and emotions that had accumulated in the smoke-filled room. I decided not to react. I'd wait for him to repeat his demand, and then I'd get up and reanimate that old shit. The armchair creaked. He stretched out his right arm and reached the switch of the lamp on the shelf. The lightbulb poisoned our eyes. His sweater was covered in ash. His gray beard was longer by a fraction of a millimeter and his eyes bloodshot. A yellowish-rimmed hole gaped at the edge of one of the snowflakes. The burning end of a cigarette had fallen off and burned through the wool. My father looked at the hole and stuck his little finger through it. He contorted his face as if he'd stuck his finger under his skin. "That's a shame," he said. He looked me in the eyes, thus announcing the importance of the next sentence: "Did the phone ring?" I didn't understand the question and shrugged my shoulders. "In all this time, did the phone in the hall ring?" he asked. "No, I didn't hear anything," I said and glanced toward the hall door. His question sounded as if there existed a possibility of the phone's ringing not being heard as well in the dark, as if he personally heard worse in the dark. It seemed he was still expecting a call and very important messages from the other end. I thought for the first time that he had perhaps been constantly thinking about today's phone conversation and that his condition was a consequence of the words that had come out of the black receiver that morning. Unknown, mysterious words, whose meanings I couldn't imagine. "Were you expecting anyone to call?" I wanted to know. It was clear that the question slightly disconcerted him. He lit another cigarette and asked me once more to turn on the television. I got no answer to my question.

I pressed the worn black button at the back of the large box. It started to hum, and then the green sparks appeared. "It needs time to warm up," my father said. "Louder," he added. I turned it up full bore and the orchestrated theme that introduces the news roared from the speakers for several seconds. He put his hands over his ears and waited for me to adjust the volume. The newscaster was reduced to a sensible level. He had a ridiculous hairdo and his deep voice read the news of the day: snow. The towns in the north were cut off. The side roads were blocked too—and my father had changed beyond recognition, I thought. We sat through the current affairs, waiting for a more detailed report on the white-blanketed cities and the roads with long lines of waiting cars. The conference halls sent out green rays at our walls. My father smoked and looked absently through the window. Politics didn't interest him now. But when the newscaster announced *footage of the weather situation, the woes of the rural population, and drivers on the northbound roads*, he abruptly turned his head and asked me to turn it up.

The report on the snow began with close-ups of a village house with only a few feet of its roof still showing above the blinding white. An old man stood leaning against the edge of the roof. When the microphone was held toward his face, he said he didn't know what to do, and went on to repeat the same sentence three times. He kept moving closer to the device, and the tips of his lips brushed against the foam cover. The reporter evaded him, but the old guy got up and headed toward the camera. *Here we return to the studio.* The man with the ridiculous hairdo said that what we'd just seen best illustrated the distress of the vulnerable rural population trapped by the masses of snow. The next report was broadcast live. The main road that makes its way through a gorge high into the mountains of the north was almost paralyzed. Long lines of cars were at the mercy of snowdrifts that had cut the road in several places. The reporter stood in front of one of those hills interviewing a certain head of a certain agency, who was trying hard to keep his cap on in the gusty wind. A large machine in the background worked to push the banks of snow straight into the river. There was also a murmur of people asking when they'd be able to continue their journey. The guy said self-confidently: *Everything's under control, we can move off in ten minutes*, and then he repeated the sentence twice more. Finally the reporter got into his car. He headed back south, and for several minutes the camera filmed the long queue of vehicles, complemented here and there by groups of travelers deliberating what to do next. My father moved closer to the television and turned up the volume some more. There came the crackle of snow under tires and a loud discussion at the roadside. The beam of the camera's light lit up the vehicles one by one and zoomed in on smiling children's faces glued to the car windows. During this time, my father stood in front of the television, riveted, like in a trance, and attentively followed the developments on the screen. He managed to frighten me one more time: I was perplexed and didn't know what those images meant to him. What did he really see in place of the scenes of a snowstorm? When the report was over, my father went up and put the flat of his large hand on the glass surface. "What on earth are you doing?" I asked, trying hard to restrain my anger. "What's wrong with you?" I blurted out and then realized the horrible meaning those words could have. He was pale and unsettled as if he'd just seen something on the screen that shook him to the core. He stood in the middle of the room and turned his head, looking now through the window, now at his feet, and then at the ceiling. "Get me some water," he said and sat down in his armchair. I came back with a glass, and he indicated for me to put it down on the table. He sat for a few seconds with his head thrown back, as if he was making a decision that would be confirmed when he lowered his head again. Then he shifted abruptly and sat on the edge of the armchair. He drank a sip of water. Now he looked me straight in the eyes. It was a conscious expression for the first time today, unclouded by derangement and madness. "Now listen to me, I need you to help me," he said and rubbed his forehead with his hand. I nodded. "Did you come by car? Of course you came by car," he knew, and quickly got up. "Let's go then." But he sat down again and lowered his voice. "There's one very important thing. Very important . . . You have to promise me something," he spoke slowly and quietly, with self-confidence. I moved closer to the table. "Don't ever—got it?—don't EVER ask me to explain. What we're going to do . . . it's simple. A few hours' drive and that's it. When we come back we'll make coffee and rest from today. But never—please, my son—NEVER ask me what I was searching for this evening. Understand?" I nodded. We stood up together. He put his hand on my shoulder, squeezed hard and affectionately, and asked: "Are we going?" When my father had put on his coat and shoes he went up to the phone and lifted the receiver. He held the thing to his ear for a few seconds. His finger was prepared to turn the dial, but he changed his mind and gently put the receiver down. He ripped out the December page of the wall calendar, took a look at the scene, and tore the sheet in four. "Ready?" I asked and opened the door. "Cigarettes," he remembered. He went into the living room and he came back with two packs of Winstons. "My sustenance," he said, pointing to the golden-yellow packs.

I believed our mission was in some way linked to the phone conversation that put him in this unusual mood. But I didn't have the slightest idea who my father had been talking with.

We went down the stairs. There was no light from the entrance. He stopped on the landing of the third floor and lit a cigarette. On the stairs down to the second floor a couple stood in the ecstasy of kissing. Their thick nylon jackets rustled. They didn't interrupt their pleasure when we passed. I once used to stand in the same place with my ex-wife, I thought. Before going outside, my father did up all his buttons, raised his collar, and energetically opened the metal door. Cold air and snowflakes hit us. But the wind had dropped. Tracks of cars were sketched on the road. Traces of children's hands were sketched on the parked cars. I forgot where I left the car. I inhaled the chill air deeply and felt calm for the first time that day. Whiffs of a sweetish smell spread between the buildings. At the bottom of the street a garbage container was smoking. Burning garbage always smells nice, almost idyllic. Columns of smoke rose vertically from the houses nearby. Druids and shamans were able to tell by a glance at the smoke rising from a house how many people were ill beneath that roof and which ailments they had. I read that somewhere. We found the car. I started to clean off the snow. My father shifted the cigarette to his left hand and joined in. We got into the car with freezing hands. I rubbed mine together. The palm of one of my father's hands was still quite red. My calm vanished because I knew that, when I started the engine, I'd have to ask which direction to go. The Opel diesel engine rumbled into life. The vibrations pervaded the inside of the car and our bodies: things rattled and shook. I drove through the parking lot and stopped at the intersection. I swallowed and asked: "Which way?" My father shook off his ash down near his feet: "To the right . . . Head north . . . Out of town. Over the big bridge . . . Across the river," he said, without mentioning the names of the streets, the name of the bridge, and the river. As if he was talking about all bridges and rivers, I thought. As if he was reciting a poem. I stepped on the gas and turned on the radio. A clear woman's voice announced a concert for piano and orchestra. Snow was falling thickly on the windscreen, but the wipers were doing their job impeccably. My father's smoke filled the space. My father filled the space. We left the city. When we crossed the bridge, I slowed down and looked at him. We were driving between the tall cliffs of a canyon. He looked around and held an expression blurred by the curls of smoke. He nodded, which meant I should continue on. I stepped on the gas again and nestled my back into the seat. The white line in the middle of the road was freshly painted. Not a single car could be seen. With every mile there was more and more snow on the road. That didn't matter because my new tires kept a good grip. My father tucked up his coat and leaned his head against the window. The cigarette between his fingers had burned out. He fell asleep. I turned down the piano passage and threw his cigarette into the ashtray. Now everything was in its place, I thought. Things were changing for the better. I'd drive for as long as I could: until the car came to a halt by itself, and until my father woke up and told me what we were searching for that night.

# The Harbinger

"I'm going to bed," she said at eleven.

"It's not late. Wait a bit longer. I think he'll come. When he came the first time, it was at nine. Yesterday it was ten. Why shouldn't he come an hour later today? He simply *has* to come," I said.

"Has to?" she looked at me, and her eyes filled with tears.

He didn't turn up. That evening we didn't hear the whistling that suggested "Strangers in the Night" and the rustling of cellophane with cheap flowers. If it had been raining or a storm had been blowing, Irena would have been able to find reasons for his not coming. But as it was, she sat in the same chair, a wooden rocking chair, where I found her that morning too. Awake even before sunrise. The creeping August heat brought on her delirious forebodings. And now it was the end of the day, the end of sweating and the humid wind. A dark cloud of emptiness came from the sea and descended on the town, the four-story stone building, and the marble table we sat at, waiting for Maurice.

"You met him in town, didn't you? You met him down at the monument by the shore. Afterward you strolled together eating ice cream and talking about me. I know it. He told you . . . He told you everything. You know, but you're a coward and you're afraid to say it," she railed.

She began to cry. I went to the bathroom and washed my face. I shaved although there was no need: it had a calming effect because I really can't bear Irena's tears. After half an hour in the bathroom I came out again, trying to make no sound. She was sitting with her hair undone, her forehead in her hands.

"Do you want tea? I'll bring you some. Hibiscus?" I said and went into the kitchen, not waiting for a reply. It was cooler there than in the other rooms, with the marble-tiled wall and no windows—none of the red window frames that Irena had been sitting at for days. And waiting. Inevitable architectural facts became the framework of the pain she gives herself up to. Her eyes seek Maurice's silhouette that slinks along the streets, up the hill, to our building. But that evening he wasn't there. Only occasional couples and stray dogs came to a halt by the lampposts.

"I don't want any tea," I heard her say.

The light trembled to her voice. And that flickering continued for the next few minutes. The fridge ceased its humming. The record player in an apartment off the next courtyard fell silent. The cheering of a group of drunken tourists resonated out on the street, accompanied by several bestial shrieks. Silence followed: the portent of uncertainty.

I knew she wouldn't try to get up. Everything was quiet. And every movement would have meant a new sound and an unpleasant surprise. On the other side of the street and farther down the hill, the black holes of windows turned to a fabric the color of apricot. Candles were lit and the shapes of people swayed above them. The window frames, tables, and old radios—they were now altars where light found refuge. The candles guttered and burned low. But we had no candles. That forced us to sit in darkness and sift through the remains of our nervous thoughts as we waited.

The silence lulled the town. An occasional light sparkled down in the harbor. Ships studded with red and green lanterns seemed like castles scattered over the sea. She spent a few minutes on the balcony watering the geraniums. I heard splashing on the cobblestones down in front of the building. While she poured, always too much, she looked to the left and then to the right down the street, and then over the roofs, over the town, all the way to the harbor. She came back in because there was no more water in the can. Then a quiet knocking began at the door. First three times. And then again, three times more. A cold dew of sweat covered her face. But Maurice would have given up the idea of coming in a blackout. And yet he might have been in the neighborhood the moment the power went off. Walking in the dark in an unfamiliar town is always unpleasant. And that's why he decided to come after all. Now he stood at the door, straightening the lapels of his woolen blazer. He smoothed down his eyebrows. Besides, in the semidarkness of the moonlight he wouldn't have to look us in the eyes when he spoke. When he *made his announcement*, I thought.

I heard her muted moans. She didn't have the strength to cry anymore. Tears were a luxury in situations like this, I thought. I wouldn't open up. Not for him, Maurice. But the knocking continued. It was repeated every ten seconds or so, and it became tedious and unbearable. I quietly felt my way along the wall to the door. Irena's face was scarcely visible in the pale light by the window. Then: the key, the door handle, and a creak.

"Sorry to bother you, sir," came a child's voice from the bottom of the stairs.

"Hi, junior," I replied cheerfully, glad it wasn't Maurice.

"I live down on the first floor, but . . ."

"I recognize you," I said. He was a boy of about ten and had pronounced dark rings under his eyes.

"Would you be able to lend me a few candles if . . . if you have any, sir?"

I'd met his mother at the beach the day before—a woman with huge buttocks and breasts. She smiled timidly when I went up to her, not knowing what to say or why I spoke to her at all. She was sitting on a red towel. And reading.

"How are you?" I said.

"This heat," she gasped, taking off her hat, and long curly hair spilled forth with the smell of sandalwood. A slanting scar across her forehead changed the expression of her face when she smiled. It cut across her left eyebrow, inscribing a sternness.

"You're new here," I said.

"In a manner of speaking. We've been on the first floor since

February. Before that we were down by the harbor, and before that . . ."

"Yes, yes . . . That old misanthrope was still living there last summer," I said.

"What?"

"My father," I added as the red-bound book slipped from her hands.

I bent over to lift it up and my leg brushed her shoulder.

"Sorry," I said.

"That's all right. Do sit down," she offered.

The mark of another wound ran from the middle of her right thigh and ended somewhere beneath her bathing suit. She noticed I was looking.

"It's a long story. Much longer than the scar," she said, looking out to sea. I apologized, blushed, and muttered something incoherent. The sand was seething hot. I got up after a chat about the weather and the harmful effects of UV radiation.

"Have a nice swim. We'll see each other again, won't we?"

"Perhaps," she said, opening her book again. The gold-lettered title flashed in the sun.

We didn't have any candles, and our young neighbor started off back down the stairs straightaway, embarrassed by the evening encounter with me, a stranger. I offered that he stay until the electricity came on again.

"My mother has gone into town. I wouldn't want her to come back and not find me at home. But thank you, sir," he said, while I stepped out to light up the stairway for him with one of our five matches.

The matchhead crackled and hissed. Flash. But the flame disappeared again in an instant. I only managed to see my own fingers and his silhouette with his back leaning against the wall. The second match burned calmly. I raised it high above my head, going down a few steps.

"What's your name, young master?" I asked cheerfully.

"Enzo. That's what they call me," he said, watching the flame. The curve of his lower lip continued in the fine prominence of a scar stretching almost to his left ear. Red embers trembled in his frightened eyes. Again darkness. I would have lit another, but he was already on the floor below, near the door of his apartment.

When I closed our door and headed back, Irena was standing in front of me.

"That was Maurice, wasn't it? He told you. He told you everything."

I put my hand on her naked shoulder beaded with sweat. She pulled away and returned to her chair.

"Admit it!"

"Try to get to sleep. He's not coming tonight. It's late. Please calm down. Nothing terrible is going to happen. I feel in my bones that everything will be all right," I said. I often used to say this.

But I was unable to have a presentiment of this or anything. Things change too fast. Moments of good mood and happiness recede before the feeling of reality. Two days before coming here to the coast I watched her stroll naked about the apartment. She felt better, she said. She offered me coffee and lemonade with honey. "Oh yes, that would be just right," I accepted. A little later she came up to the table. A crystal glass in one hand and a cup of coffee in the other. But her fingers began to shake: smash, and pieces of glass on the floor. She bent down to pick them up and started to sob. I said I'd do it. Irena moved back because she didn't want me to touch her. Emerald droplets of blood on her hands and the tips of her fingers.

"Nothing," came out through her tears, and she went to get dressed. "It's nothing."

Just a few tiny pricks that could hardly be seen when we were waiting for Maurice today.

The boy and his mother weren't so lucky. Indelible scars monumentally marked their bodies. Like snakes impressed on a bas-relief.

"That was Maurice!" she said, leaning over my bed.

"No, it wasn't Maurice, just our little neighbor. It wasn't Maurice!" I repeated and wanted to say something to hurt her.

Instead I just told her, begged her, to go back to bed, and I'd come and talk. If she wanted.

"Don't. What is there to talk about? Maurice alone has something to say. That's obvious, damn it! Everything else is pointless."

Her relaxed and indifferent voice revealed a double dose of sleeping pills. In a few minutes she'd lie down and dream of Maurice for a long time. She felt his presence in the town. She'd go out onto the balcony at night and watch the tiny, scattered districts that stretched all the way to the harbor. Sunken paths between the roofs of the houses: a labyrinth he was now wandering. A minotaur, I thought. A mythical beast. But labyrinth isn't the right word for streets clad in darkness.

I got ready to go out, I checked that she'd fallen asleep and quietly left the apartment. Thirty steps down to the first floor, and five more to the street. I felt my way along the fence that would lead me to the way out: ever closer to the whispers, in which I recognized the shape of words. The contours of a conversation.

I stopped at the door and then I heard everything distinctly.

"Why did you go to see the neighbor? Tell me!"

"I'm frightened of the dark. I went up to ask for candles."

"But I told you not to go anywhere, ever, when I'm not here. We don't know those people. We don't know the first thing about them."

"He was friendly to me. But they didn't have any candles."

The conversation became less intelligible. They walked about the apartment. There was a loud kiss, and then, as I was going down the last steps, like a crystal glass smashing or a heavy shower breaking loose, I heard a harsh and abrupt: "Maurice!"

Yes, she said *Maurice*. She uttered it like the name of an evil pagan deity in a bedtime story for boys. That sound echoed in my skull as I strolled for the next hour.

Maurice had told me he'd be staying at Hotel Evropa. When he rang two days earlier and announced he was coming, I offered that he could sleep at our place, although I hoped he'd decline.

"And if some female company flutters by . . . ," he said with a laugh, "a few pretty doves?" Female company was perhaps why he didn't show up.

The first night he came at nine o'clock, the next at ten. When I opened up, the ringing of a wall clock came in from some other apartment in the building—together with Maurice and the odor of basement mold. Dirty echoes of the old mechanism accompanied both visitations, I recalled.

Coincidences are unnecessary. They arouse suspicions and deaden rationality, I thought, as Irena coldly accepted the flowers from his arms. Because we knew why he'd come. We also knew that in two or three hours' time he'd get up, say *au revoir* with a slight bow, and slowly descend the never-ending steps between the houses, all the way to the shore, and we knew we'd watch him from above until he disappeared behind the first corner, one hundred yards down the street, and think of him until he returned the next day, the last time, at around the same hour.

A conversation followed that was overshadowed by anticipation and loud music. She went to look for a vase, and within a few minutes the record player was blaring: *Summertime, time, time, time . . . child, the living's easy . . .*

I hate that song. I demanded that she turn it down, but Irena responded by increasing the volume even more. Maurice got up soon afterward and apologized in passing for his *dirty shoes*. He said he'd come and speak with us again the next day. Of course, I said, as I accompanied him to the door.

But he didn't turn up this evening. He was probably panting in the dark in Hotel Evropa, kneading the breasts of some unhappy prostitute. On the way back from my stroll, I stopped again at the door on the first floor. The power was still off and the town drowned in the night. In silence. I didn't hear a thing. They'd fallen asleep. My scarred neighbors were sleeping. Perhaps on the same bed which my father spent his last few nights on, I thought. He'd managed to drag himself to a presentation of his last book, only to then guzzle whiskey by the bottle and hasten the deterioration of what remained of his liver. When they sent him home after three weeks in hospital, he knew there was nothing more to hope for. He stopped swearing, but also talking to anyone. Seven days before he died, he kicked out the nurse responsible for his health, or for easing his death, and with the last of his strength went on to drain quart bottles of Johnnie Walker. They found him dead in the bathtub full of water—water full of feces, his books, and manuscripts. If he were still alive I'd say there was no essential difference between the two substances: the same old shit. That's what I'd say, although I've never read a single page of his writings. They laud his short stories, criticize his novels, and shower abuse on his poetry. He wrote a lot. He published all sorts of things and didn't care about criticism. As a boy, I'd peek into his book-filled study and was most often driven off with a roar: "Get out, you hoodlum. I'm writing!" he used to say, aided by alcohol.

"Father's writing; don't bother him," my mother whispered.

At his funeral there were just a few decrepit literati of his generation: grotesque figures steamrolled by modernism, packed away in comfortable apartments and senility. And Maurice. It was there that I made his acquaintance. He joined me under my umbrella, rubbing his shivering hands together.

"Don't worry. He didn't suffer," he said.

"What are you talking about?" I looked at him in confusion and noted that he was standing up close to me although I didn't know him at all.

"Sorry, I'm Maurice. Your father must have told you about me."

"Yes, yes, he did," I lied, wanting to end the conversation as soon as possible. I hadn't been in touch with my father since I was fifteen. He left after a fracas with my mother, after the fist in her face, which broke her nose and resulted in five stitches below her right eye. That could not be undone. I came home from school and found her sitting on the bed with the sheet crumpled over her face. White mottled with red. And crying. Tears seasoned with blood. He gathered up his things, manuscripts, and books, and left.

"So you're his son who adores spaghetti and hates soccer?" Maurice asked at the funeral.

"Amen," spoke the priest and interrupted the conversation.

He managed to push his business card into my hands and smile enigmatically before saying a curt goodbye and vanishing among the cypresses, glancing back at me and Irena.

She'd gotten out of bed again this evening, too. I could tell because the front door was locked. I didn't have a key, so I'd have to knock. She'd think it was Maurice, lock herself in the bathroom, and cry. Just now I heard her sneaking fearfully down the hall.

"Open up. It's me."

She kept silent. In the apartment next door a clock struck three. A dull *ding* and a more piercing *dong* hung in the air. But Maurice wasn't there.

"Speak louder," she said. She didn't recognize my voice deformed to a whisper.

"It's me. Irena, open the door."

"Louder . . ."

"Come on, stop this!" my voice rang out on the landing.

"Sing me something," she said and then I heard her laugh hysterically, swooning from her huge doses of medication.

I had to leave her in peace. After several minutes of hysteria she usually fell asleep, exhausted by fear and lulled by solitude. I'd go for another walk and wake her when I came back. And then, refreshed by sleep, she'd forget Maurice for a moment, hear my voice, and unlock without hesitation. I went out onto the street again. The cobblestones gave off heat, but my hands were cold and clammy. The night watchmen were sitting in the dark below the porch of a cafe—outside because the power was still off. They were keeping watch: seven sleepy old men, who from time to time lazily raised their heads. Cats on the square. No one on the streets. There were no longer any passersby in these hours when the darkness becomes densest. When nightmares are dreamed. When Irena dreamed of Maurice.

She first felt discomfort a month before. She woke up racked by stomach pain and took a few antacid tablets, not wishing to go to the doctor's. The following night her shoulder ached, and then the left breast, and after two days' respite the pain came in her legs and the back of her head. She developed huge dark rings under her eyes and her skin started to smell unusual—a sweetish stench. She showered ten times a day but couldn't do anything about it.

"Gawd, I'm decomposing. I stink like a corpse. I'm rotting." After such words I'd go up and hug her, hiding my fear-stricken expression. I didn't want to admit to myself either that I could smell it in her hair, on the sheets, in the air, and on my tongue.

One of the business cards in the pile I accidentally knocked over one morning while she slept on the couch between bouts of pain read: *Dr. Maurice, Clinic of St. Nicholas*. It was signed like an Egyptian witch doctor or oracle might, I thought. The great Dr. Maurice healed completely, and for a small surcharge you could get a prediction of the future over the next five years. If you paid for ten years, there was a twenty-percent discount. But it didn't say anything except *Dr. Maurice, Clinic of St. Nicholas*, and the phone number, which I dialed half an hour later. I was met with exaggerated, husky-voiced amiability. He purred like a cat, I thought, as he explained me the way to his office. We could come at five that afternoon, he said, but if that didn't suit us we could visit at any time of the day or night, he added cheerfully.

"No need. We'll come today at five. It's about Irena, my wife."

"Yes, yes."

I asked why he said yes and if he perhaps knew that she was ill, not me. And how he could assume it was to do with an illness when I hadn't indicated that in any way. Why didn't he assume that I wanted to talk with him about my father, for example?

"I'm a physician and I usually deal with the living," he said. Now I felt there had been a rude impertinence in my voice.

"Please forgive me. I'm a little excited and impatient," I conceded. "We'll come at five if that doesn't interfere with your commitments."

It didn't interfere with his commitments. But I had to tell Irena, she who stubbornly refused to see a doctor, that we were going to a clinic. I'd try to avoid her questions: "Who

is Maurice?" and "Why are we going to see him?" And if necessary—forced by my sick wife's insistence, which was not to
be refused—I'd reply with outright lies. Because all I could say
about Maurice was what I knew he knew about me: that I love
spaghetti and hate soccer. That's correct.

Long summer afternoons followed. We sat in the dimmed
apartment, waiting for the sun to go down and for the night
to bring some fresh air. She was gradually losing her wits. After
the medical examination at St. Nicholas's things only got worse.
Maurice told us that day to go home and wait for the results.
Detailed analyses of all bodily fluids had to be done, and that
would take a little while, he said. He suggested we go and rest,
and take a break from the city. He asked for a phone number to
contact us when the results were ready. I told him we were going
to the coast and planned to stay there for a month. Then we said
goodbye. Irena's face was pale. She complained that she was cold,
and she shivered.

"Go home, don't worry. Everything will be fine," he consoled
her. She didn't believe him.

When the blackout ended I was next to a neon sign for Lucky
Strike. Tints of green and red blinded my eyes, accustomed to the
darkness. At the same time, people woke up, startled by the flood
of light. When the power goes off, we never remember which
position of a switch turns the lightbulb on and which turns it
off. The lights went off again as I was going up to our apartment.
The flame of a candle was still flickering on the first floor, hidden
by the window frame. But there was no light upstairs. Irena was
still sleeping, I thought. Unless she'd unlocked the door, I'd have
to knock. Her illness and fear of Maurice put many obstacles
between us. The enigma of her illness spread like the carpet of an
unknown language or an ancient, long-dead alphabet, because
it was impossible to reach it with words. No comforting, prayer,
or suggestion could elicit a reasonable response.

The door was locked. I still didn't want to wake her. Tomorrow
I'd sleep a little on the beach. That's always bracing: I wake up

bathed in sweat and covered in sandy dust. And with the aureole of sleep in my eyes I lay my body in the sea. It was June when we last visited that place together. The water was rather cold and clear. Far from the town's bathing beaches. And beyond the reach of tourists' indolence, souvenirs, and orange-juice sellers. Fifteen people at most. Real quiet and rest. That was where I met Enzo's mother, and still I couldn't describe the feeling I had after that conversation. Something grave? Worrying? That was guessing. Now I held my ear to our door but didn't hear anything. Then there was a rustle and the smooth surface of an object that shouldn't have been under the brass lock. I saw it was a white envelope. A sealed white surprise. Anxiety and fear rose in me as I turned it over and over in my hands. I looked for a sign, some mark that would explain what was inside. Inevitably, I thought of Maurice. That was the only thing I could do that evening because everything unknown, fatal, or liberating was tied to his name in those days. All substantial matters, our lives, and moods were condensed in Maurice's words, which we awaited. Morning was drawing near. The letter was in the inner pocket of my blazer. It would remain there until I sat down on a wooden chair on the terrace of the hotel that opens at five, ordered a coffee, and read the newspaper for a while. Until I'd breathed enough fresh air. It would be out of place to remark that the sun was rising, I thought. But the yellow gleam of the sea really did invigorate me that day: salvation from the agony of insomnia. From Maurice, who I knew in some strange way could appear only at night. Long after the setting of the sun.

The waiter brought me coffee and a glass of lemonade. That reminded me of Irena, who was now dreaming the last scraps of a nightmare. Not for much longer. Not for much longer . . . The light would wake her. And then it would start all over again and last until evening: "You met him on the beach. You strolled together eating ice cream . . . He told you everything. Admit it! You know everything, but you're a coward and afraid to say it. Be a man for once, for God's sake. Have some guts. I knew all along what was coming . . ."

Three night watchmen, tormented by the battle against sleep, sat down at the next table and flung out their heavy legs like ducks. Their faces were the same. They waved hello to me: perhaps the darkness hadn't been so thick as I stood in the square during the night. I nodded back. Cats came along behind them. Equally old and lethargic creatures. They sleep during the day, hidden from the blazing August sun that had already begun to throb: a drumming in the epicenter of the town, concentric circles of heat that swept over everything, penetrating bodies, streets, and the cut stone of houses. I held the letter up to the sun. It revealed the outlines of a folded piece of paper. I also felt a paper clip at the bottom—something was attached. My coffee steamed. Here was the cigarette vendor. Today I needed something very strong and flavorsome. Through the gray rings of smoke there also came the newspaper boy.

"Murder, sir. Hot off the press," he said. I reached him some money. He thanked me for the tip and moved on. The old guys were already leaning over page three, shaking their heads. They didn't know the man in the picture. But they blamed the mayor for the frequent blackouts.

"It's dangerous at night," I heard their hoarse voices.

"There are all sorts about. Starting with the stevedores . . ."

Working at the square allowed them to feel like hellhounds of the street, at least for a short while. Of the seven of them, three had been doing the same job for nineteen years, they said. And Petar for twenty. He'd seen all sorts of things. He remembered everything. The square used to be a peaceful place, he said, until the ships started coming from Mexico and Argentina—and until the tourists started pissing in the corners.

I opened the envelope and put on my glasses. In front of me was a page torn out of a medical magazine. Under the title "Healing Hands" stood Maurice, leaning over a sleeping child in a hospital ward, in a green smock, his head turned toward the photographer. He looked considerably older, with grizzled brows and exhausted eyes, his eyes red from the flash. A note was attached with a paper clip and read: *Scar.* An arrow pointed

came back, there would be only one thing left to do: to sit in the dining room or on the balcony and wait for Maurice. For the last time.

Our neighbor lady climbed out of the water to sit on the seaweed-covered rock, shivering with cold. She radiated hidden thoughts. She didn't want to look me in the eyes but stared out to sea, and her hand traced the orange streak of the scar on her thigh.

"The water is cold today. We'd better go back," I called.

"Yes. It is cold."

I lay down on the sand. Elvis looked at the sun. Red Elvis looked at the sun, while Maurice slept the sleep of the dead in one of the dank rooms of Hotel Evropa. He lay with crossed arms in the shade of the heavy stone walls and waited for night. When, bleary-eyed, he'd drag himself outside and walk up the cobblestone street sluggishly to our building.

I was woken by drops falling on my back. Only now had she come out of the water. With a towel around her head, she was like a caricature of a nun.

"You can keep on sleeping," she said.

"No. It's enough. Are you going?"

"I might stay a little longer, I don't know . . ."

I suggested we drop in at the Alexandria together.

"We could have fish if you like."

"Okay. Yes, fish is okay," she said. And after a minute's silence, "Please, I don't want to talk about Maurice. Don't ask me to."

"Maurice?" I blurted out. "He's coming to see us tonight—"

She interrupted me: she knew that already, or at least she assumed it.

"I saw him the first night. He was going around in the court-yard. And then he headed up the stairs."

Her fingers moved toward the scar again. Toward her fore-head. Hesitation, and then:

"The envelope at your door . . . the white envelope . . . That was me—" she said and stopped. She put on her glasses.

"I took it up last night. During the blackout. I wanted to warn you, so you know who you're dealing with. This scar—look at it again, please. It's clear for all to see. But of course, you don't know . . . He doesn't mean anything to you," she said and pointed to the scar, as if that were Maurice.

"He pushed us through a glass door while I was holding my small son. You can see the result on my legs and forehead, and with him across his left cheek. Did you notice? Then he cut into his own biceps. Imagine him grinning as he did it—as he rent his own flesh! You can't, of course. You're a decent man," she said.

She picked up her book, shook the sand off the cover, and put it in her bag. Once again, I didn't manage to read the title.

"That was his alibi for *an accident,*" she continued.

"He'd point to his left biceps and say all three of us had tripped over toys scattered on the floor while we embraced and fallen through the glazed balcony door. He told the same story to everyone: friends, the police," she said, as she squeezed herself into her tight jeans.

"I didn't want to take him to court," she sobbed.

"But even today I live in fear of him coming back with that same rage. It's a good thing my boy doesn't remember anything. He was just a baby," she said.

She hadn't seen Maurice since that night. She thought he'd insist on them living together again, but after he'd spilt the blood of her child it would be unseemly to do something like that and agree to live under the same roof as that monster, she told me.

While we walked along the narrow path between the olive trees back to town, to the Alexandria, she was silent and looked around with eyes wide open. It reminded me of Irena and the way she was shadowed by the same kind of inarticulate fear.

With the first glass of wine she continued to talk about herself, as well as the boy and Him, whose name she only ever spoke in a hushed whisper. A specific tone of whisper was reserved for Him, which was felt more by the body—a kind of prickle or irritation—than it was heard.

"We lay there in bandages. My boy could hardly breathe. The first morning in hospital they took me in a wheelchair to see him. He was in the southern wing of the building. The doctor said the gash was deep but I needn't worry. Everything would be alright. The blood loss could have been fatal for a child, you see," she said.

"I leaned over the aluminum bed and realized that his little hands had been tied to the bars. 'They have to be, so he doesn't touch the wound,' the doctor said. Imagine, he thought that was necessary! The little tot lay on his tummy and rolled his delirious eyes with crusts of dried tears . . . For heaven's sake!"

She fell silent, her gaze fixed on the wall. She came alive with a start after a sip of wine and looked at me with eyes full of Maurice.

"My God. I don't understand how he can have any friends," she said. And after a few seconds' silence, "Sorry, I was forgetting about you. Maybe it's different in your case. But I—" she faltered, "I really don't know how he can have any friends."

"He's a bad man," she whispered. "He works at the Clinic of St. Nicholas and speaks the death sentence to incurably ill patients. And I think he does that because he likes it," she continued.

"Our wrangles and quarrels culminated when the unfortunate people started coming to our place. He'd spend hours with them before he told them the truth. And then he'd leave them in excruciating uncertainty. One afternoon, a bald fourteen-year-old girl turned up at the door looking for *Mr. Maurice*. I couldn't stand it anymore. The poor child. I told her *the doctor* wasn't there and would be gone for several days," she stopped and lit another cigarette.

"He found out and was furious. He went stark raving mad. It was that night that the scars happened. We couldn't stay together anymore. For goodness' sake: dying people walking about our apartment with that freak, touching everything, leaving traces . . . I couldn't take it. Everything reeked of death. He even took them in to my son's cot so they could look at him sleeping and stroke him on the head."

"You know, each of them had a . . . how should I put it . . . a very specific smell," she said and started to cry, and I knew very well what she meant. We finished our lunch. She wiped away her tears with her napkin. She noticed I was looking absently through the window.

"Are you still there?" she asked.

"Yes, yes, I'm here," I said with a smile induced by the simple pleasure of good food.

"I don't know how he can have any friends," she repeated.

I thought of my father. And of his funeral. Maurice stood beside the coffin. He held his arms crossed behind his back and from time to time wiped his glasses with a hankie. I tried to remember Irena's face. She wore a black coat, and the lapels of her silk shirt were showing. An embroidered rose was on the left. Or maybe two roses? Her face eluded me. I remember her hair was tied up in a ponytail with a lace ribbon. Black. Was she wearing glasses? I forget.

The waiter brought a candle to the table. She said it was time: the food had been nice, but now she had to go home.

"Shall we go back together?" she asked.

"I'll stay a bit longer," I said and escorted her to the door. They offered me coffee, but I decided to go back to the terrace of the hotel and wait for the sunset there.

The old guys were in their place. At the same table. They chatted less than in the morning, still drowsy from their daytime sleep. The sea took on an orange hue. The sun set behind our backs. Irena, I imagined, was now on the balcony watering the plants. The guys got up, stuck their rolled-up newspapers under their arms, and looked into the sky. They exchanged glances and nodded. Time to leave. They slowly got up and headed off for the square.

On the way back I called in at a bakery. I bought some fresh bread, which no one would eat, but the smell spreads through the rooms and it becomes more agreeable: almost *familial*.

As I climbed the stairs I broke off some small pieces from the end and nibbled them with my front teeth. No one was home on the first floor. The neighbors had let down the blinds and turned off the lights. She mentioned that she'd be going into town with her son that evening. She'd take him to the circus and then to an Italian restaurant for dinner. They did that once a week, she said, although I believed they were only going because of Maurice, who might be around that evening. Close at hand.

Irena heard my steps and opened the door while I was coming up the stairs. She clapped her hands, happy to see me, but I was blinded by the light that came from the apartment and couldn't make her out properly. The fluttering silhouette of her dressing gown let through narrow beams of neon. She shut the door with a crash.

"He was here," she chirped. "Everything's all right, thank God! He said everything would be fine and nothing's wrong with me. Gawd . . . Can you believe it?!"

Big dark rings under her eyes. Blue lips. I looked in her bleary eyes that for the first time in ages radiated joy. A false and bloody joy. She rushed up to hug me and stayed in that position, flush against my body, for a few moments. I realized that if she let go she wouldn't be able to keep standing, and a little while later she vomited a substance the color of rotten cherries.

I went to look for Maurice the next morning at Hotel Evropa, but they said he'd left before dawn.

"He left a letter, sir. For you . . . 'For the man with the gray sideburns.' That's obviously you," the receptionist said.

Another letter. Again, cats and old guys out on the hotel terrace. Except that this time things were explained. Another walk to the beach. I didn't meet anyone this time. Later, after returning home, I told Irena we had to go back. To *our* city. I had some urgent commitments at work, I lied. Didn't I consider this town *ours* too? she wondered. "No, I suppose not," I said. She didn't ask anything more.

The rainy season begins at the end of September. From our eighth-floor apartment in the city center you have a view all the way to the park speckled with hints of yellow. Irena doesn't like trees. If you lean over the railing of the balcony you can also see the centennial cypress at the southern edge of the well-treed park, to the left. It's my favorite. She's much more fond of flowers. She says they're more intimate and delicate. The geraniums she grows on the terrace wither and enter a phase of hibernation. Just like the memory of Maurice, who we didn't mention until the last evening at the sea. But as we sit dully staring at the television and cracking our sweaty knuckles, each for ourselves, I feel we're thinking about that. I remember the corpulent lady downstairs, her boy, and the scar. My father's selected works have been on the shelves for a little while now. I'll start reading them when all this is over. Page after page, book after book, slowly, as if I'm burying him one more time.

    I watch Irena as she wakes up. She says she's hot. Pains. I open the window, and she throws off the woolen blanket. She rubs the now noticeably rounded, shiny skin of her belly for a long time. I thought the illness would be faster. *She has less than six months left*, Maurice wrote. And that is also how long our children have, twins, whom Irena tenaciously bears.

# All That

DANILO SHOULDN'T GO, I said. *Those rituals are a terrible experience. Children shouldn't go there. They don't realize what it means when someone dies. Death confuses and frightens them. So why try to explain it in such a brutal way?*

*You're right, Marina replied. He can skip going to the house. He'll be going to the cemetery on Sunday anyway—that's enough. But imagine: this morning he asked me for a black shirt. "Mom, I want to wear a black shirt," he said. "Why?" I asked. "I have to look sad tomorrow," he answered. It's a half-day at school today. He shouldn't go. There's enough upsetting things in store for him already, Marina said. We'll ask him, I said. I think that's best.*

"Danilo."

"Yes?"

"Come here for a tick."

"Would you like not to go to school today?"

"I don't know."

"Just have a think. If you don't want to, that's all right . . ."

"It's not all right."

"What makes you say that?"

"I don't know."

"We can go to the lake if you want. We'll roast chestnuts and go fishing. Mom will make us a packed lunch . . ."

He never refused a trip to the lake.

"Great, can we go straightaway?" he beamed.

"Right away, young man," I said.

We tanked up the car and set off. It had been raining all week.

And it would be the same today, I thought. But I'd promised we'd go fishing. There are usually no fish in weather like this. If there's mist low on the water, it's risky to go out far from the shore. We'd just row around the islands and then make a fire on one of them. Our favorite pastime, I thought. I was glad he wasn't at school today.

"Dad, have you ever been to a cemetery?" he asked while we were driving.

"Of course I have."

"What did you do there?"

His seemingly simple questions demanded careful answers.

"I went for a walk."

"Why there, of all places?"

"Let's say I needed some peace and quiet, young man. You and your sister make one hell of a racket sometimes."

"You went to the cemetery because of us? To have some quiet?"

"Yes."

"Weren't you afraid? So many people lying there in silence?"

"What do you mean 'lying there in silence'?"

"Well, when a person dies they're silent."

"Yes, among other things," I said, trying to end the conversation. I was starting to glimpse his concept of death and dying. We had never talked about that. Perhaps we should have. But this wasn't the time. He explained that at school they wanted him to carry the wreath. Marija and Ana would walk behind him.

"Dad, they're not going to carry anything. I'm the class president," he said looking toward the village. Its roofs were growing ever redder, ever closer.

"Danilo, do you know what happens there?"

"Dad, can we drop in at Petar's first?" he asked, avoiding an answer.

"No. We're going to the house. We'll call him from there."

That was a mistake, I thought. The wrong words. It's hard to talk about death. And even harder to explain to children the rituals that accompany it in this rotten country. When my father died, I was just six. A chip off the old block, people said with

sighs and tears coming on. I only remember it vaguely: my sister
was crying, my grandmother held me on her lap, endless can-
dies and cuddles for the whole year to come. My mother passed
away seven years later. Her death was much worse. She lay in a
hospital bed for three months and in the end gave up the ghost
without a whimper. If she'd gone like my father—suddenly and
violently in a traffic accident—I think it would have been easier
for me to take. As we were holding vigil over her beside the coffin
at home that first day, as I stood there with sweaty palms at her
head, Uncle Petar, my father's eldest brother, came up. "Stop that
wretched sniveling, for God's sake!" he hissed furiously through
clenched teeth. "Go to the bathroom, I'll stand in for you. Go
and wash. I don't want to see any more tears. You're the head of
the household now, you mustn't cry!" he said sternly. People kept
coming like a river. And I was a little white pebble that didn't
dare to budge beneath that torrent. I stuck through to the end,
without another tear. After the funeral, silence was the way out.
But I guess I still hate Petar today. I've never told him that. Now
he lives in the village, not far from our weekend house, and rarely
comes to the city.

"Petar!"

"He's not coming out. He's probably in the forest collecting
wood. I'll ask him to lend us a few logs."

"Petar! Maybe he's sleeping."

"Grouchy old hermit."

"Don't call him that, Dad. He's good, and old. He said he
was seventy."

*Good, and old.* And *seventy*, he said. As a matter of fact, he's
sixty-three. Not one year more. My father didn't speak with him
for the last ten years of his life—a banal family argument over
inheritance. When I was a boy I often met him at Grandma's.
My mother liked me to spend Sundays there. Petar, me, and
Grandma would have lunch together. And everything was all
right until my mother's funeral.

"He's my *bro* in the village," Danilo said, looking at the red
roof at the foot of the hill. There really was something appealing
about the old guy. When we got back from fishing, I'd let him

go for a visit. He's obsessed with the boy. I'd send along some cigarettes too. He was poisoning himself with the locally grown tobacco.

"Danilo, bring the oars. So, young man, it seems we have everything here: bait, tarpaulin, sandwiches, matches . . ."

"All hunky-dory, boss," he said cheerfully.

Sycamore leaves were scattered over the smooth water. A mist was falling. But we'd row between the little islands and make a fire on one of them. Danilo loves going in the boat. As we glided through the silence, he leaned over the bow and tried to pick the water lilies. He rolled up his sleeves and dragged his arms through the water. There was no wind. The air was balmy. The shoreline of the island could be glimpsed.

"We'll land there and make a fire."

"Fog. I hate fog."

"Why now *I hate fog*? I mean, you don't have to like it, but why does it bother you?"

"It doesn't bother me. I just don't like it. Just like I hate bean stew."

"All right, Danilo, moody prince of darkness. Let's row a bit faster to the desert island."

"I don't like it when people die . . . and all that."

He doesn't like it when people die *and all that*. The generalization is disturbing. All what? But I think I know exactly what he wanted to say. I felt a hundred words on the tip of my tongue that could explain all that. Or a hundred shapes, a hundred secrets, fears, a hundred inarticulate feelings compressed into one. Into one? I felt all that at my mother's funeral, with a dry face and eyes. My attention split between the dark coffin descending into the ground and the trembling vigil of the multitude of black shapes. On the left—as I realized later—was Aunt Marta; diagonally to the right, next to the white gravestone, a man with a hooked nose chewing on a straw; straight ahead, a cypress obscured the face of a woman; on the right, wrinkled hands crumpled a handkerchief. A crucifix dangled on the priest's chest.

"Danilo, the cord."

The lake has no surface currents, so boats aren't tied up at the shore. I do it for him, for fun. The simulation of an adventure: a small, harmless flight from reality, I thought. A mutiny on the *Bounty*.

"We'll sit here, and make the fire over there."

"It's damp. Dad, it's better we make it here and sit under a tree."

We laid out our things on the tarpaulin.

"Bait, sandwiches, matches, chestnuts, sandwiches, more bait. It's all here, Dad."

"And now, off to hunt monsters."

He brought the box of worms, but carefully, as if he was carrying an ancient relic. The red box looked much larger in the boy's hand. He smiled and pensively rummaged around, trying to find the one that would go down best with the voracious fish of the lake. An experienced angler. An old laker.

"Here . . . a tasty little worm."

"Good choice, ol' laker."

We cast out and then lit the fire. With its soothing crackling behind our backs, we waited for the fish to bite. The fog was thicker. The lights in the village faded. We should have brought a gas lamp so they could see us better from the shore if we missed the mooring. But it usually disperses in the evening.

"Dad, I'll be carrying the wreath," he said all of a sudden.

"Okay. And?"

"Nothing else. I'll carry the wreath, and Marija and Ana will walk behind me."

"Uh-huh."

He'd carry the wreath, and Marija and Ana would walk behind him. The way he said it suggested he had no idea what he was supposed to do. As if he was going to put the wreath on his back and walk around the house with it. It's cruel to burden children with this kind of nonsense. Why should they come to know death as a ritual—a rustic ceremony devoid of meaning and simply morbid?

"And where are you going to carry the wreath?"

"Somewhere there."

"Please be more exact. That's no way to speak with your

father. Admit that you don't know where you're going to carry it. I want to help you!"

"I know. Marija and Ana know what happens there. They've already been to a funeral."

"Good." I wanted to say: Do you know what it all looks like? Do you know what it all looks like where you have to put the flowers?

His rod began to shake. Concentric circles spread out across the surface of the water and disappeared in the mist.

"Pull it in, boy. It's yours!"

"It's huge, Dad! Look!"

Disappointment followed. The rotten branch really was large. Springs at the bottom stir up the fall's layer of silt and rubbish. If you fish close to the shore, near the hills, these things can happen.

He put his rod down on the ground. He took the branch, threw it into the fire, and watched as it crackled and popped. It burned, hissed, and turned to ash. His little revenge: the execution of a shameless cheat. We cast out again.

"Marija said we'd see some strange things. But we needn't be scared because it's normal. I mean, it's normal for adults to behave that way. That's what she said. I asked her what she'd seen there. 'I saw women in black with black scarves around their heads kissing the dead body and screaming. And crying. And then everyone stood in a circle, and everyone cried. And they laid their wreaths around it. Lots of tears.' She said we have to go around that circle, shake hands with everyone, and be sad. She didn't do that but she watched the others."

Some blue showed through. Within half an hour the mist would be gone. You could feel the silent movement, the tiny particles of water vapor creeping. Mist slithers like a python after slowly digesting its prey, I thought.

"Mist slithers like a python after slowly digesting its prey."

"What did you say, Dad?"

"Nothing. We have to go back. It'll get dark soon."

"Are we going to see Petar?"

"No. You can go and see Petar. I'll wait in the car."

He clapped his hands and got up to hug me.

"Let's go, young man. The journey begins! Untie the boat and unfurl the sails."

I rowed with my face toward the hill. I didn't know it was so tall. The mist turned to haze, and the haze to an old church with a crumbling bell tower. Here was also the cemetery, at the top. Ash-gray fragments of crooked slabs, stone contours of rituals, and paths between empty graves. *My condolences*, you're supposed to say and mechanically hold out your hand. A throaty sob in response. And again: my condolences. And again. And again. My condolences.

"Petar!"

"Can I go?"

"Wait."

"Petar! I'm sure he can't hear me. I think I see a light . . . Yes, there's a light. Can I go now?"

"Hang on. Take the cigarettes. And here's a pencil and paper. If he's not home, leave a message."

"A message?"

"Yes."

"What should I write?"

"For heaven's sake, what could you write?"

On Thursday afternoons he was alone at home. On Thursdays we visited Natalija and Simon: cooking day. We'd spend a few hours preparing a new dish together. We'd been doing that for months. On Thursdays Danilo went to his English course: he came home from school at three and left the house again at five, so when we came home at six he wasn't there. On the dining-room table, this time, there was a neatly written message: *Mom and Dad. Hana has died. Danilo*, he signed at the bottom. Usually he wrote: *Dear Mom and Dad. I've gone out. I'll be back at seven. Can't wait to see you.*

The girl had leukemia and came to school until the very last day, in her wheelchair. When he came home, we didn't want to mention all that. Until he said: "Mom, I have to wear a black shirt."

"Why?"

"Tomorrow I need to look sad."

"Do you need to look it, or are you really?"

"I don't know," he said and started to quietly sob himself to sleep.

Why was he taking so long at Petar's? It had been forty minutes since he went up.

"Petar! Danilo! Petar!"

For days after my mother's funeral I'd wanted to go and see him and start to cry just to spite him. But my anger left no room for tears. Even in front of the mirror it didn't work. Later all that passed. I feel more at ease now and think of my mother's death and the funeral much less often. When I meet Petar or go to the cemetery.

"Petar?" I called and knocked on the door. "Danilo?"

I pushed down on the handle.

A smell of roast quinces filled the space. The house was empty. An icon of Saint Nicholas next to the window. The window next to the icon. And in its frame two lights that came bobbing through the darkness.

"Hi, how are you?" he asked from the door.

"Fine. Well enough. Where's Danilo?"

"Out the front. He's got a flashlight. Are you staying?"

"No. We have to go back."

I made for the door. He thanked me for the cigarettes as he crammed wood into the stove.

"You're going straightaway?"

"Yes."

"See you then."

He slammed the stove's hatch hard.

"Take the flashlight with you. It's dark. When you get to the car, leave it under the water can."

The narrow path wound down the hill. Then past the lake and the old fishpond, back to the village.

"Dad? Can we go via the cemetery?"

I never liked going there without a reason. I took flowers for the anniversaries of my mother's and father's death. I came to funerals when one of my relatives died. Once or twice a year. Condolences. The funeral. The third morning. Forty days after death. The ghastly decorations of mortality. Deformed quotes from the Bible. Because when you hold vigil at a person's grave three days after their burial, you're doing nothing other than waiting for their resurrection.

"Can we go via the cemetery?" he asked again.

I shone my flashlight in his face, turned, and kept going. He didn't come after me.

"Wait a tick. Can we go via the cemetery?"

"Why, Danilo?"

"I don't know."

"There you go again! It seems you don't know anything today."

"I think I'll find out if we go that way."

"Stop going on about it, please. What do you think you're going to find out if you get the spooks up in that bumpkin graveyard?"

"I'm not afraid. Petar took me there this evening. We were sitting on a slab and . . ."

"What are you saying? Petar took you to the cemetery?!"

"He said I should imagine him dead. He lay down, crossed his arms, and closed his eyes. He taught me what to say and how to behave at the funeral. He's kind."

"We're going. Turn off the flashlight."

I realized I ought to do something. When we got home to the city I'd suggest that we spare him the unpleasant experience. He didn't have to go. We'd come to the lake again on Sunday. And I wouldn't let him talk to Petar.

"He says he's going to die very soon, Dad."

"Oh, don't you worry about him!" I said as we were driving back to the main road. The lake drowned in the night. There was no mist over the wide road. The white dashes glided past in the middle of the road. Crisp and clear. Soporific. Marina would be making dinner now. Something tasty. I could just imagine her flour-covered hands. Danilo fell asleep. I'd drive more slowly. The beams of passing headlights lit up his face and his arms folded on his chest. His eyelashes trembled and his eyes rolled wildly beneath his eyelids. He was dreaming.

The crucifix beneath the blurred rearview mirror danced mutely as we traveled toward the city.

# Rats and Writers

*Hum! Hum! said the king. I have good reason to believe
that somewhere on my planet there is an old rat. I hear him
at night. You can judge this old rat. From time to time
you will condemn him to death. Thus his life will depend on
your justice. But you will pardon him on each occasion;
for he must be treated thriftily. He is the only one we have.*

ANTOINE DE SAINT-EXUPÉRY,
*THE LITTLE PRINCE*

*. . . and so Lozano looks at the floor and allows the words
to play on their own while he waits for them, just like
Calagasta hunters wait to catch the giant rats alive.*

JULIO CORTÁZAR, "TARA"

PEOPLE, AS A rule, are irresistibly reminiscent of their pets. They
take on their looks and habits. They begin to piss and to eat at
the same time. They turn in for the night and go outside together.
One man kept a rat in his one-room apartment for years—a gray,
gluttonous animal that he fed on chicken. Fritz the rat had only
one incisor. He broke off the other as a baby when gnawing on
a Coca-Cola bottle, I said, but no one was listening. Stories
about Fritz, endless narrations about his red eye and almost
human habits no longer interested anyone. Now I resign myself
to silence. I write. Orgies of worn-out words and events in the

life of one rat have become a part of memory that people no longer speak about with passion while smoking and drinking. Every rat has its hour. An expert on the application of psychoanalysis to animals, our friend Dr. Osvald Petričević, got to know Fritz in detail through several one-hour sessions. Whenever he left his office with the rat on his shoulder, he'd only talk about one thing: "Fritz—the triumph of form over content! Fritz—a man among rats! A postmodernist in the sewer of modernism!" All this time, Fritz would let out shrieks of contentment, already prepared for an abundant feast of fresh chicken. But as I said: no one is interested in stories about Fritz anymore. Besides, they tell me I'm incorrigibly egoistic. Exactly. Because the sentences I've just deleted resembled the famous words, *I am going to talk to you about myself on the subject of Shakespeare.* That's an impermissible and harmful manner in prose writing. I started to speak about Fritz and at the same time—like an infatuated high-school girl—identified myself with the main character of the story, the most charming rat to ever walk the earth. He had something of Wilde's daintiness and Bogart's refined elegance. But I say: Play it again, Sam! Repetition is the mother of learning, Sam, but the evil stepmother of literature. You've been telling the same story for years, and you haven't realized that no one says those words to you anymore, *Play it again, Sam.* I think it's a very exciting story. But still I'll avoid telling it for the umpteenth time now, as if I had no other stories to tell. The dark stain in Fritz's biography is one of the main reasons for the silence I've vowed to keep. It's hard to write about dark stains. Such things usually fade to a blemish, a minor bruise on the body of brilliant narration—Fritz's vita, his biography. The only other detail I'll disclose is that Fritz's master was my lover and that we were no less passionate about each other than old Jorge and María. A blind love bonded us, seasoned by the titillating gray hairs of Fritz's fur—whenever we discovered them on the tips of our tongues, they aroused us to an ardor. I could tell you as much about rats as I can about my parents, with the distinction that the tale about the life of Branislav and Kaćuša would be much less interesting. I owe them a debt of gratitude for bringing me up well. Without the subtle manners of the upper middle class and an ample private library I'd definitely have needed much longer to arrive at an understanding of what it means to love and be loved. But those days are past. I used to love, and now I don't love anymore. I used to be loved, but the phone's been silent for days like a dead rat in the basement. My salvation is in writing, I said, and I was right. That's how *Rats and Writers* came about, my first novel, which will never be published. There are many reasons for this, but most serious criticisms are to do with its evident documentariness, which I was unable to break free of to the desired extent. There were enough other scandals in 49 K. Street that I was unable to cope with. Publishing *Rats and Writers* would only have poured oil on the fire, and my intentions were obviously very different. I started writing for Fritz, to wash away the dark stain, although in the end I saw it was indelible. I started noting things down for my dear friend, whose caresses I still feel on my flesh. I started writing because they are both deep under the ground today and deserve the redemption I promised them at the grave, and perhaps I haven't lived up to that task. Every night I pick up the manuscript, four hundred typed pages, and weep. *Rats and Writers* is essentially a beautiful novel crying out to be read. But I dare not go back on the word I gave to myself. I'll also tell you that Fritz and his master—my close friend—died the same day under rather strange circumstances, to say the least. Strange to you perhaps, but not to me, since I've been initiated into the secrets of the dark basements and passages of the city's sewers, with red eyes that temperamentally gleam in the dark, and ghastly, dread-filled screams. *Rats and Writers* reveals some of the mysteries clad in the furry gray pelts so pleasant to touch. And I'd say that my four hundred pages have turned into a good-hearted shaggy monster that hides away, having realized its power and the ruinous consequences should it ever be revealed. Let things stay that way. Manuscripts don't burn, but they are eaten by mice. It's different with my text because if a rat greased its chin, that would be reminiscent of cannibalism. Not to mention the self-destructive obliteration of their illustrious and largely unknown ratological history. In one of his lectures, our dear Dr.

Petričević wisely inferred that the myth about rats as a metaphysical evil spread not thanks to the bubonic plague in medieval Europe but most of all because of the mistaken belief that the red eyes, which in truth only a quarter of the race have, were a sign that Satan had a hand in their creation. Fritz had one red and one black eye. As did Pope Pius XII, Petrarch, and Erasmus of Rotterdam. Need we say any more about such Satanic insinuations? Rats are also ascribed an ignoble role in the Cold War and the spread of nuclear waste in the countries of Eastern Europe, as well as a plethora of crimes as dubious as they are bizarre. *Rats and Writers* explains this in detail, along with many other incidental quandaries, as I've said. Unfortunately, no one wants to listen anymore. Repetition makes stories uninteresting but at the same time lends them a patina of myth and legend, which to an extent is soothing and gives hope. The stories stagnate in dank corridors of text. Years pass, and then they emerge again in full glory, ready for new ears, new eyes, and a new Hollywood. Centuries pass, tinged with nullity, epochs torn by decline, and they return lavishly ornamented with new meaning. That is the fate I wish for *Rats and Writers*. Dr. Petričević had the honor of reading a few excerpts, which I pretended were from the manuscript of a good, anonymous friend. He asked if he could keep them—a request I was unable to fulfill. I believed he suspected something, although he knew I have no authorial pretensions. He gave the pages back three days later without a single word of criticism, and I resisted the temptation to ask, aware that I was writing for future generations and that people's petty conceits mustn't hinder me in that. New civilizations are already sowing their seed, and I will reap the shiniest spikes of grain. You can hardly speak of any *shine* today. All just ordinary stories, which I still couldn't circumvent when creating *Rats and Writers*. They too sometimes contain fragments of palimpsests of ancient times when the forests shone with a red gleam. Several specimens really do deserve an author's attention even if everyone knows about them and children talk about them out of boredom, laughing about the grotesque death of *a rat* in a bathtub of boiling water or the famous pornographic film where a black dwarf fucks a large male. Do you see now why I spoke of the *dark stain* in Fritz's biography? The rat chronicles of K. Street also can't boast of any particular imaginativeness. Everyone talked about the same things, blind to Fritz's exploits and the subtle charm of his rattish aristocraticness. They were more interested in the story about the author of the book *100 Ways to Kill a Rat* than in Fritz's post-structuralist exercises in style. They preferred to listen to the tale about the rat that gnawed through a tin of biscuits and stayed there until it had eaten every single one, down to the last crumb, after which it was so bloated that it couldn't get out. When they opened it, they found the rat sprawling on its back, queasy and rolling its eyes, and raving deliriously, immobilized by the huge quantity of food, and vomiting. They devised nineteen more ways of killing that they afterward elaborated and sent to the author of the disputable book, hoping he'd include them in the following sixth edition. My neighbor from number 22 was especially proud of his discovery. You take an ordinary bathing sponge and pluck it apart into pieces half the size of a pack of cigarettes. Then you soak them in wine vinegar and the acid makes them shrink to the size of sugar cubes. Roll these in bread-crumbs and put them in a rat-infested corner of your choosing. The voracious creatures rush up and swallow them whole, it was believed. Since a rat's gastric acid is one of the most powerful chemicals in the world of living organisms, it neutralizes the acid in the fateful morsel and the sponge slowly begins to spread, spread, and spread, while the unfortunate creatures run around in a frenzy. The stomach bloats to bursting point, and then a painful "Acidic Death" ensues, which is the name of the recipe. Another method of execution promotes heroin as the method-ologically most efficient means of eradicating rats, as opposed to the much less advisable use of cocaine, which changes the nor-mally good-natured rats into beasts—primed bombs ready to take it out on a Bengal tiger and a rhinoceros together. "Death Comes in a Yellow Coach" elaborates several ways to first get a rat addicted to narcotics, and then you radically curtail its satis-faction. The most complex option demands the prior establish-ment of a minifarm of well-nourished turkeys that you turn into hardened addicts by injecting them with a steadily increasing daily dose of heroin. Rats' appetite for poultry is well known, so after slaughter the turkeys are expertly carved and the tissue cleanly separated from even the tiniest of bones. This method of cultivation allows a level of up to five percent heroin to be attained in their blood and meat, which the rats devour with delirious pleasure. If you reduce the rats' daily dose, their craving for heroin becomes unbearable, and the only meat that contains it is their own: the epilogue is clear. Fritz liked only very young chicken and you couldn't entice him with cheap processed meat. He had a nose for good things, I said, but there's no one who attentively looks me in the eyes and nods from time to time. There's no one to listen anymore, not even when I start to tell the story of the infamous Horatio Ognjenović, whose fame spread far beyond the bounds of K. Street. The old guy had very deft fingers. Some of the rat traps from his workshop even came under the hammer at Christie's auction house, and it was rumored that one of them, a real masterpiece of Horatio's imagination, made it onto the shelves of a Smithsonian museum. I can't corroborate that, but whoever had the honor of seeing Horatio's rat traps certainly doesn't need much convincing to believe stories that are even more illusory. The workshop was located in the old nuclear shelter at the very end of the street. The large hexagonal space was adorned by three symmetrically arranged Corinthian columns, while the walls were decorated with stylized reproductions of Roman mosaics in volcanic glass, which Horatio devotedly polished. On the wall opposite the door was a painting of Dionysus with streams of red wine flowing from his hands stretched heavenward. An unraveled Hebrew scroll lay on the ground by his legs, with seven rats around it immersed in reading. Old Horatio always used to pose with his rat traps in front of that scene when he was in a good mood and allowed one of the annoying television crews to enter his subterranean kingdom. Rat traps, plural? Perhaps it suffices to speak of just one to fully understand the essence of Horatio's poetics. He considered it his masterpiece, and it could only be viewed by the handpicked guests at Horatio's annual banquet traditionally held on March

15, the day of Caesar's death. When I was invited for the first time, the central marble pedestal was occupied by a huge block covered in fine red silk fringed with gold, and the front shone with the words *Caesar Gaius Julius* embroidered in silver, and on the line below, stitched in somewhat smaller letters, *Orbi et Urbi*. The pleasant chatting and assorted gossiping, in which Fritz was a very frequent word, were interrupted first softly, and then ever louder by the rumble of Wagner's *Twilight of the Gods*. The lights changed from a milky sfumato to a bright red, dimming, and when the music became unbearably loud *he* would appear at the door, cloaked in a black mantle, his face pale from the finest powders: Horatio Ognjenović, *god among rats and apostle among people*, as a critic from our country's most prominent monthly review of literature, culture, and social questions noted. The beam of a spotlight hidden in one of the columns focused on Dionysus's head and then moved slowly to the rats' Hebrew epic. A hitherto unnoticed door opened and out of the scroll came one of biggest rats my eyes have ever seen. From its tail to the tip of its snout, Maximus was as long as a standard computer keyboard. Obviously I'm not claiming all this happened spontaneously. We can assume that Dionysus concealed some kind of backstage operations well guarded from the eyes of the public. Horatio's assistant was probably hidden behind the Hebrew text and would simply give surly Maximus a kick in the ass so that it theatrically traipsed up to Caesar with a diamond-studded crown on its head and consented to be caught. People also said there was a space behind each of the six mosaics with a special function in the show; rumor had it that the man in the black vestment with the white face wasn't the great Horatio Ognjenović at all but a well-trained actor, and that he was supported by a group of artists who were the brain of the whole project. Or so people said. Yes, but no one is interested in my masterfully structured narratives anymore. As soon as I start to recount the legend of Horatio Ognjenović, they interrupt me mid-sentence because they're itching to know so many things: How does Horatio's rat trap work? How does Maximus move his legs when he's walking toward Caesar? What does Horatio mutter when he takes the red cowling off the machinery? I curse their curiosity! Fritz and my lover were completely different. They'd lie reclined among the colorful cushions on the floor and listen to my gradually unwinding tale seasoned with brilliant digressions for hours with immeasurable enjoyment. Horatio's rat trap was like an embodiment of Michelangelo's most stupendous projects and a nuclear-powered washing machine—in symbiosis. Swarms of bright little lamps, large and small screws, springs and microchips, vast labyrinths of electrical circuits and optical cables, spherical mirrors and electric motors, plaques of the finest gold and diamond conductors, fine neon tubes and cylinders, miniature electronic displays, rays of red, green, and blue laser light, speakers with bird chatter on one side of the gadget and muted organ melodies on the other, functioned in perfect harmony. If the Almighty had wished to give Adam and Eve an electronic paradise, I believe Horatio's mechanism would resemble His miniature. Everything was set in motion by the almost imperceptible pressing of a brass button on the floor near the edge of Caesar's marble pedestal. The machine roared into life and the maestro raised his arms to the heavens, and when the contraption was steadily chugging the old fellow would withdraw into the shadow of one of the beautiful Corinthian columns and wait for Maximus, whose snout just a moment later lunged at the decoy. All the mechanical droning and cranking served to propel two varnished arms of a tree. One held an "apple" formed from dried meat, which Maximus would greedily snatch, while at the same time the other arm with its two rigid fingers began to swing a pocketwatch on a long chain. Occupied with its food and seated on its hind paws, the rat attentively watched the toing and froing of the object until it took the last mouthful and crashed to the floor under the influence of hypnotic slumber. According to our dear Dr. Petričević, the point of Horatio Ognjenović's ceremony was the symbolic *return to Eden of those expelled from Eden*, and he tried to persuade me that we put Fritz through the same procedure. With all due respect for the old master, I must say that Fritz was above such things. After all, he was in no doubt as to his origins: he knew that his line, as well as the genealogies of all of his more or less slow-witted relatives today, reached back several thousand years to *Epimys rattus alexandrinus*. Only a few insist on such roots nowadays. The others vigorously deny the existence of the small Alexandrian population and have tried to prove that their ancestor was actually *Epimys rattus rattus*, an authentic Eastern European creature in no way linked to the ancient inhabitants of the library that was reduced to ashes. That's a fiction at least as banal as the death of Horatio Ognjenović, the creator of perfect death rites as complicated as the nature of death itself. The old fellow died in a sewage maintenance hole full to the brim with the concentrated gunk and junk of civilization, which led the malicious to remark ironically that he departed *in a civilized way* after all. Inappropriate remarks, I said, but there's no longer anyone who sheds a tear for the heroic days in which it really did make sense to resemble a pet, proud Maximus, or the gentle aesthete Fritz. I speak about that time, but the others just sneer, raise their pointy snouts and howl at the moon, which tonight is red—red like the rats' eyes of old. They clamor like a thousand dogs invoking oblivion. While I ink in the last remains of paper, my *Rats and Writers* slowly disappears to the rasping of rats' sharp jaws. The reprobates eat gluttonously, turning their own history into dull belching and the smell of droppings, where once there was text.

# In the Wrong Place

THEY RAN ACROSS the smallish square with suitcases in hand and then sat down on them, wet but sheltered from the rain, in the portal of the cathedral. They gulped in air, with open mouths, staring at the chairs scattered over the worn stone slabs of the square that shone whenever the lightning flashed above the city, high in the hills. As she inhaled the moist air, she counted the twenty-nine chairs on the square and then glanced at her chest. Drops trickled into the deep décolletage of her dress and ran down between her breasts, forming a circle in the middle of her belly. Her wet and flattened black hair made her face seem longer than it really was. When she gathered a thick lock and tried to wring it out, only a few big drops fell onto the pavement, scented with perfume. "This is never going to dry," she said and shook her head vigorously. "You're spraying," he complained from beside the other suitcase, a red one. He'd been bringing her things from the car, and as they were running across the square he heard the muffled chink of her cosmetics bag. He didn't like the perfume she'd been using for the last few months. It lingered pungently, changing the taste of cigarettes and creeping between sheets and the pages of books. He wiped the tiny particles from his face with his hand and smelled traces of the familiar smell. "So many chairs!" he exclaimed and licked his lips, hoping he wouldn't collect any more molecules. "Twenty-nine chairs," she said, annulling his thoughts. "You've counted them?" he tried to distinguish thin shapes in the semidarkness. "Twenty-nine," she emphasized, searching for his eyes. She looked at him as if that number meant something special.

Strewn over the square, some turned on their sides, others with crooked legs pointing toward the sky, they resembled large insects battered by the rain. A croaking woman's voice made both of them suddenly look into the unpleasant darkness behind their backs, toward the door of the cathedral. "It's best to never have your hair cut on a Sunday. And it's good to avoid Mondays too. If you cut your hair on a Tuesday, you'll live a long life, but it's best to have your hair cut on a Friday." They could only make out the silhouette when its owner moved and raised her hands to straighten her kerchief. The old woman was sitting in the corner, to the right of the black door. "Never on a Sunday. Never . . . ," she said and nodded anxiously toward the sky. "What am I to do with all the wet chairs now?" She pursed her worried lips and her eyes pointed to the square. "As soon as the rain started, they scattered, the devils—and left me the chairs," she cawed and reordered some of the things on the little stool at her knees. "The whole day and nothing!" she lifted up a handful of tiny crucifixes attached to a wire tied around her thumb. On the palm of her hand stood a plaster replica of the cathedral. "Buy the cathedral and I'll give the young lady a cross. Buy three crosses and you get a cathedral for free. Today's your lucky day. Come on, why hold back? I can see you want to," she said, moving the model toward his face. But he didn't as much as glance at the plaster cast. He stared at the very long, blackened thumbnail that stuck out above the belfry of the miniature cathedral. He shook his head and looked away. "Won't you either?" she asked, turning toward the young woman, who was sitting on the smallish black suitcase containing his things neatly folded. As they were running across the square, this suitcase had slipped from her grasp among the chairs and gotten all wet on one side. As she picked it up, she thought she would probably have laughed loudly in different circumstances, simulating a panic-stricken flight before the large drops of rain. She also thought about that as she looked at the face of the hunchbacked woman with her crucifixes and cathedral. When she pronounced: "No, thank you," with forced courtesy, the old woman angrily jingled the relics. Then she scratched her tongue with two fingers. "A hair," she exclaimed, holding her thumb and forefinger together. "A mouth full of hair," she said and spat away to the side. "Can you help me with the chairs then? Come on, come on. I see you want to . . . The rain's all but stopped." She looked toward the clouds. It was still pouring. What did she need the chairs for? He got up from the suitcase. The old woman immediately vanished into the darkness. The heavy wooden door of the cathedral creaked and let out the smell of stale cold air and candles. "They belong inside. Put them in there. On the left . . . Are you going to or not?" Rows of pews and massive alabaster columns appeared in dim outline in the depth of the blackened space. He rolled up the sleeves of his wet green shirt, glanced at the young woman on the black suitcase, and shrugged his shoulders. She raised her eyebrows and whispered, almost silently: "She's repulsive." He strode out onto the square and took hold of the first chair by its iron legs. It was heavier than he thought. With effort, he reached for another and leaned its wooden backrest against his chest. He paced awkwardly and felt the greased, wet bars slipping from his grasp. He clenched tighter, before deciding he had to drop one of the chairs. The loud crash lured the old woman out of the darkness and woke a few pigeons hiding deep inside the porch. He put the other chair down on the pavement too. He felt large raindrops hitting his back and face. He spread his fingers and gaped at the palms of his hands. Long black hairs were wound between his fingers. He shook his hands hard in disgust and then noticed there were somewhat lighter, dark hairs on his shirt, particularly around his pockets. Drops of water dirty with rust dripped from the tips of his fingers. He had to restrain himself from swearing out loud. He sniffed his hands and clearly sensed the smell of metal mixed with the gloomy odors of other people's hair. For a moment he felt a surge of nausea and a scratching in his throat. An open pair of scissors lay in a small, dirty puddle. The old woman watched from the door, anticipating his next movement. Despite everything, he decided he was going to carry in the chairs one by one, twenty-nine times. He hoped that would give him at least a brief sense of completion and calm. He needed to feel something like that. The young woman lit a damp cigarette and crossed her legs. The wet circle on her belly slowly assumed the shape of a face. He wiped his forehead with the back of his hand and gripped the rusty frame even harder now. He rushed into the cathedral, determined to finish the work reliably and fast. Utter darkness was what he found. Flickering spots of flame behind distant columns made the blackness unbearable. He put down the chair, expecting that unpleasant face to emerge at any moment; he expected the voice that would set his coordinates, but nothing happened. He was more disconcerted by the complete absence of sound than by the darkness. He took a deep breath and immediately started imagining the people whose smells and hair he now bore on his body and clothes. "It's best to never have your hair cut on a Sunday, Mother is right." It was a man's voice now that came from the right. "She's gone to pray. Don't worry . . . She's here somewhere, among the pews," it said, moving closer. It all seemed like a gruesome trap, he thought, and retreated toward the door. "Don't worry, I'll show you what to do with the chairs," the man said and appeared at the door, turning the big wheels of his wheelchair. "Hello, miss. Could I have a cigarette too? Surely you've got one to spare?" He rolled himself up to the black suitcase and reached out his hand. She clenched her cigarette between her lips and searched for the pack in her handbag. "There you are." He took the pack and shook out two cigarettes. "One for later, too. After dinner. Why not? Mother's cooking tonight," he said. He rapped the suitcase twice with the thin cane that lay across his lap and then returned the pack of Marlboros. "Thank you, miss. A nice suitcase. But dirty. What's inside?" He laughed quietly and licked his red lips. They were younger than his face, the young woman thought. He came up even closer to her and examined both of them with an impish eye. For a moment she believed his hand was moving for her knee and recoiled slightly, but he only briefly took the edge of her dress and then carefully lifted his clenched fingers to his face. "Deuce and thunder! Just look. Hair everywhere," he said. "That's a bad sign. Never on a Sunday, never on a Sunday," he added as he blew and brushed off the hairs from his hand. Then he turned just the left wheel and spun the wheelchair around. "Are you going to finish the work or not? If not . . . forget it." The young man now stood in the middle of the square, ready to continue the task. For a moment he was frozen with fear, as well as a feeling of hatred and disgust: at the chairs, the cathedral, and the suitcases, at the old woman and her son; and also at the woman on the black suitcase with his things, whom he'd stopped loving long ago. He grabbed one of the chairs and hurled it across the square with all his strength. While it was still in the air, he stormed off toward the cathedral as if heading for a final showdown. The chair hit the cathedral wall high up and fell to the pavement with a dull crash. He tried nervously to get the hairs off his shirt and decided he'd later throw away that green rag saturated with other people's smells. But now he had to get out of there as soon as possible. He had to run away to somewhere safe, warm, and light. By himself, or the two of them, it didn't matter. He snatched his suitcase and said: "We're going. Now!" He squinted to stop the rain getting in his eyes and ran off across the square in the hope of hitting on one of the alleys that led out of the Old Town. Taking a chance, he entered a rather small, vaulted way and soon came up against a wall with a heavy wooden door and a rusty padlock. He went back along the cul-de-sac, slightly slower now but still sufficiently fast that he didn't notice the bald, freshly shaven heads that started to look out of the windows from behind curtains and flowerpots; that slowly emerged from behind the windowpanes, like nocturnal toadstools with eyes that followed his movements. Whitish heads of children and red heads of old people, their crowns rubbed with lavender oil. Long, pale faces of women, vaulted with wrinkled foreheads, with no brows or hair. He stopped near the chairs and tried hard to slow his breathing. The door of the cathedral was shut. The woman was now alone, sitting on the suitcase with her hands together in prayer. It seemed to him that her body quavered. He turned one of the scattered chairs upright and sat down in the middle of the square. He needed a few seconds' rest. He noticed that the pale lights of the surrounding houses were shining in the tiny puddles on the smooth-worn stone. He raised his head and with a little effort looked all the way around, studying the windows. When he saw the bald apparitions, he felt his body slowly lose strength as it changed and adapted to secret laws. Then he slowly but firmly closed his eyes. He thought there was nothing else he could do.

# Cut, Copy, Paste

*Got to hurry on back to my hotel room*
*Where I've got me a date with Botticelli's niece*
*She promised that she'd be right there with me*
*When I paint my masterpiece*

BOB DYLAN, 1971

HE TURNED UP at the door that morning: "I've come for the paintings." Actually he said, "I've been sent for the paintings." And when Andrej asked, "Which paintings?" he thrust his hand in through the half-open door and pointed, "Those ones there, the red ones." He said, "the red ones," although only one had red on it. It was a close-up of strong male hands with two fingers pressing a deeply slashed wrist. Spots of oil color, some tiny and indifferent, others large, bright, and malevolent. The right arm was bare, smeared up to the elbow. Blood trickled down the canvas. The sleeve of his white shirt was neatly rolled up in the middle of the left forearm. Andrej waited a few seconds, took another look at the wall, and then opened the door wide and gave a wry smile to the man who had requested the paintings. He said his name was Todd, and that instant a white envelope guided by his right hand passed in over the threshold. *I need the paintings for an exhibition*, the big letters read on a small piece of clumsily folded paper. The pen had punctured the paper in the bottom left-hand corner, at the end of the signature, so Andrej thought his former wife had drawn up this ultimatum on her lap. He smelled the envelope and the piece of paper but found no trace of anything except the typical odor of industrial cellulose and paper. He thought the tone of the message was in sync with its smell, and for a moment he even wanted to sniff at the man waiting on the other side of the threshold so as to round off the picture. "Your wife sent me, you know . . . Everything's probably explained in the letter. I haven't read it, believe me. I'm to pick them up and go. Paintings are paintings," he said and took an insecure step, setting his heavy black shoe on the threshold. Andrej withdrew in front of his body and caught the metallic smell of sweat mixed with an air of cotton and shaving lotion. "Can you describe how my wife looks?" he asked as if he wanted confirmation of her identity, but he only said it for a bit of fun. He'd never heard a description of his wife in the words of another man. He hoped the guy would start to analyze her body and that he'd be vulgar. "If you don't believe me, call her," was his laconic reply, and he produced a phone from his pocket. He was trying to make the impression of being a professional. He took another stride and now stood with both feet on the dirty tiles, nervously regarding the paintings through the glass door of the living room. Andrej moved aside and gave the man a hand sign that he could go on in and take the paintings. They were the last things she'd left behind. In the first months after they split up she came once a week with her younger sister and, without a word, emptied cupboards, bathroom shelves, and kitchen cabinets. She took everything, including a half-empty bottle of body lotion, the coffee cup with Dalí's moustache, the tweezers, nail scissors, and incense sticks. She collected those things as if to conceal all evidence of the tragedy, all trace of the catastrophe that ravaged a city that it's better now to wipe off the face of the earth completely, to abolish its artifacts and open the doors to the elements of oblivion. Her smell was gone from the apartment two weeks after she left. The room in which she painted and never wanted to call her atelier was the last to be cleared out. She turned up one morning with two tipsy workers who tossed her painting utensils into cardboard boxes haphazardly together with rubbish, small pieces of furniture, and clumps of paint that had stuck to the parquet. When they'd carried out the boxes, they came back with two tins of freshly mixed white paint and did the walls. Andrej sat in the living room all the while, trying to concentrate on his sips of whiskey and Sibelius's Concert for Violin in D Minor. He watched them going in and out, looking through the smudged glass that still bore some of her fingerprints. Through the glass on which the man who would take away the last traces had also left his marks, Andrej thought. The tips of our fingers are the most intimate parts of the body, bundles of nerve endings that define the tangible world with all its foreign shapes. When the paintings were gone, he'd take a cloth, soak it in methylated spirit, and brighten up that glass. He believed that would bring him some sort of calm. He leaned back in the armchair and watched the man who looked at the paintings from close up for a few moments as if deliberating which to take off the wall first. "Whoever painted this stuff—" he sniffed, looked at Andrej, shook his head, and resolutely grabbed the first in the series. He worked quickly and skillfully, with the efficiency of a hangman with four death row-ers to drop on this shift. Removing paintings from walls was what he'd devoted his whole life to, Andrej thought, watching as he carefully laid the frames on the parquet floor. When he took down the third in the series, he held his burly male hand close to his face and tried to make out the cut on the canvas that the blood was coming from. "This guy is a goner," he said, glanced at Andrej, and laughed. "Wounds like that don't heal," he added seriously, acting as if he'd just voiced an important insight. "I'll be off then," he muttered, put his hands around the frames and headed for the door. Andrej looked at him and wanted to say something, but then he began to feel a commotion of his thoughts like a million maggots that in a few minutes, hours, or days, would take shape as a monster made of sorrow, loss, depression, and death. He realized that fighting it would be a losing battle; the last little pieces of meaning that sustained his life were leaving with her paintings. He didn't love that woman anymore and had made a clean break with the past several months earlier. Occasionally he'd imagine her naked and try to masturbate, but his erection was forced and short-lived. He

toward the wall. He pressed on the wound with two fingers and rested his smeared forearms in the outlines of the frame in an effort to be faithful to the original. That similarity defined metaphors he was unable to turn into words. Thin red streaks slowly ran down the white surface of the wall, and all that Andrej could think of at that moment was that the painting was coming out of the frame—finally breaking free, revealing its true nature, and defining some kind of meaning. Abruptly he felt a heavy sleepiness coming over him. Tiny green sparks flashed before his eyes. Their color changed with every blink of his eyelids, and between those colors Andrej believed he could see the black limbos of an ancient warmth that would absorb his body at any moment. When he took his arms off the wall, the prints of his hands remained in the outlines of the frame: lasting and eternal, he thought, trying hard to control his steps. He staggered to the armchair from where he'd be able to peacefully observe the wall and the new meanings on it. Along with all that, he wished to hear a gentle whispering: a calm voice explaining events and things. He tried to keep his eyelids open, but when he wanted to rub his eyes he realized that his hands lay motionless with the palms turned toward the universe. He looked at them like foreign objects that someone had taken off the wall and placed on his lap by mistake—like freshly painted forms that had been put aside to dry. After that thought, Andrej breathed in and out seventeen more times.

# Free Sugar

WHAT MUSIC GOES with this kind of dance? Ivana Dedijer asked herself as she hopped about on the sidewalk in front of the gallery. And why dance if there's no music? She simply had to move around, to dance, as she looked through the glass of the high-hung chandelier in the form of beans that spilled with every movement of her head and became another kind of vegetable. The director opened the door. He nodded briefly and was then lost in the crowd of workers and exhibits they'd just unpacked. The plastic floor creaked as if there were living people in it who groaned and shrieked under the stabs of high heels. What drinks go with these clothes? And what to drink if there's no alcohol? The tap water from the gallery's smelly toilet. Yes: they ought to drink that water because a fine jet of it from that brass faucet might become art by the touch of an artist who would take a pee at the gallery and then wash his hands and frown at the smell of the soap with the scent of rotten cemetery flowers. Or any other flowers. What kind of job goes with studying painting? There should at least be a comfortable couch in the gallery. A high-sided armchair where a person can recline and read Cioran. Or have a nice masturbation session. The armchair would be quite sufficient. The director's office would be locked, Ivana assumed. Several plastic chairs were stacked up against the wall, under the exhibits, which after a few hours would turn everyone's spine into a rotten tree. But work was work. She had the task of spending the night in the gallery: to guard the fragile castings from envious souls and burglars, and to be paid for it—not much, but enough to be able to drink and dance for two days somewhere else. An offer Ivana Dedijer couldn't refuse. The opening was the next day. A stampede was unavoidable. All the vacuous looks and ungainly expressions would erode the display beyond recognition, even without things being touched. No one can save them, she thought and sat down on the floor. It was damp and cold, false and garish, covered with tiny droplets of condensation that had gathered in the course of the day while the artist carried in the works with several dutiful workers and the director. She looked around, wiping the sweat from her forehead from time to time as she watched the hands that vigorously grasped the exhibits and the serious faces set atop powerful shoulders, for which every load was just a load, nothing more. Ivana Dedijer was sitting in the corner and putting out her cigarettes on the small plate with Van Gogh's portrait. At least she made an effort not to stick the burning ends straight into his blue eyes. The large sculpture of a muscular man cast in sugar took pride of place. On a pedestal one and a half feet high, with arms uplifted and taut biceps the color of the setting sun, it resembled a bizarre combination of a classical masterpiece and a shopwindow dummy—a latter-day Adam, Ivana thought, a being out of the confectioner's, where she as a girl had bought candied apples and never dared to steal one. That was men's business, she thought. As she regarded him from behind, looking at the fleshy calf muscles and bottom that supported a powerful, symmetrical back, she couldn't understand why the workers were whispering to each other and exchanging smiles. Only when she sauntered to the trash can to shake the cigarette butts and ash off Van Gogh's face did she see the upwardly slanting phallus underlined with large balls. The sugar body was tempting to touch. A moistened finger or the tip of a tongue in any place, up the inside of its thighs, across its groin and between its legs, around the navel with sweet crystals and farther, all the way to its neck, lips, and the back of its head: that was Ivana's conception of freedom. She sat down and lit another cigarette. A black imprint of ash was on the left of Van Gogh's semi-profile and it looked as if his missing ear had regrown there. After several hours, the works were in their places. The director put his palms together as if in prayer and then leaned back slightly and spread his arms to express his enthusiasm about the whole setting. He stared at the large television screen that reflected the windows and the chandelier, and he gazed with a creased forehead as he watched the animated film in which Gustave Courbet's big, divine vagina gave birth to an animated Adam, frightened and with a rather shriveled cock. Ivana had the impression that the artist was observing the director's ear during this time, where a large pimple was growing on the top of the red auricle. When they'd finished with the TV, the three of them strolled up to the transparent soccer table, where one team, instead of androgynous, armless bodies, was made up of chesty silicone beauties. The other team, on the remaining four rods, consisted of casts of modest, kerchiefed ladies in long dresses and with boring chests à la Ivan Meštrović. The director scratched his ear and then asked condescendingly if he could play a game and if the artist would be kind enough to join him. He spoke as if that would be the incarnation of his dream of modern art, creation in motion, interaction, an escalation of the desire for an artistic act, in a word: an absolute delight, the most significant moment in his career to date, and a big event for the gallery. He took his camera out of his pocket, quickly called Ivana Dedijer, and thrust it into her hands. "Give it all you've got, honey. Come on . . . Record the moment. This is history!" he exclaimed and grabbed a rod with the silicone casts of well-endowed women. The artist went and stood on the other side, the director called, "Ready?" and rolled the ball into the middle. "Take it now, love. This is the moment. Here goes . . . ," he said. The artist blinked at the camera and everything was over. "Fantastic photo. I'll send it to you as soon as I can. Just lovely," he crooned, gaping at the screen on the back, until the artist scorned: "I knew you'd choose the silicone ones. I'm a good judge of character. You like them buxom, don't you?" He let the camera slip back into his pocket and blushed. "What? Do you think I . . . ? No, no. It was a pure coincidence. Believe me, there was no intention at all. Really. That goes without saying," he shook his head and gazed about the gallery with an absent expression. "But nothing in art is coincidental. You know that. I don't blame you for picking the big Brunhildas instead of the boring matrons with long dresses. If I were a man, I'd have done the same," the artist mocked, doing her best to conceal her laughter. The director bent over to pick up a few scraps of paper and two crushed-out cigarette butts. You can give them to me, Ivana said, and he looked her straight in her eyes. Then he saw Van Gogh framed in fresh ash. He nervously lifted the plate and started to speak: "I gave you this job. A lot of money for nothing. Literally for nothing. Did you know this is a valuable present? A gift from one of my friends? Not any old plate or even an ashtray, God forbid!" He blew in the middle of Van Gogh's face and the ash flew in all directions. When that dry snow had settled on the ground, he continued, "You're a student, aren't you? A prospective artist? Well, doesn't that expression mean anything to you? Vincent Willem van Gogh, hey! From Groot-Zundert, son of Theodorus van Gogh and Anna Cornelia née Carbentus. And I have to leave you here with all this . . ." He made a semicircle with his hand and cast a glance at the artist. "Let me go and wash it and the matter's settled," Ivana said and got up, ready to pour a little water—no, a lot of water—over Vincent's benumbed face. "Like hell you will!" the director snorted and stuck the small plate into his pocket with the camera. The workers gathered their things and left the gallery without saying goodbye. The artist was telephoning out on the sidewalk, walking about in front of the large glass facade. The director sat down on a chair next to the sugar Adam, wiped the sweat from his neck with his sleeve, and scratched his ear once more. His breathing was slow and heavy. He undid a few buttons and turned toward Ivana. "Are you alright? Would you like some water? I'll bring you some," she asked and quickly walked to the water dispenser with the plastic cups. When he held out his hand, the swollen fingers were pale and trembling. He tipped the water down his throat and made a circle in the air with his forefinger, which meant: more water. "I don't know what the hell's happened . . . I took my insulin on time, plus it was the good German stuff. German . . . Oh yes, made by the Germans . . . Just take Dürer as an example and you'll know," he spoke between shallow breaths. Ivana waited with the full cup, but the director looked at the floor, resting his hands on his knees: "Tell me where she is. I don't want her to see me like this." Ivana said: "Out the front, on the sidewalk. She's been on the phone for ten minutes." The director gasped: "Good. Give it here." He took the cup and drank half of it and then turned around and slowly surveyed Adam, from his feet, via his thighs and groin, up to the head. He pointed his finger at the sculpture and said: "All my life I've avoided sweet things. I flee from sugar like Malevich did from figuration, and now *Wham* in the middle of the gallery. So much sugar! Instead of sugar-free I get *Free Sugar*! But I'm not allowed to even touch it. Not even German insulin would help me." A small but growing puddle of sweat spread on the floor below his head. Ivana took the empty cup and went to the trash can. The artist tapped on the glass facade and beckoned her to the half-open door. She covered the phone with the palm of her hand and whispered: "What's up with him?" Ivana said: "The director? Nothing. Just power napping, don't worry." The director hastily rummaged through his pockets, sticking his hand now inside his blazer, now into the slits at the sides. He took out his camera and the small plate with the image of Van Gogh and grumbled about sugar: "The little green box . . . I had it in my pocket. It was right here, and now, just now . . . *Senza zucchero!* This can only happen to me. Have you got anything sweet with you, child? I need it urgently. Otherwise . . ." Ivana shrugged her shoulders, and then both of them glanced at the same time at erect Adam. The director's head started to shake and his pupils disappeared underneath his eyelids. He slid from the chair and threw back his head, and only the whites were still to be seen, with red capillaries that reminded Ivana of a network of rivers on photographs from space. The plate fell to the floor and broke in two: Van Gogh's face was split between the eyes, and the director began to tremble convulsively while clenching his trouser-legs. Ivana Dedijer didn't expect the balls to come off too. She thought that only the glans would break off and the damage in that case would be easily repaired. Hypoglycemia was a serious matter, she knew, and his sugar level needed to be restored as soon as possible. Every minute counted. She ran off to his office with Adam's tool in her hands and started to rummage through the cupboards, throwing around heaps of catalogs and monographs. High above the piles of magazines, set aside on a separate shelf, Ivana noticed a cup with a reproduction of Klimt's *The Kiss* and a small ceramic spoon of the same hue. She threw Janson's *History of Art* onto the floor, and added Lubarda's monograph for good measure. She stretched up on her tiptoes and managed to grab Klimt. As she ran back, the spoon played three notes as it knocked against the porcelain rim. Adam's cock clung to her left hand and sweet syrup trickled down her forearm. She filled the cup with water and then headed with large steps back to the director. The artist stood at his head, staring at the whites of his eyes and his lips that muttered unintelligible words. "I'm sorry. There was no other choice," Ivana said, glancing at mutilated Adam. "Don't worry. He looks even better this way. Just give the man some sugar now. The role of art is to help people, to raise their awareness, isn't it?" the artist declared as she held up the corners of his mouth. Ivana quickly crushed up Adam's cock. The glans plopped into the water and she started to stir it. She put the rest aside on the small plate with half of Van Gogh's face. When the sugar had dissolved, she raised the director's heavy head, trying to breathe in as little as possible of the smells of the sweat-drenched body. The sweetened liquid flowed down the man's swollen tongue, and after just half a cup he cleared his throat and could use his palm to prop up Ivana's hand. "Drink. You have to drink it all. That's it. You'll soon feel better, I'm sure you know," Ivana said and gently lowered his large head back onto the floor. The two women stood together, waiting for the tiny pupils to appear in place of the whites and for something other than nonsense to come from that sticky mouth. The man's feet settled down and his arms relaxed alongside his body. He blinked several times, closed his eyes tight, and then raised his eyelids to look in astonishment at the world above him and the spiderweb that stretched between the chandeliers in the form of beans. "Bravo! Now everything's okay again. We gals have earned ourselves a helping too. Isn't that right, Mr. Director? What's that favorite term of yours? Interaction, of course. Interaction," the artist said and raised the half plate with the pieces of Adam. They each took one of the balls and pulled hard, each in her direction. The scrotum burst in half and several grains of sugar ended up on the floor. As the crystals crunched loudly between their teeth, the man looked at one woman's mouth and then at the other's in turn, at their tongues going round and round, and at their pointed teeth breaking up the remains of the formerly shiny and rounded member. Then he looked at Adam and decided he'd stay lying for a little longer until the spirits had calmed, the spiders had retired into their dark corners, and the two women had gone out and left him alone to have a good cry like a real man.

# Family History

## 1.

DANILO KNEW THAT his great-great-grandfather had cut off several well-groomed Ottoman heads, and that he later grabbed them by their rose-oiled hair and raised them to the sky while speaking the name of God, whose face he imagined to have the features of the current ruler. He simply couldn't get that image out of his mind. He presumed that his ancestor swiftly returned to the family and their stone house, furtively sniffing his fingers still greasy from the rose oil, in the hope that a few of the molecules would remain on his hand so that his children would be able to smell it. His great-grandfather, on the other hand, bought that same oil at the marketplace in Kotor, carefully taking out the silver coins hidden between the layers of his uncomfortable woolen clothes. And his grandfather, Maxim Dedijer, remembered well where Danilo's great-grandmother—Maxim's mother, Stana—secretly kept a little bottle of that oil, which she guarded like the greatest of treasures. The seal of the Venetian glassworks is still visible on the bottom—the stylized initials of the artisan and a four-leaf clover—but Maxim wasn't able to see that detail in the years before his death and eternal rest at the village cemetery. Neither the convex lenses of his glasses, the precursor to blindness, nor the massive Russian magnifying glass and the straining of his heavy eyelids were of any help. He'd twist and twirl the little bottle in his fingers, trying to evoke a gleam: purple rays of crystal exposed to the sun, his mother's fingers, and finally a sweet breath of rose oil, which never really smelled of roses at all. Danilo's father, Nikola Dedijer, the son of Maxim Dedijer, committed suicide by shooting himself in the head with his grandfather's wartime trophy, a Walther P38 pistol that Maxim Dedijer acquired by prizing apart the cold, stiff fingers of a German soldier with a hole in his forehead; the man had committed suicide leaning up against the bole of a large oak tree with magpie nests hanging from it. He, Danilo, grandson of Maxim Dedijer and son of the metallurgical engineer Nikola Maximov Dedijer, who had been resting at the cemetery for fifteen years, was now in the possession of those mute pieces of memorabilia: the little old bottle and the pistol, whose barrel seemed to have been put to a skull with suicidal intent on two occasions.

## 2.

When he looked at that gun from up close for the first time as a boy, with his father beside him, and stared into the darkness of the steel barrel slightly from the side, Danilo imagined the corpulent German beneath the shaggy magpie nests and gave him the most Germanic-sounding name he could think of at that moment: *Friedrich*. That's what he thought when he saw the gun for the first time. Danilo held his face up to that piece of finely crafted iron and took a deep breath. The smell stirred obscure emotions and drew futile tears, which, he thought years later, had announced that his father, Nikola Dedijer, would disconcert their dozy neighbors one scorching June afternoon and print a gory constellation adorned with fragments of his skull on the bedroom wall. When Danilo returned, he found relatives and local children clustered in front of the block. Uncle Martin took him around the corner so he wouldn't see the body being carried out. Many important questions remained unanswered in the years that followed, but it was always quite clear for him why his father pulled the trigger. He never transformed that knowledge into words and never defined that realization in his mind. And when he thought of his father, he always imagined him in a German uniform, sitting with his back against a large, partially rotten tree with magpie nests dangling from it. He imagined him slowly and calmly taking off his cap, wiping the sweat from his forehead, and carefully positioning the barrel between his eyes, before gently pulling the trigger.

### 3.

The Walther P38 vanished from sight and only reappeared sixteen summers later. Danilo's mother, Marija, decided he was *ready* and *mature enough*, at the age of twenty-eight, to take on the burden of the bloody family heirloom wrapped up in a floral towel. When Maxim Dedijer prized open the stiff and cold fingers of the German soldier without much hesitation sixty-six years earlier, there had been three bullets in the magazine. The fourth was lodged deep in the bole of the oak. Danilo didn't remember his grandfather, who used another one of the bullets on January 12, 1978, sitting on a wooden block in the stable behind their village house. He put aside his glasses because everything was clear and cloudless where he was going, and pulled the trigger. His aunts retold the story for years about how their mother, Danilo's grandmother Zorka, took the Venetian vial of rose oil from the wardrobe and spread the last thick drops on the lips and face of her husband without crying a tear. His aunts also remembered that his mother wrapped up the pistol in the floral towel and took the baleful bundle out of the house. Zorka Dedijer was buried several months later; she left the tragedy behind her and didn't say a single word about it before her death.

### 4.

Danilo remembered the afternoon he visited the cemetery with his father, and afterward they went down into the dank basement together and carried the heavy chest encrusted with bird shit up to the decrepit stairs at the front door of the village house.

Nikola opened it, turning his head away because of the dust, and without hesitation Danilo thrust his hands into that cold limbo of rotten family history. His boyish curiosity was satisfied because, groping around beneath the dirty woolen blanket, Danilo Dedijer found several firm objects. First he took out a delicate Venetian vial, and then he produced a smallish but heavy bundle. He was startled when his father grabbed it out of his hands and tore off the linen band around the floral towel. Nikola Dedijer took out the magazine, which contained two shiny brass cartridges. He closed the chest and laid the Walther P38 on the black lid soiled with bird shit. Danilo didn't dare to touch the gun. He looked at it with a mixture of admiration and uneasiness because his father fitfully moved his lips, whispering unintelligible curses. They knelt there on either side of the black chest until Nikola swiftly returned the magazine into the body of the pistol, wrapped it up in the dirty towel with the flowers, and then held his breath so he could squeeze the bundle between his leather belt and his belly. The cold, sour smell of the awakened steel whirled around their heads, Danilo pronounced *Friedrich* in a whisper, and the Walther P38 disappeared from the family's history until June 3, 1986. It slept covered in synthetic blankets and tablecloths, between pots and pans and heaps of unnecessary things that Danilo's mother, Marija, accumulated for years in the belief that everything had some sense and purpose.

5.

An acute bout of depression preceding Nikola Dedijer's suicide was a logical basis for rational explanations with which people tried to console Marija and explain why he took his life while she, reclining on the couch in the living room, was reading the last pages of *Buddenbrooks*. Danilo listened to the adults' unintelligible explanations and wondered why none of all those clever and wise people who spoke about death had fully unraveled the paths of the family labyrinth which three generations of the Dedijers had passed through. In his childish thoughts, the solution was more than obvious. The past always imposed itself in a few clear images. Danilo believed that their bad luck, which he later called a curse, and then the inevitable hand of fate, had been evoked that very day when Maxim Dedijer turned from the dusty mountain path and went up to the tree with the dangling magpie nests.

6.

Marija rarely spoke about her late husband. She took away the photograph of the summer family idyll from the top of the television because it showed a close-up of Danilo pointing a water pistol at his father's chest. She decided they had to leave that death-imbued apartment as soon as possible, and so the very day after Nikola's suicide, before leaving for the cemetery, before the ritual of the funeral, she daubed the bloodied wall with a thick layer of green paint. She resolutely declined the aid of relatives, and when she'd finished the task she sat down on the edge of the bed gaping at that *deed*. Aunt Marta sent Danilo into the room and then he too, after kissing his mother on her salty cheek, sat down on the same bed. They looked at the freshly painted wall and inhaled the sharp smells of chemicals. Before he got up, Danilo noticed a bitter smile twitch on his mother's face. Marija thought at that moment—because she knew nothing is ever over—that the traces had only been covered up once more by a thin veneer of reality, and that things happened and would continue to happen following a well-oiled mechanism of the Dedijers' family history, which no one could stop anymore.

7.

Marija Dedijer, the wife of Nikola Maximov Dedijer, died on May 14, 2007, from the complications of a stroke that made her eyes fill with blood, and her carotid arteries hardened and turned black. She lived alone after Danilo's twenty-third birthday, doing her best to conceal her frail health through her proverbial good mood and the rich Saturday lunches, which she cooked with great devotion. Lulled by routine, Marija even allowed herself the impermissible and believed life had taken on identifiable outlines again, that it had formed a cocoon of immutability, and that this constant would enable her a calm old age free of abrupt turns. It was that shortsightedness that made Marija Dedijer saunter to her bedroom after the main course of one Saturday meal with her son and get out the bundle from the pile of things on top of a cupboard, which she later placed on the table beside his plate. The Venetian vial was empty. One bullet lay in the magazine of the Walther P38. They continued their meal and neither of them mentioned the gun.

8.

The final chapter of the Dedijers' family history was written on the rooftop of a seven-story residential building. Danilo Dedijer, the son of Nikola Maximov Dedijer, committed suicide on April 19, 2009, and thus culled the bad seed that lay between the springs of the Walther P38, the pistol that Danilo's grandfather Maxim had obtained by prizing apart the cold, stiff fingers of the German soldier with the hole in his forehead. Danilo Dedijer's suicide was seen by his friends and relatives as the logical consequence of the structure of his inherited DNA.

# The Vampire

*I'm used to the nightly life*
*I sleep by day and romp at night*
*Even God's given up on me*
*I don't care—I live how I like*

TOMA ZDRAVKOVIĆ,
YUGOSLAV FOLK SINGER

*Death is not what people call death*
*Real death is that which I must endure, sorry me . . .*

LJUDEVIT PASKVALIĆ,
16TH-CENTURY POET FROM KOTOR

HOW MUCH LONGER is it going to take for my aged mother to comprehend: Miomir Krstov Živković is over thirty and doesn't need to be woken at the crack of dawn when half-dead pensioners are queuing for milk, children are on the way to school, and Podgorica stirs, wrapped in haze. The sun here is merciless, Mother dear. So this morning, too, when you stroke my forehead with your wizened hands in the hope that I'll soon get up and go to work, I mutely beg you not to do that. After the sun sets, my senses are buried beneath the surface of deep and forgetful sleep. I don't dream anything. I simply shut my eyes before dawn and open them again when the last rays sink behind the hills in the west. What remains in my head is the dark droning of the previous night and the vague contours of the one coming. Everything is black. Everything is empty. The summer heat hits me hard. My native city will be the death of me. For five nights in a row the temperature hasn't gone below eighty-five, and my blood demands a cooler state. Of all the red-hot asphalts on this earth, Podgorica's radiates the hottest. I roam the city center, the dusty suburbs, and even farther, I take refuge from packs of stray dogs, and the soles of my feet sting as if they are melting. The streets bulge from the heat and you feel they're about to burst under the pressure and that lava will come streaming out of the cracks. The only thing that brings short-term relief is the old cemetery below Gorica Hill, near the Church of St. Djordje. That place instills hope in me. The main entrance toward the church and the church's overgrown courtyard with its drinking fountain are frequented by Podgorica's young apprentice drug-gies, who sit there in circles. Since the door of the church is invariably open in summer, the smell of incense mixes with the heavy odors of hash and cannabis. That annoys me. You simply don't know who's toking—promiscuous urban youth or sweaty Orthodox monks. It doesn't matter. Psychedelic substances don't interest Miomir Krstov Živković. He's a sworn straight-edger. He always bypasses the main cemetery gate. His path is on the other side and goes past the greenhouses for growing flowers, alongside the athletics stadium, and the row of twenty-year-old cypresses. It's quiet here. You come across little stone slabs mark-ing the graves of children; you find humble anonymous graves filled with dust and brambles. The nettle trees nearby are tall and strong. Next to them stand cypresses, Scots pines, and the occa-sional stunted olive tree. And while Podgorica suffocates in the heat, Miomir Krstov Živković inhales the cold indifference of the run-down cemetery which the fresh air of the pine forest on Gorica Hill sweeps over. Gravestones climb up the hill, all the way to the rusty wrought-iron fence with spikes on top. Chiseled socialist stars alternate with crosses, Cyrillic inscriptions with Latin, worn epitaphs with remains of old plastic flowers. And then: Coca-Cola tins, Spam cans, the remains of candles, and the sickly-sweet scent of moss. I assume that this cemetery—like all others on the planet—has been soaked with tears for decades and centuries. So you'll conclude that there are no pieces of earth more thoroughly salted with that substance. From so much crying, so much grief, and so many secrets. Last night, as I was sitting and resting against the eternal home and family crypt of a certain Nikola Đuradev Martinović (1845–1903), the flame of a candle sparkled at the bottom of the cemetery. Several minutes later another was lit and I could make out the hands affixing it to the finely hewn stone. Then they left the yellow circle of light again and I had no choice but to speculate who was keeping me company at this late hour—me, the night owl Miomir Krstov Živković. A little old lady visiting her long-departed husband? Some kid obsessed with death? Even things like that leave M. K. Živković cold because, to judge by all I've read, seen, and heard, I'm condemned to eternal life. And I needn't take an interest in the marginalia that flow past my eternity like forlorn souls on the River Styx. Within half an hour the candles burned low and went out, and the dark, stooping silhouette headed off toward the gate. That was a relief. Goodbye, until next time! I stood up, and my knees creaked. It was one forty-five. I should stretch my legs a bit before dawn. Podgorica teems with life on Saturday evenings. Sculpted buttocks, vulgar young girls from the suburbs, rivers of perfume: altogether a parade of young flesh. I walked through Gorica to Slobodan Škerović High School. Two young male bodies gleamed on a bench near the basketball court. Faggots, damn them. I would so much have loved to beat the shit out of those perverts. But faggots are no longer what they used to be. The one twit was kneeling and deepthroating the other's nightstick. He was six and a half feet tall and had biceps that could send Miomir Krstov Živković flying straight into the nearest trash can. The other was smaller and slimmer but had an intimidatingly deep bass voice: "That's it, tomcat, that's the way, king of kings," which spoke of experience and latent violence. So I hid behind a nearby pine, looked for a decent-sized rock, and threw it at the shits with all my might. The yell that followed—"Owww . . . fucking hell, what was that?!"—and the reaction of the one on the bench—"Hey, you jerk, what's up, what's wrong?"—told me I'd hit my target. The bewildered cock-sucker wiped his slobbery mouth while the smaller guy pulled up his trousers. "Owww . . . I'll fuck his damn father when I catch him!" Fat chance, you animal. To bang *my* father, Krsto Milošev Živković, you'd have to dig up grave number 325 at Čepurci cemetery. But believe me, you'd find nothing there but an empty coffin. If you wanted that man, or at least his bones, you'd have to go a lot farther. It's like this: You get on the Sveti Stefan ferry, Tuesdays and Sundays at 10 p.m., which takes you from Bar to Bari. You wait two days until the peeling passenger ship *Magellan & Brothers* arrives in the harbor. A one-way ticket costs 352,000 lira—181.79 euros—and then it's off to Lisbon. There you find Hotel Paradizo and ask for the Old Man. You slip the shaven receptionist a hundred-euro note and he reaches for the phone with a smile, exchanges a few words, and notes something on a slip of paper, which he amiably hands you, tell-ing you to look for the address: Cafe El Greco, the table beneath the etching of a sailing ship, 11 p.m. You enter the cafe exactly on time, and then you can fuck Krsto as much as you like, stud. If you've got the guts, that is! The dark shine of my honorable father's eyes, the hypnotic smile on his face, his long, pale fingers, which move as if they were spinning a cobweb, fatefully beguiling and instilling awe . . . Unfortunately I haven't inherited a single one of those diabolically charismatic features, I thought as I crouched behind the tree. After they hopped from the bench, the faggots dashed off in a zigzag through the darkness with muffled curses until the taller one said: "Listen . . . There's no point. He's long made it into town. I'll be off then." The smaller one instantly grabbed him by the forearm and challenged him: "Just a minute, bro. I think we had a deal. You know what they say: no cum, no mon. You're gonna give back the dough or else . . ." The tall one hesitated for a few seconds and then made a move to run, clutching the bloodied back of his head. But he was soon caught by two surprisingly strong hands, and a few moments later by feet as well, which proceeded to thrash him and kick him in the kidneys, the back, and the face. "Trying to fuck me over, eh, you ox?" His nose crunched. "What sort of fool do you

take me for?" A kick in the stomach. "You insolent bastard!" Both
feet stamped on his back. The vicious imp didn't stop until the
big wretch started to groan, took out the money, and returned it
to him. "That's right, you bandit. Let that be a lesson to you." He
snatched the money and sauntered off into the dark. It became
clear to me, crouching behind the tree, that biblical guilt had
fallen on my shoulders. I was the sinner who had cast the first
stone at the prostitute. Fucking hell! That had to be atoned for.
I went up to the body that wheezed as it rolled in a pool of
blood. I knelt down and took him by the shoulder, but he wailed
and tried to crawl away, expecting more maltreatment. "Don't
be scared, you poor thing, I want to help you," I said. I took my
hankie out of my pocket—my pedantic mother replaces the dirty
one every morning—and wiped his face. So much young, fresh
blood! It smelled irresistible in the hot summer night. It shone
purple as it dripped slowly onto the concrete of the basketball
court and enticed M. K. Živković to reveal his true nature. I
wiped his neck and the gash on the back of his head, and the
hankie became noticeably heavy. So as to use it once more and
help the poor guy, I needed to wring it out somehow. I swear
that my motivations were in no way linked to the logically and
consciously articulated movements of my hand, which rose up
above my ready and waiting lips, above which the hankie began
to exude dark, sticky drops. A new moon hung over Podgorica
like a scimitar, I remember. I watched it with my bloodshot eyes,
thinking of my cinematic colleagues. They do it so much more
elegantly. Instead of making do with a hankie, Nosferatu would
have drained the guy's jugular to the last drop. He would have
sunk his teeth into a bulging artery and kept guzzling until the
wretch was puckered and dry like a vacuum-pack of peanuts.
Miomir Krstov Živković didn't have the good luck of going to a
dentist's regularly. When I had to go, I went solely to have teeth
pulled. They removed everything that was in any way serviceable:
my incisors, my eyeteeth of the upper and lower jaws, and they
even took out some of the premolars and molars, so now I
couldn't even suck a jellyfish's cock, let alone this big, swollen
body. "You fucking queer shit!" I swore and started to thrash him

long and hard, and then I wiped him with the hankie and wrung it into my mouth. After five or six rounds, the clod lay unconscious on the concrete. I can't say I felt sorry for him, dejected and sprawled out on his back like that. It seems my sort is not inclined to lugging the weight of biblical rights and wrongs after all. Still, I felt the worm of conscience gnawing at a tiny part of my cerebral cortex. When I washed my face with cold water at the high school's drinking fountain, that tiny thread of remorse joined the spots of congealed blood to be rinsed away irrevocably down the drain. All in all: a beautiful night that should be used to the full, I thought, because days and months had passed without a drop of fresh blood. But such is life: a mother to some, a stepmother to others. And to some neither one nor the other. Now it was half past two. I cheerfully skipped along beside the high-school fence, then under the Budućnost stadium to Sloboda Street. I followed the white line on the asphalt that I loved to walk along even as a boy. My father would hold my hand and I'd place one foot in front of the other all the way to the end and back. And then once more. His presence gave me a sense of security. He never talked much but was always ready to send an affectionate smile. The last time we saw each other he didn't touch me at all. He looked at me without a trace of fatherly tenderness. It was 1996: via Podgorica, Bar, and Bari to Lisbon, and then Hotel Paradizo, the slick receptionist, Cafe El Greco, the table beneath the etching of a sailing ship. "Hi Dad," I said with eyes full of tears. He was silent. I moved to hug him, but the meaty arm of a waiter intervened and returned me to my chair. They brought me a big crystal glass of red wine. Carlos Gardel howled from a gramophone in the corner: *Adiós muchachos, compañeros de mi vida, barra querida de aquellos tiempos . . .* My father looked at the floor, and I took the wine and drained it in one go. The next thing I remembered was the blue sky over Lisbon, the large castle above the city, and the gulls. I recalled all that becoming farther and farther away, I remember rocking on the deck of the *Magellan*, where I woke up, and the children of the passengers running around everywhere. I was to discover what happened in the meantime over the years to follow.

Explanations would come all of a sudden, in brief flashes that emerge from the electric black engulfing my being and my time like tar. It was 1995. I was sitting on my bed the evening after Krsto's funeral. My mother was seeing out some boring aunts in black headscarves. Our house in the Old Town has a long spiral stairway connecting the basement and both stories. A few soft steps were heard, and the door creaked as it opened and closed. All the relatives were now gone and my mother came in to say, "Sleep tight," and give me a kiss. "Good night, Mother," I said. And she wiped away her tears and went to bed herself. Through the window I saw the illuminated minaret of the Osmanagić Mosque. A warm and gentle night. I drowned in sleep, overwhelmed by weariness and having stood at the cemetery for so long. Everything went as it should have. Protocol was observed down to the tiniest detail. The report of the pathologist, my father's old friend Dr. Senadin Hadžiahmetović, revealed two heart attacks in the space of just a few minutes. No one was able to help. Alija Dervišević's children found my father. He was leaning up against the fence of the mosque, so the kids thought he was drunk and had simply fallen asleep there. That would be nothing new with Krsto Milošev Živković, the old Podgorica bohemian who had emptied thousands and thousands of glasses. "Hey, Pa, come on out! Uncle Krsto got stone drunk and fell asleep by the fence." Alija and his brother Fahro then carried him home; they laid him on the bench in the courtyard, felt his pulse, and realized he was dead. My mother came running down and began lamenting: *Oh, you have robbed me of all beauty, my falcon / My heart is dealt a bitter wound, O Krsto fay / What is there left in life, my husband and master / But to boast with a hero's memory, O Krsto / With a lifeless brow, O woe, O misery me / You rest at Čepurci, this fate has frowned on me / Where all your line is buried, in the grateful earth*, etc. The end of the story. We buried him the next day. Grave 325 at Čepurci cemetery. But it's better to say that the whole story just begins here. The third morning brought together quite a few people from the neighborhood, as well as cousins, distant uncles who I met for the first time, and several slobbering, equally unknown aunts. They carved smoked ham, there was homemade raki, store-bought cakes, wine, and even a bottle of Scotch. Around two o'clock we visited the cemetery, no wreaths were laid, and then everyone went back to their business, and mother and I—straight home. I remember I watched the whole second sequel of *The Godfather* and fell asleep in the armchair. That evening my gang from the street dropped in and finished off the bottle of Ballantine's. All that remained of my father was a closet full of worn-out blazers, a few pairs of shoes, prescription glasses and sunglasses, and a modest-sized valise beneath their double bed. My mother fell asleep around eleven. I waited until she was sleeping soundly and then quietly got out the suitcase. I opened it on the table in my room after smashing the flimsy lock with the ashtray. I was met by a sweetish, musty smell. Papers, papers, papers . . . A mass of letters. Addresses: Lisbon, Lisbon, Lisbon. Everything in Portuguese. I knew he'd been to sea on a Portuguese tanker for three years between the ages of twenty and twenty-five. Here were several old photos with other crew members. A celebration on St. Nicholas's Day: lots of fish in earthenware ovals, the table ajumble with bottles of red wine, and the head of the table dominated by a slim silhouette in a captain's uniform with dark, dark glasses. I came across two old pipes, a half-empty pouch of tobacco, an ivory fountain pen, and a small bottle of Spanish perfume. More letters, newspaper cuttings, and a bundle of depreciated Portuguese banknotes. At the very bottom lay an ebony box with the engraved countenance of an African demon with sharp teeth. I had quite a battle to properly remove the red post-office wax the lid was sealed with. In the box I found 650 American dollars and a return ticket from Podgorica to Lisbon, a miniature envelope with directions from Magellan & Brothers, Hotel Paradizo, and the rest, two of my father's photographs from his youth, and, finally, a short letter addressed to me: *My dear son . . . It is night on earth. And I am no longer a stranger in that night. Before you rein in your excitement at the thought of your father, Krsto Milošev Živković, still being alive, you must realize one thing: death screams from every cell of my tormented body; it wakes me up at night and sings a lullaby during the day. I've been buried, true. Not beneath the ground, however, but on the surface. Forever. If you wish to see me one more time, everything must remain a Secret. Follow the instructions exactly. Adieu.* The end. I asked myself how he managed to do all this. I didn't understand who we had buried. But those 650 dollars were the main reason why I didn't rack my brains much. I'd never seen so much money in all my life. The next spring, I packed my things, told my mother I was going with my gang to Kotor, and flew the coop to Lisbon. How could I have known what awaited me and what the consequences would be? As I've said, we had a brief encounter, which was followed by a hungover awakening on the *Magellan.* Then the bright light started to bother me. The discomfort began as a mild form of porphyria, and today I dare not expose even an ear to the sun. No more swimming in the Morača River or hanging out on the Sutomore beaches; I can forget long morning coffees in outdoor cafes in town. During the summer I just have the hot Podgorica nights, which easily become tedious. Fortunately, that night was a striking exception. It was now two fifteen, and I wondered how the big, beefy faggot in the high-school courtyard was faring. I could go back, kick him a few more times, and wipe him with my hankie, of course. But who cares about the distress of others? From around the corner, opposite the barracks, came loud music and the laughter of drunken teenagers. I like watching them, so ruddy and obsessed with their bodies. Fifteen-year-old high-school girls getting down to "Losing My Religion." They don't wear bras. Their thin, white, beer-soaked T-shirts emphasize their budding breasts and erect nipples. A sign on the door of Cafe Biblioteka read: *Rock Party.* One loudspeaker had been plonked outside, so the music rang down the length of the street. I went in and sat at the bar beneath a large map of Europe. "A beer, brother!" I yelled out to the waiter, who was as white as a sheet and squeezing his way through the wildly bobbing crowd of youngsters. Everyone was jumping and smiling with their eyes closed. What's so damn cheerful about that song?! I sat up straight on my chair to get a better view of things, and in the corner I noticed a girl with pigtails, whose skimpy top revealed the top of her tits every time she bounded. Super, girlie! That's the way. Hop, hop, hop. Thank you for giving Miomir Krstov Živković these precious moments of joy. The record hit a scratch just when Michael Stipe pronounced his, *Every whisper of every waking hour I'm choosing my confessions*. And then *choosing my confessions* was repeated twenty-seven times. "Waiter, give the man another one of whatever he's drinking," I said, pointing at the DJ. The guy realized that the frenzied repetition of Stipe's words was leading the teenagers into total ecstasy; he didn't interrupt the fun but turned it up full bore. The girl was hopping about like mad. Exactly twenty-seven times I saw the exciting gleam of her young and firm breasts, and twice I caught a flash of rosy nipple. There was applause at the end and DJ Gligo got up onto the table, triumphant, and toasted the throng with a bottle of Nikšić beer. After that delirium a sudden hush fell and commotion broke out. The youngsters crowded together in a circle on the dance floor. I came up, weaving my way between the sweaty bodies. The kids soon got out of the way themselves because Miomir Krstov Živković with his thirty-five years is no schoolboy anymore. The girl lay sprawled on her back. Her pigtails were half unbraided and tossed to the side. Her chest heaved convulsively. Bright, red lights went on in Cafe Biblioteka and a few frightened teenagers ran outside. I called out for a glass of water with lots of ice and a wet cloth for her forehead. I raised her head, hoping I could pour a few sips into her mouth. That's actually no use, but they do it in the movies. The girl coughed unconsciously and flailed with her arms. The water trickled from her mouth and ran down her breasts, making her T-shirt wet and almost transparent. Pure eroticism. But I couldn't allow myself to be turned on in moments like that. Dozens of wide-open eyes were watching me, expecting a miracle. "What do you want, you fuck-faced little turds?! Has missy here spoiled your party?" I took her limp, cold body in my arms and carried it outside, into the fresh air. I went and stood like that on the road, and all the onlookers stopped on the sidewalk. The kids soon got the miracle they'd been waiting for because the hysterical, flashing blue light of an ambulance appeared from around the corner, coming closer and closer. It was obviously on a call. The driver frantically blew the ambulance's horn while I stood in the middle of the street. Then he leaned out the window with a cigarette between his lips and waved: "Eyyy . . . Are ya out of yer fuckin' mind?! Eyyy, you . . . Y'll get run over, ya dickhead!" Then another voice came: "Maaax! The guy 'ere's dyin' on us!" The brakes screeched and the ambulance came to a halt just a few yards away. A chesty nurse came out first and turned to the driver: "C'mon, turn off the light, blockhead! It's damn well blindin' me." The lights went off and then the driver arrived with a stretcher. "Put the girl down so we can see what she's toxed out on," the nurse ordered. "Why don't ya take better care of 'er, ey? Looks like she's smacked 'erself up," she muttered as she felt the girl's pulse. "Veljo, let's load 'er in here," chesty nurse said. The driver took one end of the stretcher: "What are ya waitin' for, damn yer eyes?" he snapped. "Bend down and lend a 'and!" The nurse went to make room. A man's body lay under a white sheet hooked up to several infusion tubes. She strained to shove him aside and pressed him with her knees: "Owww . . . Heavy old carcass!" The wretch groaned and lifted his right arm, which then went slack again and fell to the side. "'Ere, chuck 'er in," the nurse said, pointing to a sheet spread out on the bare metal bench. I wanted to go back to the Biblioteka, where several of the most persistent onlookers out the front were waiting, but the well-endowed lady swiftly jumped out of the ambulance again and stormed toward me. "Where the 'ell are you goin'? Am I s'posed to take 'er home when she comes round?" Now it was three seventeen, and I was riding in the ambulance with two half-dead bodies. A small window separated us from the front seats and revealed the driver's meaty hand on the nurse's breasts. "Oh, Veljo, no, don't," she moaned. "What's wrong, Natalija? Am I no good no more?" the driver grumbled and stepped hard on the gas. He kept grumbling: "Ya prefer that livin' corpse of a guy . . . Dr. Popović, is that it?" She straightened her coat and said: "I swear he never touched me, I swear by all that's 'oly!" Veljo drove like a madman, racing ever faster through Podgorica's streets. Natalija whined: "Don't, Veljo, y'll get us all killed!" I held the head with the pigtails, with eyelids that trembled, and two forlorn, dark eyes looked out from beneath: "Where are we now? What's going on?" Veljo braked sharply. The covered body slid and pressed against us. Patches of blood showed through on the sheet. The girl screamed. Veljo accelerated again. The nurse seized the steering wheel to try and control the vehicle, and the tires squealed and shrieked and screeched . . . a mighty crash. The girl's head hit the floor and she fell unconscious again. Fuck this life! Using my legs, I managed to push away the man under the sheet. Infusion liquid was dripping on my head. Deep silence punctuated by the shrill calls for help of our injured fellow passenger. I pulled back the bloodstained sheet together with the tubes—and saw the familiar, disfigured face of the faggot from the high-school courtyard, whose tongue was licking fresh blood. I saw his big, frightened eyes that drew me into their maelstrom of fear as he recognized me and shrieked: "Heeelp! He's here. It's hiiim!" I tried to quiet him and explained that I had no desire to harm him, but he flung himself about like a hysterical woman, banging into the sides of the ambulance. The girl woke up again and added her voice to the general chaos that was leading Miomir Krstov Živković to the brink of madness. I reached for the small but fairly heavy fire extinguisher in its mount beside me. Two or three dull blows and the faggot was made to accept the facts. Just as he deserved, I thought, wiping his broad, bloodied forehead with my hankie. And the tepid drops tickled my palate again. And again I heard the distant whisper of my honorable father; words that echo like thunder through the dark halls of memory: *My dear son . . . It is night on earth. And I am no longer a stranger in that night . . . Death screams from every cell of my tormented body; it wakes me up at night and sings a lullaby during the day. I've been buried, true. Not beneath the ground, however, but on the surface. Forever.* Now it was three forty-five. The exhausted girl sat on the ambulance floor, and I explained that I had to beat up the faggot because he tried to attack her. It all hung together. She understood the situation and nodded. She took some cellophane out of her pocket, unwrapped it, and vigorously snorted the yellowish powder. Clever and pretty child. I kicked open the large double door. "Come on out, honey. Just take it slow," I said. She could hardly stand. She talked nonsense and mumbled. We went out into the darkness. I realized that we'd crashed into a pole not far from the Petrović Palace, near the hospital. I peeked into the driver's cab. The mussed-up, chesty nurse was busy on Veljo's cock, and he begged me with his hands to go away and wait a bit, and then we'd continue the trip. Thanks a million, you imbecile. Just go ahead and enjoy, you damn low-life, I thought. I grabbed the girl around the waist. My fingers felt the soft beginnings of her right breast. We set off through the park near the Sports Center. We staggered along Lenin Boulevard like fallen angels heading for the heart of darkness. When we turned off through Njegoš Park, my hand slowly climbed, and my fingers met hard young nipple. We passed along the barracks and Cafe Biblioteka, where there was no one any-more except the weary waiters gathering up glass and cigarette butts. The girl moaned with pleasure. I kept kneading the sweaty, hot flesh. She took my hand and led it over both her breasts. As we walked toward the high-school courtyard, I teased her moist vulva. Now it was four twenty-five. Day would break at a quarter to six, which meant time was gradually running out. Night was departing, and with it the black spirits that incarnated my vital-ity. I cursed my gap-toothed jaw unable to deliver an effective bite. We sat down on the same bench the faggots had used for their disgusting business. The girl got on her knees. She unbut-toned my trousers and tried to arouse my sleeping mouse. But he, too, felt the ominous proximity of dawn and only timidly righted himself, just enough to be able to stay in the woman's warm throat. Don't worry, little fellow: ruddy dawn has not yet broken. Besides, the cemetery is near. It was easy to hop into one of the empty, well-conserved graves that are reliable wardens of the dark. I could wait without panic because the girl was doing her job brilliantly. No need to interrupt her. But the light was inexorable. The eastern sky above Podgorica reddened, the moments of gratification soon passed, and Miomir Krstov Živković had to find a dark place beneath the sun. I moved her head away. "Let's go somewhere else, love," I said. Her bleary, bloodshot eyes were half open above her flaccid, pale body, and her lips tried to come together in words. I grabbed her under the arm and we tottered across the high-school courtyard and onward, through the forest of Scots pines on Gorica Hill, all the way to the Church of St. Djordje and the old cemetery behind it. I imagined my old mother sitting anxiously on the terrace in front of our house, hoping to see Miomir's thin silhouette that usually comes into view behind the Osmanagić Mosque, opens the gate, hurries to his room, closes the shutters thoroughly, and goes to bed. Oh, Mother dear! Tonight I'd surrender to a womanly embrace in a different bed. Now it was five twenty-seven, I had to find a safe refuge fast because my eyes were already stinging and my skin smarting as it was splashed by the faint morning light. *My dear son: The purple nights will become your boundless seas. I tell you, it is our destiny to seek solace in the darkness like fallen Odysseuses . . . alive without life, crying without tears: death is our distant Ithaca.* My father talked all sorts of nonsense. Now let him explain how I'm supposed to shift the heavy stone slab and slip inside. The girl seemed to be pointing to tell me that she ought to head off home, but she'd do no such thing. Just imagine she died somewhere along the way, and Miomir Krstov Živković would be charged with the brutal murder of a female minor after unnatural acts with her. No way! My poor old mother's heart would break. The tips of my fingers hurt as I tried to scratch out the small, wedged-in stones. I had to make one of the slabs budge. At the far end of the slab, as the day gently broke, I noticed some melted yellow wax and a few candle ends that had burned in a stranger's hands. I'd watched them there, at the bottom of the cemetery, together with the dark outlines of humanity that waited for the flames to go out and then slowly walked away through the darkness. Now it was five thirty-nine. I had no choice. The girl was already sitting slumped against the grave in deep heroin slumber, and with the last atoms of my strength I managed to move the stone with its barely legible letters. We'd hop into this former eternal home of a diligent postman. *Here lies the departed of blessed memory Filip Androv Marković who betrayed naught that was written*, it read. The marble slab screeched, and before me lay a dense, enchanting piece of cool darkness. When we got settled, I'd move the slab back into place with my legs and finally rest after an unusually turbulent and ghastly hot Podgorica night. I threw in the girl, and she sighed sleepily. I lay down beside her and repositioned the heavy cover. Now it was a quarter to six. Not a trace of light. Everything was done properly. I found a large, blunt stone that would come in handy if the girl woke up and got hysterical. It's not exactly nice to be alive in a grave. I needed the stone sooner than I expected: she started to yell and wriggle just as Miomir Krstov Živković was falling under the spell of the sweetest velvety sleep. I took as much swing as the restricted space allowed, *bong*, and silence returned to our humble home. Now the girl slept like an angel. And outside my beloved streets came to life. While thousands of miles to the southeast, by the sea, the vampire city of Lisbon sighs: a vast labyrinth of scattered squares, dim stairways, and shady, thick-walled cafes. The clatter of closing shutters resounds in the empty mornings. The shades depart underground to feed and readily await another night of lust. My dear father is part of that splendid pandemonium. Like most Montenegrins, he did well for himself abroad. I believe he voraciously sucks the blood of the occasional French faggot or prettier-than-average prostitute. I like it here; I'm not complaining. But sometimes the smells and sounds of Cafe El Greco ring in my head, the gulls on the *Magellan* call, and then the spectral whisper of Krsto's voice visits me: *My dear Miomir, accursed days are coming, a time of tears and wandering without end . . .* What the hell?! I really didn't know what that mystification could mean. I tried to get to sleep while licking the blood from the neck and forehead of my girl, but an old song echoed in my head: *Forgive me, Pa, for the harsh things I've said / It's now just like yours, this life that I've led / Forgive me, dear Pa, 'cos now I agree / I look at your picture—it's me that I see.* The girl woke up twice more that day. Both times I put her to sleep by hitting her on the head with the stone, but I took care not to seriously injure her. No blows on the temples or the back of the head—that's the rule. You give her a little knock on the top of the head and her body sags straightaway. Her pigtails become soaked with blood, and you simply stick them in your mouth, squeeze with your hands, and suck. What a delight. Sheltered like this from the intolerable Podgorica heat, lying next to a young body with lots of fresh blood, I felt a love for the whole world. And hours later I woke up with that love after a salutary sleep. Seven thirty-two in the evening. The sun would set at three minutes past eight exactly. The pulse on the young woman's neck was faint. She'd lost a lot of blood, the poor thing. But there was no rush. Fools rush in where angels fear to tread, as the old folks used to say. We'd laze a bit in the lovely deep shade of the postman's grave, and I'd wet my whistle once more before going out. Bon appétit, Miomir. Your old mother was now sitting anxiously in the lounge room, smoking one cigarette after another, and watching inane Channel 2. Two days ago she baked a baklava like you've never had before. She was probably asking herself now: What on earth has happened to her Mio if he can't smell his favorite treat. Oh, Mother . . . If that wonderfully sweet filo pastry was soaked with blood, things might be different. But no, I couldn't insist on that. We all know what baklava is. Just as the simple fare of my kind is known. As I greedily slurped once more, I felt the girl's blood growing cold and thickening. It stuck to the roof of my mouth and I felt a pang in my stomach. You can get chronically bad digestion from the blood of a druggie. Therefore I had to pause for a few hours. In five minutes it would be eight o'clock, and I wanted some fresh air. That was the first time I'd spent a day in a grave. Now I pushed the slab impatiently, trying to get out. At last! Encrusted with the girl's congealed blood, I peered into another night. Freedom at last! *Avanti popolo, alla riscossa, bandiera rossa trionferà*, I sang under my breath. I stretched my arms and my back as I stood there on the slab. *Vogliamo fabbriche, vogliamo terra. Ma senza guerra, trionferà*, resounded along the docks of Bari while I waited to board the *Magellan*. The port workers were on strike due to the introduction of an additional tax on income from the sale of shellfish. I spontaneously joined the masses and sang deep and loud amidst grimy workers' jaws and the smell of fish. I almost missed my ship. If I had, fate might have been kinder. And I wouldn't now have jumped back into the grave imbued with fear, hauled the heavy marble slab over it, and looked up through the crack at the dark silhouette that, like the previous night, approached holding a burning candle. Its eyes shone beneath a thin hood of black silk. My hand was over the girl's mouth. I needed to keep her hidden because it really would be no good for them to find me in a situation like this: me and the girl in a deserted grave; her shot up with smack and covered in blood, and Miomir Krstov Živković sated with the same substance. I'll be damned! All of Podgorica would enjoy the retelling and cheap mystification. The whole city would be buzzing with questions: Have you heard about that guy and what he did near the church? His poor old mother dishonored and the Živković family name sullied for all time? Therefore I squeezed the girl's mouth shut even more resolutely to prevent any screams or calls for help. I heard footsteps on the slab above us and the tapping of a stick that supported those steps. The man energetically cleared his throat and then lit a second candle. He swore: "Fucking miscreants. The Inter vs. Lazio match, and I'm bumming around here like a fool. Argh . . . It's not gonna go on like this, that's for sure. I'll teach you some discipline, boys and girls!" Judging by his voice, he was getting on in years. Sixty. Perhaps seventy. That was a voice, I tell you. The man loudly cleared his throat once more and then started to yell: "Oh come on. Wake up! Get your act together, won't you all?!" He beat hard with his stick on the grave slab: "Had a nice long sleep, have we? Come on . . . Time to get up!" He sat down and lit a cigarette, while I sweated and shook with fear. If I had teeth, they would have chattered too. I didn't understand what was going on up above. But explanations always come quietly and depart into legend. Now a gentle creaking of stone slabs could be heard throughout the cemetery. Graves and tombs were opening, that was obvious. I realized that my hand had been pressing firmly on the girl's face, covering her nose and mouth, which no longer emitted a warm stream of breath. The girl was dead. I'd had it too: the slab suddenly moved, and in that sound I sensed the sad end of my existence here beneath the ground, and on the earth. From below, I watched the silhouettes that showed above the grave, and several strong hands seized me by the shoulders. Heave-ho! And I was already out in the fresh air. "Uncle Branimir, is this the new one?" asked the lips, beneath which long fangs gleamed. "Yep. This is little Krsto," the familiar voice of the old man with his stick replied. Slabs were still being shifted. Thin, stooping figures with shining eyes rose up all over the cemetery. That horde languidly shuffled up and gathered around us. "This is Uncle Krsto's son?!" asked the teeth and the pale face that appeared beneath the yellow flame of the candle. Branimir counted those present, and then again. "Is somebody gonna wake those lazy misfits? Tell 'em to get up so I don't have to come. They have to go to work," he said, pointing his stick toward the bottom of the cemetery. "'Ere we are, Uncle Brano. Don't shout." I heard movement in the bushes and steps that stopped close at hand. "I know this guy," exclaimed the newly arrived voice. "Yep, me and Natalija drove 'im. 'E took it out on some girl and then didn't know what to do with 'er. What a fool." Natalija: "Animals like this discredit us, Uncle Brano. 'E should be sent to a little dump like Kolašin or Mojkovac to mess around there. Not every dumb bloodsucker can be a Podgorica vampire. We have a reputation to think about." A commotion ran through the crowd, and then we heard another voice in the background: "Meaning you and Veljo are gonna look after our reputation? Come on Natalija, cut the crap." Veljo: "Stop insulting 'er, ya jackass, or I'll kick the shit out of ya. Filthy cunt!" The voice in the background: "Shut yer trap! Just take it easy and suck some of that tit." Veljo rushed into the crowd, but he was caught by Branimir's rod. It came down heavily on his head and he fell down unconscious. The voice in the background: "That's the stuff, Uncle Brano. Good on ya. 'E struts around 'ere, but 'e ain't got the guts to tell ya he smashed up the ambulance last night and lost 'is job. 'E's got somethin' goin' with this sleazebagette . . . 'E don't know what 'e's doin'." There was a murmur divided between approval and acute objection. The mass split into two groups that kept bandying accusations and curses at each other, growling and showing their fangs. They shrilled bestially and their eyes turned to glassy bulbs of hunger and hate. "I don't know what to do with them. They're as nervous as puppies these days," I heard Branimir's voice right next to my ear. His hand gently pulled me aside, from where we kept watching the altercation. "I let them have a good scrap. They're a little more peaceful then," Branimir said. The two hostile sides now came together loudly in a seething nebula of screams, howls, and curses. "May the sun bleach yer bones! Ya don't know what blood is, ya downtown wimp! Go impale yerself, insolent cur!" Stones whistled menacingly past our heads and we sat down in the shelter of the wide tombstone. Branimir took out his pack of tobacco, rolled a thick cigarette and lit up: "My Miomir . . . It can't go on like this. There are too many of us. Discord, vanity, envy . . . They're divided into cliques and are destroying each other. They'll rot here in this cemetery, the poor bastards. But I love them as my own children! That's my misfortune." The old man rested his head on his chest and calmly smoked while I finally tried to summon what little common sense I had left. No one got worked up about the girl, evidently. It was probably something quite normal here. Which probably goes to explain the relatively frequent, mysterious disappearances of people in Podgorica. I realized I wasn't as deep in shit as I thought when the strong hands pulled me up to the surface of the earth. I should just be quiet and cold-bloodedly observe things. The old man stubbed out his cigarette on the tombstone. He got up, looked at the seething crowd, and then sat down again: "They can have their fun for a little bit longer. When they've let off steam it's easier to keep them from going into the city. It's dangerous there these days, but I dare not tell them everything. They'd die of fear, the poor wretches. That has to stay secret." I wanted to ask what was so dangerous that it *had to stay secret*, but the old man stood up and moved resolutely toward what remained of our accursed band. He spoke loudly: "Boys . . . Girls . . . Have you had enough for this evening? Now all of you come here to Uncle Brano so we can talk about something." The crowd went silent, and a few seconds later we heard only Natalija's voice: "What scum bit me in the leg? I'll zilch every damn one of ya! My silk stockings are tattered, fuck ya all!" Branimir calmed her and said he'd buy her new ones the next day. Natalija wiped away her tears with the top of her hospital coat and sobbed: "Thank you, Uncle Brano. You've always been kind to me." The old man patted her on the head and gave her a tissue. Natalija quickly took it and then ran up to Veljo and said angrily to his face: "Why don't ya protect me, ya cunt of a man? Vampire bastard! At least ya didn't let 'em rape me." At the very same moment, Veljo's injured pride gave Natalija a resounding slap in the face, and then we watched once more as Branimir's rod came sailing down and hit Veljo smack bang in the forehead. Silence again, which let my thoughts return to ordinary topics. I imagined my mother crying because I hadn't been home for two days. I thought of my pale father sitting with his sinister, bloodshot eyes in the Cafe El Greco and recalling his native city, where there's no place for him anymore. Our warm home is rundown. The spiral staircase is decaying irreversibly, and when my mother descends she has to go quietly so as not to wake the ever-hungry worms. A moving story. But there was little time for sorrow in this deserted cemetery teeming with life. Branimir lit a cigarette. He asked for us all to sit down and listen carefully. Our fate depended on what he was about to say. The crowd silently lowered itself to the ground. Teeth gleamed and eyes shone in curiosity and fear, Branimir began to speak: "My dear children . . . We've been together for many a year. A lot of adversities have befallen us. We also cherish memories of brighter moments: times of love, unity, and understanding . . . Isn't that right?" A timid murmur of approval was heard. Branimir sighed and continued with a trembling voice: "I've never lied to you. I admit there were moments when I had to hide something, but it was only ever for your good. And now I'm going to tell you the truth, and nothing but the truth . . . It's hard." The old man stopped and blew out a plume of smoke. The crowd stirred and Branimir tapped with his rod: "My children, the Hunters are upon us!" Miomir Krstov Živković would have continued to doze, leaning against the pleasantly cold ground and attentively listening to Branimir, had not a few pained howls of fear etched themselves into his soul. Those words caused an indescribable uproar and the din left no doubt that the presence of those *Hunters* was pernicious for my unhappy brothers, and thus also for me. Two dark tears ran slowly down the old man's face, and again I felt his hand on my forearm, and now that hand drew me into the total darkness. As we observed the panic-stricken crowd of unfortunates, Branimir sobbed loudly: "My good Miomir Krstov Živković . . . black days have come upon them. They will be obliterated. You are lucky because you have somewhere to go. Your father will always take you in. But them . . . I wouldn't wish death like that even on my worst enemy! The Hunters are merciless and cause a slow death. They're not those pretty-world movie imitations with stakes, little crosses, garlic, and all that. Oh no, when a Hunter is onto you, you're up shit creek. Period. Their teeth are twice as long as ours. They don't bite your neck but go for the back of the head. They're as strong as bears. There's no escape! They suck out your brain!" Branimir rubbed his forehead, and the crowd became ever more uneasy. At one end you saw skinny creatures scowling at each other. Then they grappled with each other and rolled in the dust. A furious fight. Veljo and Natalija were sitting at the side embracing. And crying. The rest of the band was bewildered. They wandered here and there, not knowing where to go. But as Branimir said: there was no escape. "As of tonight, the Hunters are in the city. They've taken up positions and are lurking, so you don't know when and where they'll strike. They don't touch me. I survived the devastation of 1979. If you've eluded them once, they have no right to chase you anymore: they probably consider that it makes you a worthier member of the race. As I understand it, the Hunters serve to maintain its vitality. That's the way it works. The headquarters in Lisbon sends them out all over the world to do the dirty work. Natural selection? Who knows. Survival of the cleverest—that's all there is to it, my good Miomir. Your father caught the last train and fled, and from what I hear he's doing well there," said the old man and withdrew into the deeper darkness. Then for the first time I felt something like familial feelings for these poor bastards. I turned to Branimir and wanted to tell him as much, but in the place he'd been standing I found only the essence of blackness. He'd vanished. Evaporated. Desperate voices called out for him from all sides, but he was gone. Another grave opened, and out of it peered the bloodied head of that faggot. He tried to stand up. He made an all-out effort to get to his feet, but three rabid creatures came up to him from behind and latched onto his neck. They scrambled like beasts around their quarry. Without Branimir, fear of the Hunters grew into panic, and anarchy reigned at the cemetery. All the sounds, the smells, and the fangs gleaming in the dark painted a sad scene of downfall and dissolution. The end had come. I knew it, because I heard two grating voices from the nearby thicket and realized it was Portuguese. Natalija came running up all tearstained, stopped, listened and sniffed the air, and then her blood-curdling scream rang out and echoed through the cemetery: "It's them! It's true, Uncle Brano!" I jumped into the nearest grave. Fear lent me strength and I easily hauled the heavy marble slab over me, which muted the screams, death rattles, and wailing on the surface above. I thought of my mother and the pleasant smells of home I was missing more and more. I tried to forget the good-natured faces of my vampire brothers, gaunt and gruesome in death. On the sails of memory I glided toward childhood, to the sandy banks of the Morača River and the clear water full of reticent sneeps that we plunged after from the sharp rocks, trying to catch them alive. Lulled by those scenes, I managed to nod off and sleep long. Right up to dawn, when I was woken by a dull pain in my back and the distant chatter of birds. It was now five thirty. Too late for me to make it home before sunrise. Besides, the Hunters were upon us. It would be no good to become their prey at the age of thirty-five. I peered out cautiously. I listened and didn't hear anything. Then I climbed out. The graveyard was littered with bloodstained bodies. I went up to one, and then another, and touched them in the hope of finding some sign of life. Nothing. The poor wretches were now at rest, mown down by gruesome death. They'd all been killed, every last one of them—all twenty-seven of them, as many as Branimir had counted early in that accursed night. Only Krsto's words could bring me calm: "It is your destiny to seek solace in the darkness like fallen Odysseuses . . . alive without life, crying without tears: death is your distant Ithaca," I spoke to my fallen brothers and sisters. I dragged one corpse after another to nearby graves. I hauled the heavy slabs over them, burying a whole generation of Podgorica's vampires, and I comprehended that I alone had survived the purge. I will be a Lucifer who will carry the desolate light of our kind through the streets of Podgorica like the Olympic Torch, the vampire who will clear the paths for a fresh spawn of evil. I don't think I'll blacken the name of my honorable father. He'll be proud of little Miomir—the gap-toothed monster with huge blue eyes and a big nose. But above all, I want to have a decent sleep again. These weary bones need rest. Here, at the old Podgorica cemetery. But another night is coming. Soon the darkness will silently envelop the city. And in that darkness, if you look over your shoulder as you walk through Njegoš Park, as you sit enamored on a bench in the high-school courtyard, or elsewhere, as you doze peacefully on your warm bed at home, the shadow of Miomir Krstov Živković will be ready to interweave your days with fine threads of that most awful, primal fear of the essence of evil.

# The Fly

ON MARCH 21, 2006, a fly flew in through the window of my room in number five Blattgasse, in the third district of Vienna, through the large double window that looks onto the courtyard and the two big chestnut trees. I'd been trying to get to sleep for half an hour. I turned over and over, seeking a position that would make me indifferent. I'd gotten used to the metronome ticking somewhere deep in the wall. Drop by drop from the cracked central-heating pipe, and sleep gently covered my thoughts. My next-door neighbor was the athlete Fritz, who was separated from my body stretched out on the bed by a thin wooden wall with nothing in the middle. If there had been any kind of filling in that wall I wouldn't have been able to hear Fritz's energetic squirming and the thumping of his knees. When the sound of a starting pistol marked the start of a race in his dream, Fritz's legs writhed and the wall shook, and a sad whimpering came from my neighbor's throat. And all because, in his dreams, the sound of the starting pistol wasn't that of a starting pistol but presumably a deafening Kalashnikov burst or even the blast of an atom bomb, whose pink mushroom with the Adidas logo rose above the stadium. He gets up early, quickly leaves his room, runs down the corridor, and then charges down the stairs, as cheerful as a puppy. His atavistic remnants of a tail try to wag to the left and the right, and Fritz's tongue becomes redder and longer as he gallops along the sidewalks of the third district. He returns to room 22 two or three hours later after going quite a few miles. Then almost nothing can be heard from his room. Fritz is tired.

He doesn't have the strength to take a shower but flings himself onto his bed, sweat-drenched as he is, and sleeps the sleep of the just, dreaming of a sidewalk that extends all the way to the first stars and farther on into space. Thomas Bernhard says that sport is the most deplorable of all ways people try to convince themselves that life makes sense. I contemplated how my young neighbor would react if I woke him up in the middle of the night and tried to explain Bernhard's definition to him. But if I had to choose the company I'd spend the rest of my life on a desert island with—if I had to choose between the athlete Fritz and the fly that has just flown into my room—I think I'd still decide in favor of my next-door neighbor, without much hesitation. Above all, Fritz would teach me the basics of German. Then, if a ship suddenly appeared on the horizon, Fritz would easily be able to run up to the top of the hill and light a fire to attract attention. All this time the fly would be busy licking feces. I tried to ignore its ominous buzzing and not let myself call to mind the repulsive nature of that insect, a reproduction machine, the last link in the food chain, which swallows others' shit. But in vain. The fly occupied the space, spreading its charisma. There could definitely be no cozy sleep now. The first evening of spring would pass in insomnia. I thought how lucky some people are to see the swallows migrating from the torrid shores of North Africa as the first sign of that magnificent time of year, or the delicate and fragrant flowers of snowdrops. My herald was a fly, an unavailing form of life, ordinary, dull, and incommunicative. In a moment of romantic passion a person can address a bird, a snowdrop, a rhinoceros, or a dog and expect some kind of response, but a fly simply eliminates the possibility of any dialogue. I got up in the darkness, pulled aside the curtain, opened the window wide, sat down on the bed, and lit a cigarette. I believed waiting to be the best way of combating this blight; I thought the insignificant black spot would soon quit my room and leave me to enjoy the privacy of my dreams. As I blew out rings of smoke and their molecules merged with the universe, the question rang in my mind: Are Austrian flies the same as Montenegrin ones? Or rather: Can any national characteristics at all be ascribed to flies?

Suddenly the buzzing stopped. I thought for a moment that the creature had picked up reverberations of my thoughts, that it felt the flickering of an idea and then died, conscious of the magnitude of the moment. I held my breath and thought for a second that this was the end of the story. But the small black spot, blacker than the darkness of my room, turned up again and began to buzz right in front of my eyes, clearly visible for the first time like a crass misprint on one of the eminent pages of world literature. The time of decision had come. *Death and Mercy in Vienna*, I thought and laid hold of Thomas Pynchon's book of stories that lay by the head of the bed. The paperback edition became a fearsome weapon. I switched on the light, surveyed the room, and waited for the animal to fly toward the source of light because excrement and lightbulbs are an irresistible destination for these creatures. Just like Ithaca for Odysseus, I thought, and started to sneak around, carefully inspecting the walls. Nothing. I moved closer to the jumble on my desk. I looked over the laptop and my eyes eventually came to rest on the heap of scattered books on the shelf at the side. My chin quivered and my eyes filled with sweet tears: the fly was strutting on the open pages of Bernhard's novel *Concrete*—my favorite book by that Austrian genius. Why the tears and all the emotion, and also fear? Because I was certain I had closed the book before going to bed. I'd smoked for several minutes and thumbed through it, skimming my favorite pages, and then shut it and laid it on the shelf beside the table. It simply could not be otherwise. Books themselves mean as much to me as the words in them. I'm embarrassed to reveal this purely materialistic and very male collection fetish. Words really mean so much to me that sometimes I sniff individual passages like cocaine, line after line, and then red-eyed, as befits the habit, rub my nose with satisfaction. Well-bound sheets of paper, margins, and stylized titles—all that together made me a meticulous custodian of books. When packing my things to come to Vienna, I painstakingly chose what to take with me. *Concrete*, *The Loser*, and *Frost* were definites. They went first class, right next to my underwear. Carver, Pynchon, and Paul Auster likewise traveled in style and comfort, and I bashfully squeezed the manuscript of my new novel in between them. I recall what happens to books. I even remember which underpants I laid *The New York Trilogy* on when I was packing. And therefore I couldn't find a single good reason to believe that I left Bernhard's *Concrete* open on the shelf and that it hadn't just been opened by the fly. I carefully nudged the chair closer. The little creature humbly groomed its wings as it stood next to the large letters at the beginning of page fifty-seven. I'd never seen a fly on a book before. Moreover, I'd never thought of those two things together. I wiped the sweat from my forehead and took a closer look at the nighttime visitor. Then, to my great surprise, that little miracle started to walk along the lines, slowing down when it came to a comma or a period. I read, first in a mumble but becoming ever louder: *If I go away, I shall be going away from a country in which the towns stink and the inhabitants of the towns have become coarsened. I shall be going away from a country in which the language has become vulgar and the minds of those who speak this vulgar language have for the most part become deranged. I shall be going away from a country [. . .] in which the only model of behavior is set by the so-called wild animals.* The fly stopped. I was astounded by its choice. It's no feat to open one of Bernhard's books and find a passage like this. But this was literally the only place in the novel *Concrete* where his petulance so explicitly fires a blast at Austria and its people. I'm a decidedly literocentric person inclined to strictly subjective fantasies that I find it very hard to depart from. Ever since I read the first page of *The Loser* in high school, Austria and Vienna have always indelibly been a country and a city whose president and mayor is Bernhard, in spite of all the Mozarts, Musils, and futile Elfriede Jelineks. Some people may think Bernhard's books aren't the most appropriate guide for a person visiting Austria for the first time, but it's thanks to precisely these pages that I developed an ingrained affinity for this country. So the first place I ordered a *kleiner brauner* was Cafe Bräunerhof in Stallburggasse. The large faded poster in the window just near the entrance annoyed me slightly: Thomas sitting cross-legged and with his hands in his pockets; a pile of newspapers and his glasses on the table; a bar and a few people hazily visible in the background. Bernhard had an innate facial expression resembling a smile, so an uninformed American tourist might well consider the picture a piece of conceited self-promotion by the cafe owner in the photograph. It was clear that the interior had remained the same. The photograph originated in 1986, but the minute pores of the shabby plush booths perhaps still contained a few of Bernhard's grizzled hairs. On top of that, the Bräunerhof has the strangest waiters you can imagine. My favorite is a rather old gent with close-cropped yellowish hair, a crafted bristly beard, a pocked face, and John Lennon glasses with indescribably thick lenses. In addition, he is very impolite and slow, so you wait at least half an hour for your *kleiner brauner*. I was nervous at first, but then I concluded that a waiter who served Thomas Bernhard for years must be allowed to be arrogant and unfriendly. All the more so if he's read all of Bernhard's novels, and I believe he has, so his attitude can at least partially be interpreted as a tacit homage to the black but brilliant cynicism of the great writer, and to his blooming and complex misanthropy. When leaving the cafe after my first visit, I analyzed the photograph again. Back then, in the peripheral conduits of my mind, I noticed along with a few other details that there was a small but distinct black spot at the very edge of the table, on the right, that could be nothing but a fly. I took a look from closer up and thought: "Yes. There are flies everywhere." Back then it was easy to avoid the fact. But today, as far as I'm concerned, the window of Cafe Bräunerhof sports a photograph of Bernhard and a fly. Whom the writer may have summoned by name, and whose descendant was now strutting on the pages of *Concrete* in my room two hours after midnight! I began to feel an indescribable fear. It was as if my childhood dream had come true and I finally had evidence of the existence of God. Or the Devil. One or the other. My perception of the world changed instantly. The false self-assurance I'd used to nourish my writer's vanity now evaporated, and looking at the creature I asked myself: Who here is really the fly? Who is watching whom, and what will be the epilogue of this nighttime visit? I suddenly wished to say something. My mouth opened by itself in that desire. But that was all. I broke out in a cold sweat when I realized I'd almost started speaking to a fly. I lit another cigarette and wanted to run outside, but I stayed in the same place and nervously finished my helping of nicotine, drawing the acrid smoke of the blue Gauloise deep into my lungs. I hadn't felt so insignificant and vulnerable for a long time. And then I thought that coming to Vienna was a big mistake. Writers do their creative work at a desk in a room. Did it make any difference if that room was in the third district of Vienna or in some Montenegrin backwater? Paper is always equally blank, wherever it is. I'd lightheadedly accepted the kind offer of my hosts and exposed myself to this peril. When your worldview is shaken by a civil war or the death of a person you love, you still stay within the rules of the game, in a way. But when you are put out of action by one little fly, you are catapulted into an unknown realm of mysterious interactions, where the theory of relativity is pure fiction. People normally think that writers long for unusual occurrences to give them inspiration for their textual exhibitionism. Writers perhaps wish for that, but this *Writer*, or rather the writer's *Ego*, wants only an ordinary life coddled in pleasant rituals. In my case that's the daily coffee at Cafe Prückel and several beers before midnight. No flies, new social contacts filled with triviality and broken English, the appearance of the Virgin Mary in St. Stephen's Cathedral, or the passage of Halley's Comet. No thanks. Vienna offers me exactly what I've longed for: boundless meditation under moderate doses of caffeine. That's an immeasurably valuable psychiatric treatment. Plus the dignified Austrian refusal to introduce a smoking ban in public places, which represents an almost revolutionary act of resistance in today's times. I enjoyed watching the little old Viennese ladies who, half-alive, drew puff after puff of smoke into what was left of their lungs with relish. Whenever I had the opportunity, I got up and lit a cigarette for them, and they rewarded me with a warm smile. Then I thought: hold your ground, Austrians! A society without small, salubrious doses of anarchy, even if the price be lung cancer, fast becomes boring. It starts to rot without you even noticing it. At the end of April last year I was walking in the park in the center of Oslo in a break between two lectures on "Literature and Reconciliation." A mass of imbecilic phrases poured from the mouth of a university armchairist who passionately capered about on the rostrum and advised the peoples of the Balkans that they needed to read as much humanistic-minded literature as possible. In simple terms, if a Balkan idiot who still keeps a Kalashnikov under his bed attentively read Hermann Hesse, the Kalashnikov would rust because the Balkan idiot would realize after a good read that killing other people—one's acquaintances and neighbors—is senseless. What creative genius! It should definitely be put into practice. In other words, the territory of the so-called enemy should be bombarded with Hesse's collected works! However, the unhappy peoples of Palestine, Chechnya, Afghanistan, and Iraq will pirate the technology. Secret underground printeries will be opened, and suicide bombers will strap carefully chosen titles to their bodies. When a Chechen suicide bomber, for example, makes it through to a Russian army garrison, he shouts: "Long live books!" and swallows a cyanide pill. The soldiers then seize the entire print run and wake up the next morning as inveterate pacifists who reflect on the meaning of life and the nature of God. These thoughts entertained me as I strolled through the central park in Oslo. A delightful turquoise-green bench beneath birches bursting with fresh green leaves seemed an ideal place for a cigarette. Children were racing around after a ball, and mothers after the children. Birds sang and people were happy. But the harsh metallic sound and the flame of my Zippo instantly upset the balance. Two mothers with two beautiful, blue-eyed little girls were sitting on the bench opposite. Straightaway, the women riveted their glances at the objects in my hands, and when I bit into the cigarette and started to move the lighter and the flame closer, those Norwegian mothers hurriedly covered the eyes of their daughters with their white hands. I turned into dog shit and immediately got up and left the bench, accompanied by expressions of contempt and relief. I clenched the cigarette in my large teeth and invoked the mighty spirit of Knut Hamsun. I smoked my cigarette beside a phone booth, and then went back to the auditorium, ready to brave more well-intentioned stupidity about literature and reconciliation. I forgot to mention that the Latin name of the creature meditating on the pages of Bernhard's book is *Sarcophaga carnaria*. Latin terms always make things sound serious. When you call a maggot *Cochliomyia hominivorax* it grows to the size of an elephant. When you call a fly *Sarcophaga carnaria* it becomes a prehistoric, carnivorous reptile. But when you give a fly a human name it remains a fly, and you become an idiot. Not wanting to let the chance go by, and all the time staring at the black spot that spread its tiny wings, I first quietly, then once again, louder, said: "Hello, Thomas." To my surprise, the creature began to buzz and did a circle around page fifty-seven of *Concrete*. I immediately put that down to coincidence, of course. But the one speck of suspicion that makes our lives more interesting caused me to get goose bumps, raise my eyebrows in surprise, and open my eyes wide. I decided to deepen our acquaintance. I held out my thumb and moved it up to the book. Without hesitation, almost cheerfully, Thomas flew up and landed on my nail. The next question was logically: Should I catch the precious little animal and keep it in a matchbox or take it to the window and let it out into the night? If I caught it, perhaps one day it would begin to speak and reveal pages of unrecorded thoughts. But in doing that I'd be acting against my imagination because it would probably turn out to be a most ordinary representative of the race that's drawn to fresh shit rather than good books. That grain of suspicion would then be irrevocably destroyed, and I'd remain forever without that profound spiritual experience. And so Thomas walked around on my thumb. I got up, taking care not to disturb him, and opened the window wide. A full moon shone above the city. Bats circled the spires of the cathedrals. I held my hand right out into the night and raised my thumb to the sky, like Caesar granting life to a brave gladiator. I felt a gentle stream of air on my fingers and heard a humming. In gratitude, Thomas first landed on my forehead and then beat his wings with all his strength and sailed away toward the moon. I felt sad. Because tonight the world had shown itself to be a wonderful place.

*

That night I dreamed Thomas Bernhard and I were sitting together in Cafe Bräunerhof. Large bowls of beef goulash steamed in front of us beside mugs of Budweiser. The cafe resounded to the laughter of a group of models of all nations and races. They were sitting at the next table and nodding to us bashfully. At the piano in the corner, Rachmaninoff was playing his Prelude in C Minor. The waitress was Jennifer Lopez and the waiter John Fante. At the bar, Joyce was just finishing off "The Dead." Flies were everywhere. They whirred cheerfully and complemented the scene. I sat there enjoying the spectacle, and Bernhard unconditionally claimed that my novel *Hansen's Children* was just about the best thing he'd ever read. Then Mikhail Bulgakov appeared at the door of Cafe Bräunerhof with an enormous black fly on his right shoulder, an insect the size of a cat. He ambled up to our table. Bernhard amiably offered him a chair. Mikhail waved sternly to say no. The huge fly started to bark and silence fell. The Master stroked the ghastly animal to calm it. He looked me in the eyes and asked: "What the devil are you doing here?"

Only then did I realize that we are all futile and dead, and that outside a black snow has been falling for centuries.

## Raymond Is No Longer with Us—Carver Is Dead

THEY WERE DRINKING juice. Watching TV. The old set could only pick up two channels. She was expecting to give birth by the end of the week. He was an accountant at a sock and underwear factory.

"Perhaps I'll go round to Vladimir's," he said.

His wife was leafing through the newspaper and didn't raise her head.

"Perhaps?" she said a minute later.

It had been raining for three days without letup. He'd read that very painful births were seventeen percent more common in humid weather. Medically unproven but true. He believed in statistics. And hoped the statistics would bypass them this time.

"The phone number's on the fridge. If anything happens— just call."

"Do you have to tonight?"

"How do you mean—*have to*?"

"Do you have to go out?"

"You know where I'm going. What's the problem?" he said as he put on his coat.

He had no idea where to go. The only thing for sure was that he usually ended up at Vladimir's. He lived alone and went to bed late.

She supported her back with her hand as she walked. She went with him to the door so she could lock it afterward. Her full belly looked healthy. At the hospital they said hers was a "textbook pregnancy."

She believed the doctors and liked the "bookish" comparison. She straightened the collar of his coat and said:

"Bring me a book. Let Vladimir choose. I want to read something exciting. Okay?"

"Of course," he said, checking the umbrella.

She kissed him on the cheek and locked the door twice.

The stairs stank of urine. The rain wouldn't stop that week, he thought, and looked up—the sky was the color of a dead TV screen.

He would stroll along some neighboring streets and then take the boulevard to Vladimir's. He wouldn't have to avoid the puddles. He had good, watertight American boots. His socks would stay dry. The socks made by his firm bled dye when they were wet. You had to keep them dry.

When he went round the corner he thought of the baby and tried to imagine how it would look. But he could only picture pale skin and helpless arms waving. An unborn child—a nameless being, he thought as he entered the drugstore. He would buy a bottle of whiskey for Vladimir and try to stay sober tonight.

"Twenty, please."

He searched through his wallet—he only had fifteen.

"I'll put the whiskey back then," he said.

"You'll have to," the cashier affirmed, punching the buttons of the cash register.

If the baby came on Thursday, that would be on their wedding anniversary. Double luck, he thought as he left the shop. But he still didn't feel real joy. That was probably normal *the first time*. He thought everything would change when he saw the baby, when he held it in his arms and called it by its name. He looked to the left and then to the right, down the street.

There were no crowds downtown that day. So much water, he thought, it had to run off somewhere. He skirted the largest puddles and chose the sidewalks under the eaves. The wind snapped two ribs of the umbrella, opening it became impractical. He would have coffee in the bar on the other side and wait for the weather to calm a bit.

"Your face, sir," the waiter said, pointing to his own face.

"What's wrong with my face?" he asked, perplexed.

"There's blood on your face."

He touched his nose and looked in embarrassment at the blood on his fingers. Now it made sense—the metallic taste in his mouth in the last few minutes.

"It's my blood pressure," he said and pulled out his handkerchief. "It starts bleeding just like that."

They brought him napkins. Lots of napkins.

In the bathroom only one lightbulb was working. As he washed himself with cold water a man and a woman were arguing. They paid him no attention.

"You could at least have asked. I was the father."

"You pig."

"That's murder!"

"It's my business."

"Is that so?"

"It sure is."

He turned off the tap and wiped his hands with the last napkin.

"You think our child is just your business!"

"Yep, it was inside me, and it ain't no more. Simple enough?"

Instead of answering, the man slapped her hard in the face. As he was headed back to the table he heard it again.

He finished his coffee and waited for the two to come out. Maybe he should have done something. He was sure he would never hit his wife. He loved his wife and knew it would destroy him.

It began to thunder. Every explosion made the image on the TV screen above the bar disappear. Humphrey Bogart and Ingrid Bergman were blanketed in electronic snow. The waiters swore.

First the man came out, several minutes later the woman. She was busily leafing through a smallish bundle of banknotes. Large dark glasses covered her face. He saw them once again the same evening, arm in arm under an umbrella and staring into a store window full of TVs. The central screen focused their faces, which were drawn into smiles. Before continuing off down the street the woman adjusted her hair; the man waved at the camera and they walked off again in silence.

Vladimir's apartment was on the seventh floor, just round the corner. Vladimir was a writer. He was forty-three and wore his age like an old man. He was divorced and had a daughter. Little Ines lived in another town with her mother and came to visit once a month.

He knocked, and behind the door he heard a "Coming!" and then an amiable "Hi bud! Roll on in."

They shook hands and patted each other on the back. Vladimir took him by the arm and led him into the dining room.

"Sit down. I'll be with you right away," he said.

He sat down and looked at the books scattered over the table. Piles of books. Instinctively he wanted to turn on the television, but his friend had voluntarily relinquished having a TV.

"I'm much better known as 'the man without a TV' than I am as a writer. Shocking, isn't it?" he sometimes said.

Vladimir rummaged in the kitchen, there came the clink of glasses.

"A sad night, old pal," he came back with two glasses and a bottle of whiskey.

"The greatest among us is no more. The great text tamer. The prince of the short story. The baron of metonymy . . ."

"Cut the baloney. Who are you talking about?"

"You really don't know?"

He poured the whiskey and pronounced solemnly:

"Raymond is no longer with us—Carver is dead."

"Oh, so I don't forget: your beautiful wife called," he added.

"What?! Are you crazy? Why didn't you tell me right away? Give me the phone. She's pregnant, you know!"

Six.

Two.

One.

He thought of the little yellow cot in the corner with the designer bedcover they spent ages choosing.

Five.

Eight.

Four.

"Come on, come on, come on, for God's sake!" he stamped his foot impatiently. The phone rang seven times. He thought he was going to be late for the birth. That she was in the hospital already or perhaps in the apartment, on the floor, unconscious.

But then her voice came, a sleepy "Hello?"

"Is it you?" he yelled.

"Sure it's me. What's up?"

"You're okay. And the baby? Everything okay?"

"Everything's okay. Why?"

"Say that again, please."

"*Everything's okay*, I said. What's wrong?"

He put his hand over the receiver. Vladimir stood leaning against the doorpost with his glass of whiskey and wide inquisitive eyes.

"Everything's okay. False alarm," he said with relief and put the receiver to his ear again. She asked why he'd got so worked up, she didn't understand. She'd called to ask Vladimir about the book. He agreed to send "a good, dead American writer."

"Carver died today, didn't he?" he asked.

"Yes, he did."

She said it was interesting to read when you know that the person—the writer far away in America—is still lying in an open coffin.

"And a wave of sadness, strange and strong, rolls in from across the ocean," she said. And then, "You weren't there when I called."

"No. I stopped for a coffee on the way."

"Did you get wet?"

"A bit."

"Ha! I can feel the baby moving. It tickles."

"That's normal. It'll be coming soon."

"Please don't come back too late. I want the book. And you're not bad to have round the place either!" she chirped.

"I'll be straight back," he said and reached for his glass of whiskey.

Carver was in his pocket. Before he left he had one more glass with Vladimir and drank to his health. There was an *American way of life*, and there was also an American way of death, he thought. It wasn't good that the summer had begun with such unpleasant weather. Warm, boring rain. She couldn't go outside, that dampened the mood a bit. So far they hadn't had any serious arguments. He thought the two of them would have a harmonious, easygoing marriage. A little more money would remove all misunderstandings. But it was good like this too, he thought, as he looked from the street at the window of their rented apartment. They hadn't bought curtains yet. All of a sudden he felt sorry that he'd left her alone. He wouldn't do it again. At least not at night. She had to be relaxed and feel secure. He couldn't give her Carver tonight for that reason. Carver's stories were unsettling. They radiated a particular kind of anxiety. They were too much like real life, he thought.

She unlocked the door, put her arms around his waist and hugged him. As she kissed him on the cheek he felt her belly against his stomach. He wasn't sure he liked the feeling. And her face was moist. As if from tears.

Usually she watched television before going to bed. She turned off the lights and lay down on the couch. The freshly whitewashed living room was bathed in the flashes from the TV screen. Hues of red and green danced on the objects, on her face. The bright reflections of the film explosions glistened in her eyes. The cool inexorability of the cathode tube.

"Did you bring the book?" she asked.

"Sorry, I forgot it. Your call threw me," he said and went into the kitchen.

"I felt it in your coat pocket. Why the lie?"

"Listen, I don't want you to read Carver tonight."

She went into the hall and got the book.

"It's cold and wet around the edges," she noticed.

"I'm afraid it's like that inside as well. Cold and wet," he said.

She sat down and began turning the pages.

"Please, leave it on the table."

As if she didn't hear him, she began to read the first lines.

"Leave the book, for goodness' sake. You don't need that

agitation, neither you nor the baby," he said, getting loud this time.

He thought Carver's stories would have a negative influence. But he wasn't sure how. There was a brilliant vagueness and a queasiness to them that he couldn't grasp. He sat down next to her, but she turned away.

"I'm going to the bedroom. I'll read there. Good night," she said and quickly got up.

He also got up.

In the near-dark he worked on her fisted fingers with one hand. With the other he gripped the book. She felt Carver going from her.

"No!" she screamed just as her hands came loose.

Today she would read. She would have this damn book.

She caught one of the covers and a dozen pages and leaned back.

But he wouldn't let go. He felt the book slipping out of his hands and he pulled back very hard.

*In this manner, the issue was decided.*

# Drops

WHEN HE LIFTED his glass from the table, a circle traced by water and a map of the world remained on the black vitreous surface, something like a map of the world, with a watery Africa, the watery outlines of Europe, and traces of South America. I said that what we had on the table was reminiscent of a map of the world, but he, with glass in hand, preparing for the next sip, stared at the parched oleander flowers that were dying in the sun not far from our heads, not far from our table. He kept silent even when I repeated the bit about the map of the world on our table. He rested the rim of the glass on his lips, and I waited for him to speak, to say that it was unbearably hot, that today wasn't a day for important conversations, that we should drink the alcohol in front of us and then order more; I waited for him to say anything at all and tried to make out the whites of his eyes behind the dark lenses of his glasses. He wiped the map of the world from the surface of the glass with his hand, poured the rest of the wine down his throat, and put the glass down on the opposite side. He took a deep breath, removed his glasses, and then breathed out and put them over his eyes again. I thought he was going to start speaking and moved my chair a few inches closer. A green fly kept circling his glass. He blew out a cloud of smoke and gave an artificial grin. He took another deep breath and flicked his ash onto the pavement. Dry flakes fluttered through the air in different directions. "Sorry," he muttered, bent over, and brushed the ash from the leg of my pants. "No trouble, don't worry," I said, and that was the beginning of our conversation.

Here under the bridge by the river, by the dry riverbed that people still called a river in August, when the hot wind blew about
leaves, the smell of decay, and green plastic bags—here an
important story was meant to happen: a conversation that would
define the past and foresee the future, answer questions, and
create lasting clarity and meaning, without black holes and awkward mysteries. The aggressive, muffled sounds of the traffic
descended from the bridge. The thumping of wheels, the rumble
of rusty exhaust pipes, hysterically blaring horns—all that fused
into a single tone that cascaded down from the bridge when the
light turned green. Then quiet ensued, and for a few minutes the
murmur of the poplars reigned, together with conversations at
the neighboring tables and children, lots of children. I waited
for that lull and waved to the waiter. I ordered a beer for myself.
Did he want some more wine? He nodded. The waiter waddled
off to get our order, and now I expected him to start speaking in
that perfect gap and nothing would be able to stop him anymore.
The cars were at rest, waiting for green. No one was sitting at the
tables closest to us. All the right conditions for breaking the
silence. The river dried up on Sunday, August 2. I knew there
wasn't a drop in the dusty riverbed. Therefore I was surprised by
the noise: a rising, crackling sound that perfectly imitated the
murmur of water. The empty riverbed was now filled by the
acoustics of a river running down the huge concrete support of
the bridge. A voice of water, pleasant and refreshing. A
road-washing vehicle inched over the asphalt above us. Workers
with high-pressure hoses pushed along the leaden grunge in front
of them. It started to drip from the edges of the bridge and for
a moment it was like a curtain of large drops that left a regular
wet line on the baked earth. He briefly looked up just to prove
how little this change interested him, how immaterial compared
to the aggregate state of his thoughts and emotions that boiled
and froze, and which would soon come thundering like an ava-
lanche. When the waiter had brought our drinks, two bedewed
glasses, and a new ashtray, he immediately lit up another cigarette and took a large sip of the wine. The same old cynical smile
wandered across his face like an ameba. It would stay for a few

moments in the corner of his mouth, then creep away to his cheekbones and eyebrows, before rising to his forehead. When the water stopped dripping from the concrete edges, it continued to pour down the gray slabs above our heads. Tiny watercourses plotted a network of rivers. I was on the verge of saying just that: tiny watercourses are plotting a network of rivers above our heads. But another geographical association would have left a deep scar in the scanty trail of meaning of our meeting, which was already teetering on the brink. I was thinking about things like that when the first drop of water loosed itself from the concrete arch, sluggishly, in heavy flight, direct in its coincidentality, and landed right on his knee, on his linen trousers, leaving a circle with a few particles of rotten grunge from the road. I expected him to react nervously, to jump in surprise at the dampness, swear, or knock his glass off the table with some abrupt movement. But he kept on staring in the same direction, motionless, as if he was gazing at a point in the distance, as if he knew what that point was. I pointed to his knee and said: "Would you like a tissue?" He raised his eyebrow a little above the top of his glasses, which meant he didn't want a tissue; that was supposed to mean that the tissue and my question were just particles of dead matter in the whirlpool of meaningful thoughts that had to be consumed here and now. The water kept accumulating in the cracks of the concrete above our heads: the drops on the arch took shape in a row, like perching birds. The force of gravity pulled the molecules toward the center of the planet, and his knee was an obstruction on that path, which didn't move even when the second drop made a mark on his trousers. Slowly he removed his glasses and put them down on the table. He shook his head and rubbed his lips. I knew this was the moment. He looked me in the eyes and started to speak. I moved the chair a little closer and listened. He said: "I couldn't have imagined that I'd put things back in place in three months—just three months. I'm glad to see you. I really am glad to see you and look into your eyes. But not so as to go on about this and that, you know . . . Not so as to earbash you. I'm simply glad to see you. Like an object, a thing from the past. You know? Like an old radio, a chair, an ashtray, a picture, a house . . . That's what I mean. You look better than ever. My compliments. How is your mother?" Another drop landed on his nose. He didn't show in any way that he noticed, but he made a rather long pause between sentences. He continued: "I know you're fine. I'm sure. I'm fine. You're fine . . . That's how it should be. A strange feeling. I can't explain it now but I have the impression that this is happening in some other reality, as if someone else was sitting and writing about everything that happened between us here under the bridge. So you probably feel I'm speaking without emotion. Without emotion? Yes, because I don't have any emotions. I mean that I don't have any feelings for you anymore. Our marriage was a blunder from the word go. But that belongs to the past. That soothes me now. The mistakes are in the past. They were made in the past, and that's where they're buried. There's no point talking about them. I hope you feel the same way. I'm so glad to see you." A hot wind blew along the dry riverbed. It came in gusts and I could feel the traces of sweat on my forehead rapidly evaporating. Carried by those currents, another drop ended up on his shoulder, and the next one on his neck. I noticed that he nervously glanced up at the concrete construction for the first time. He said: "You can call whenever you like, to have a chat. About anything. I can help you. We can talk about whatever you want. You know I'm good at solving problems. I've always had a good hand at unraveling things. And . . . I've never seen you in such high heels. Please stand up. You must look beautiful when you stand. No, no, no, you don't have to. I'll have a good look when we're leaving. Just you stay sitting. And now this: you probably won't believe me, but that other guy doesn't interest me. I don't doubt as to your choice. I just hope you'll play things a bit differently this time. Don't think I'm faultfinding. I'm saying this for your sake. I hope you've learned a few things. That's all I meant." He endured another drop that hit his cheek diagonally. He wiped his face. Now he was silent for considerably longer and looked at his wet hand. He stared up at the concrete for a few moments and continued in a somewhat different tone: "Your lipstick has smudged at the sides. I see now for the first time that you're using that clear red. Or maybe I'm seeing you with different eyes for the first time. Don't take it too seriously. That seeing things with different eyes. It's just a phrase, nothing more. There's no anxiety, agitation, or emotions. It's obvious to me that none of that exists anymore when I look at you, and that's why it's important to me that we've met up. I admit I was afraid of the meeting. But that's normal. A man never gets to know himself well enough. He can't foresee events. I mean . . . I've finally attained the peace of mind I lacked for years. And I see a lot of things differently now. Memories are no longer a bloody mess, a shambles. When I think about you now, everything's like a black-and-white movie. All the standard stuff. You know?" As he spoke those several sentences about agitation, a bloody mess, and attaining peace of mind, he kept looking up at the drops on the bridge. They were hanging in rows even thicker now, they were bigger, heavier, and ready to detach themselves. The cigarette had burned low between his fingers, and when I said: "Stub out your cigarette," he quickly lowered his eyes and gave an ugly smile. "Okay, okay, look—I'm putting it out!" he sneered and squashed the butt on the dirty bottom of the ashtray. The street cleaners had finished their work. The black road evaporated a leaden mist. The long line of cars started to move. The concrete shuddered. And they started to fall: drops, one after another, in regular intervals, hitting him now on the top of his head, on his shoulders, and hands, now on his back and crossed legs. "Do you want to shift your chair?" I said, but he then turned his face toward the concrete, lowered his eyelids, and waited. His right hand clenched the delicate wineglass. When a drop, a heavy dirty drop, crashed down on his forehead, he squeezed even harder and the glass broke without a sound. His face was spotty from black particles of asphalt dust. He kept squeezing the pieces as if he was draining drops of blood from the glass, as if invisible crystal arteries were being severed rather than his cold hand. Now the usual din of machines poured from above again. His lips moved in the twitch of a curse. He lowered his head and turned his face toward me. Then he opened his eyes wide and furiously flung the handful of glass shards into the air above our heads. A disharmony of percussion instruments was heard when the glass landed all over the concrete floor. He continued with a torrent of equally sharp words. "You slut!" he shouted, waving his bloody hand. "It's your fault, oh yes. Don't think it's not." The waiter came running up and put a pile of white napkins down on our table. After that he frisked about on the terrace, gathering up the shards and slivers. I slowly took a sip of lukewarm beer, and he continued without touching the napkins. His shirt was covered in damp gray stains. Drops of blood grew on the tips of his fingers. He went on: "Your lies and your stupidity . . . You stupid, lying bitch! I tried hard to make it work. You know I did. But then it all began: the accusations, the deceit, the distrust . . . All from you. I know why you're looking at me like that! There's a grin of contempt behind that serious face. But that's just what I deserve for allowing myself to believe. I wanted to believe the lies you poisoned me with for years. Well, that's over now!" He hammered on the table several times. He looked at his thumb and pulled out a fragment of glass with his teeth. He kept talking. But he spoke quietly now, staring at his bloody hand. Occasionally he gazed away absently to the side, and several times he glanced up at the arch which drops were still falling from, but he never looked me in the eyes again. I could only make out individual words in the incoherent diatribe he muttered to himself. Whenever a drop struck his body he'd start to stutter louder and stress the word he was speaking at that moment. He sized me up briefly and then got up abruptly. He opened his bloody hand in farewell and headed off toward the tall set of stairs. He walked slowly, a little bent like an old man, as if his body hadn't been splashed by the drops but pierced by invisible crystal sabers, which now cut his flesh and would stay there forever.

# After the Dress of Text

ANA WAS SITTING with two friends, drinking whiskey, and peeling an orange. The knife was rather blunt, and the sweet juice trickled abundantly down her bare arms to the elbows. She couldn't get the skin off properly so she bit into it like an apple, with muffled giggling and heedless of the streams of fragrant liquid. When she licked her fingers she glanced at one friend, then at the other, and all of them kept laughing. I'd expected her to be waiting by herself, and as I went up to the table and Ana waved to me I inadvertently thought of how I found him dead on the kitchen floor with an orange in his hand, his eyes half open, sprawled between the freezer and the old gas heater. His heart, the doctor said: it simply burst from the high blood pressure. And the orange still lies on the shelf next to his picture today. Shriveled and light. The lady who cleans my apartment on Sundays tried to throw it into the garbage can and then tip it into the dumpster with the rest of the trash. That was in the early morning hours. There were just a few lumps of rotten things on the bottom, between which I easily recognized the withered but still brightly hued fruit. It retained its natural color and the marks of his convulsing, dying fingers. I went up to the table, and she said her hands were soiled and sticky. She held out the back of her hand and kissed me on the cheek. "You smell like oranges," I told her. She also smelled like whiskey, cheap perfume, and cigarette smoke, but I said she smelled like that fruit and looked pretty with her hair tied back in the ponytail. "Thank you," she replied and pointed to her friends, who were getting up and leaving, and whispering to each other. "It doesn't matter. I'll intro-duce them to you next time. If we ever meet them again," she said and burst out laughing. I ordered a coffee, and she another whiskey. She got up to wash her hands. She came back serious and cleansed. After a few minutes of silence she asked if she had rings under her eyes and if she'd changed much since we last met. "No," I said. She'd put on some weight, but that suited her. The last time she'd been unnaturally skinny. "Svelte," she added. "No, you were excessively thin," I affirmed. Back when we planted an orange tree on his grave together, she wore a thin silk dress that emphasized the contours of her body and the lines of her bones; I expected she'd cry and that the memories would evoke his fig-ure—a silhouette that slowly browsed through the newspaper in the dim light of the dining room, his dense crop of prematurely gray hair, gently curved eyebrows, and gravelly voice—but she just said it was hot and that she wanted some water. Those were her only words at the cemetery. Maybe she didn't love him the way one loves a father, although outwardly it seemed she did. She'd sit on his lap and pick little balls of lint from his sweater. They went out for walks and to the theater. I usually refused the offer of us going together: my father wanted to fully gain her trust and get to know her as best he could, I thought. I was six when he and my mother divorced. She left for a certain Vladimir. I repeated that name in a whisper at night beneath the blanket, imbued with a greater dose of hatred each time—hatred for my mother, which came out when she called years later, when I answered the phone and rudely refused a meeting. Another encounter at Father's funeral, cold handshakes and awkwardness, and then goodbye: the ultimate launch into the deepest pits of memory, into the limbos of the mind, a funeral at the cemetery of emotions. I first met Ana on November 14, 1984, at midday. The day before, my father suggested we go out for a walk. He sprayed my hair with deodorant, and as we locked the door he said we were going to Cafe Bulevar. "Why don't we go to the movies or for a pizza?" I asked. "Sorry, I have to discuss a few things with a lady. It won't be boring: Margit has a daughter roughly your age. Her name is Ana," he said. Two weeks later,

Margit Eigenmacht and little Ana Ostojić moved into our apartment—the same shabby rooms full of dusty books and forgotten
objects. I didn't understand why they had different surnames.
We had three surnames in the house until my father and "Aunt
Margi" married. Afterward there were just two: Ana's and ours.
Her real father, Mr. Ostojić, demanded by court order that the
girl keep his. I remember invisible Mr. Ostojić as a voice at the
other end of the receiver—a whisper that Ana would reply to
with, "Hi, Martin, how are you?" And then, "It's fine . . .
Everything's okay. No, I didn't get your letter. Yes, I know you
love me. I promise. I'll send a photo. Do you want Mom's too?
It's all the same, we always have our picture taken together." After
every conversation like that she was silent and ill-disposed. I'd
knock on her door to try and elicit a sound, but there only came
a muted whining and a quiet: "Go away, please." She'd come out
later, her face puffy from tears and her hair mussed up, and open
the fridge, which would suffer considerable losses. It was an
unspoken rule that we were not to ask Ana about her father. That
was a private agony that she abandoned herself to wholeheartedly
and calculatingly. Her occasional bouts of depression confirmed
her status as *an unfortunate child deprived of fatherly love.* We
went along with the game, and little Ana made an effort to keep
it within the bounds of good taste. My strategy was more exact
and much less larded with emotions. I decided that Margi really
was my mother in particular situations and I consistently
addressed her as such when we were out of the house—at restau-
rants or on Sunday strolls. Within the walls of the apartment she
was just Aunt Margi. Fair-skinned, perfumed Aunt Margi had no
inhibitions about walking barebreasted to the bedroom after her
shower. I'd be sitting in the armchair, the bathroom door would
open, and Aunt Margi would pass by next to the table barefoot,
on her tiptoes, leaving a trace of yeasty warmth and fruit-scented
soap in the air. I thought her the most beautiful woman in the
world—until Ana turned fourteen and we secretly drank a bottle
of wine on the veranda, when she licked my wine-smeared lips
and kissed me on the forehead. The last fragments of the partly
imposed feeling of brotherly love for a sister sank in the

irresistible attraction of her body that was present every day, our unrestrained giggling, and the sweet smells of Ana Ostojić. Over the next year we repeated that ritual with the wine a good ten times, aware of the possible consequences. I knew that our illusion of a happy family rested on shaky legs of glass—the superficial chats, the feigned expressions of understanding, and the strolls together. I knew a situation like that usually didn't last long, at least no longer than our ability to forcibly maintain it; at some stage the glass would shatter in our midst, flinging out shiny, razor-sharp slivers ready to injure and inflict pain. The studio at the opposite end of the city, where Margi spent at least five hours a day—to then come home completely drunk in the last few months of our life together—became the subject of disagreements and rows. She'd leave for the studio at around six in the afternoon with a whole load of painting utensils, and with every day that passed she returned a few minutes later. My father would accompany her out to the car; Ana and I watched from above as they threw her things into the trunk, after which they stood and waved to each other. She went in and came out again, tut-tutting with her finger, and nervously shifted her keys from one pocket to another; my father rubbed his forehead and sighed. Aunt Margi left with a screech of the tires, and he'd go to the nearby cafeteria, where he ordered a whiskey and practiced the smile he'd appear in the apartment with ten minutes later. Ana understood what was going on. She tried to cheer him up when he sat with his head bowed in the lounge room, enduring the agony of the disintegration of yet another personal empire: the family circus, in which he played the role of clown. She warmed up stories from school, never-ending tales with an unavoidable *girlfriend* who always did *something stupid* or made a *funny face*, and sketches where the teachers came to classes with their fly unbuttoned and traces of shaving cream, which caused outbursts of laughter from the students. Every day she met another person in raptures over his last book of short stories, and her *friend from the Spanish course* said she'd never read such *moving passages about the disconsolate position of the contemporary intellectual*. While Ana gesticulated with her whole body, turning her face into a series of bizarre grimaces, my father mutely spread his mouth and raised his eyebrows, unable to extract a single acoustic signal of cheerfulness from himself, the slightest hint of laughter. He was thinking of Margi, and he'd think of her in the years to come, too. He dissected his memories like decomposing bodies, trying with the instinct of a pathologist to discover the true cause of the death and decay of their family. And he knew much more than I could have imagined at that time. His mass of unpublished manuscripts contains meticulously exact diagnoses of our lives and complicated relations. The story "Children" brilliantly depicts my and Ana's relationship: from the disappearance of the discreetly imposed brotherly love for a sister, to fictitious birthday parties that were a clumsy cover for our evenings out. We went to the Artists' Club, a démodé place a quarter of an hour from the apartment, and in a plush booth beneath a dimly illuminated reproduction of Gauguin's *Riders on the Beach* we contemplated that fatal, feigned carefreeness. "How is your esteemed father?" Simon, the club's owner, always asked when I came. "Well, thank you. He sends his best regards," I lied. A book of my father's stories with a dedication to him personally was the guarantee that my and Ana's age wouldn't pose a problem. We were the youngest in the crowd of old drug addicts, failed writers, journalists, and the shady demimonde, who transcended their fiascos and loserhood with cheap domestic wine. *For my dear friend, in memory of old times*, I wrote on the second page of one of my father's books, faking his handwriting—enough for good old Simon to quaver with delight. He kept it on top of the cupboard above the bar and sometimes showed it to guests. We had our last little party three days before I left for America and she asked, "What will become of the two of them?" meaning my father and Margi. I shrugged my shoulders. That meant *I don't know*, although both of us had a premonition that the forced daily grind of family life was now entering the darkest passageways of the impenetrable labyrinth. Margi spent nights in the studio preparing for *a big exhibition*. She wouldn't answer the phone, which my father steadfastly proclaimed could only be interpreted as dedication to her work. In those days, our whole life together could fit between quotation marks. We weren't a family but a family in inverted commas. A simulation we shut our eyes and held our nose before, lest the sour odors of decay crawl under our skin and remain there to be sensed years later. I think that's what killed my father and poor Margi: she slit her wrists and jumped from the fourth story, through the window of her studio. A small oil-on-panel painting was left on the floor, like a last will. *No name (no game)*, it read along the right-hand edge of the picture. The airy head of a child hovered over a black puddle in the upper left-hand corner; instead of a reflection of the child's face, a ghastly wolf's muzzle protruded, with red eyes under the water. On the right, next to that scene, she painted a hyperrealistic TV screen that emitted the clearly visible figures of four people with their backs turned to the viewer. And they in turn peered curiously through rents in heavy drapes covered with twisting and densely set lines of illegible text. What was all that supposed to mean? Guessing led absolutely nowhere. Margi was a taciturn woman and definitely wouldn't have been able to explain her wild visions. The picture was later sent to Ana. She locked it up in an old cupboard in the damp basement of the four-story building where she lives today. "I hope it's finally rotted," she said as the waiter served her another portion of alcohol. She nervously entwined her fingers, looked at the ceiling with half-closed eyes, and thought about us, I imagined. About all of us. Memories escaped from the murmur of people who, as the night advanced, flocked to the tables and the bar. Sweaty bodies rocked mechanically to techno rhythms and pressed against us. But we couldn't get up until Ana's tale was told. That's why we were there that day: she'd announced a story. That's literally what she said: a story. I waited for her to speak and overcome the distance between us, a landscape full of long since depersonalized emotions. "Last winter . . . ," she began and paused. "Last winter I bought a dress. For the first time. You know I don't like dresses. I look gawky in them," she told me, trying to outshout the music. "But this really was a beautiful dress. Different. I saw it in the shop window and decided to buy it without trying it on. Why? I can't say. I just knew I had to do it and that I'd feel feminine in it. You know?" And I said yes, although I didn't understand what she was talking about in the slightest. It seemed she wanted to dress the whole story in a garb of futility right from the start. "Ninety percent cotton. I wear only cotton clothes, nothing else. But they have to put at least ten percent synthetic fiber in a textile so it doesn't stretch out of shape," she explained and took a sip of her whiskey. When I announced five years before that I'd be staying in America, when I said school was going well and I'd enroll in university there, she just cried and cried over the phone and almost made me change my mind. Margi *went* the next summer and my father two years later, fifteen days after I arrived with the aim of spending my vacation here. He and I saw each other twice: once we had dinner together at the Club, where Simon fussed around the table hysterically, keyed up by my father's presence; and once we met at the apartment. We smoked in the lounge room and talked rubbish. The third time we'd speak about everything, I thought, and I'd mention Margi, as well as Ana, who didn't call anymore. But he lay on the kitchen floor as mute as a maggot, with the orange in his hand. I dragged him to the armchair, pulled the ruddy fruit from his grasp, and laid it on the open, leather-bound copy of *The Odyssey*. After the ambulance and the police had called, pro forma, spectacular headlines full of pathos appeared in the next day's newspapers, and all the valedictories began with quotes from Homer. *When the rosy-fingered morning dawns, / I gather my friends to me and speak: / Some of you shall stay here, O dear friends, / While I take ship with my companions / To view the lands and gauge the people, / Be they unruly and wild, with no sense of justice, / Or hospitable and wont to honor the gods*. The effect was achieved. During his life he spoke about a *dignified* death, of dying in decency, and the characters in his short prose pieces weren't allowed to as much as cough in their final hour. "He went like he should have," Ana said. I think she meant that in the context of Margi, Mrs. Eigenmacht, who transformed her death into an unprecedented outrage. They managed to conceal the details, so Ana didn't find out exactly what happened. But in the chapel the coffin was sealed, and I presume that caused suspicion because normally only disfigured bodies are served in that way. She had no idea that they needed to pick her mother up off the concrete. And that you could see the small spots of blood on the white facade of the building, since she slashed her wrists before jumping and flailed her arms frantically while falling. But Ana Ostojić went on talking about the dress, about its fine and delicate material printed with excerpts from the local papers. "Mid-1980s fashion is coming back again. I liked the idea with the text," she said. "Imagine you're sitting up close to a person, very close, say. The text runs all over your body: on your breasts, shoulders, sides . . . And he watches your rounded textual landscapes and then starts reading. And you let him do that; he moves from line to line, letter to letter, running his eyes along the fine black bands of printed symbols. A new line, exclamation mark, colon, question mark, comma, another new line, italic, capital letter: you feel your whole body is legible, your body is being read and becoming part of those symbols, and at the same time they become your body, coated with meaning," she said. "Yes, exciting," I commented. But I had to yell to be heard. The sour cannabis smoke from the next table made my eyes water, while Ana, leaning back in her chair, followed the beat of the music with her shoulders. "When it came out of the washing machine—" she exclaimed. She stopped and said it again louder. "When I washed it the first time and ironed it, I sat down to read. To read a dress!" she shouted and laughed. She asked the waiter to bring more whiskey. I asked if that was wise because I knew she couldn't take much drink. "That was long ago, little brother," she said and let the last drops from the bottom run slowly into her mouth. "I read it from the bottom up, from the hem at the bottom toward the neck. All sorts of pieces. A lot of boring things, idiotic titles everywhere, an epidemic of adjectives, a few stylistic glitches and typos," she explained. Her two friends were standing at the door. She waved for them to wait, she told me they had time. They shrugged their shoulders indifferently and went to the bar holding hands. She continued her story about the dress, talking faster, and now I could only make out parts of her sentences. "The text on my left breast—" she said. Her words were lost and came together again in the occasional pauses between the powerful bass notes. I stopped her and pointed to my ears. She realized I couldn't hear and moved her chair closer. I felt the warm breath of speech. She touched her chest on the left. "Here . . . Here it said that Margi . . . Just imagine, my Margi. I couldn't bear it. Those were lies," she told me and took another sip. She didn't understand such cruel coincidences, she continued. She asked herself if she had to go into the clothing store and buy exactly that dress. She asked how the news of her mother's death made it onto the fabric, and why they published all that in the first place. For days after the funeral she hadn't wanted to read a newspaper, she said. "I suspected there was some outrage and that they'd uncovered something more connected to Margi. Something more," she repeated, tapping the rim of her glass against the table. She opened her handbag and delicately unrolled a piece of fabric. "Read it. The local paper. The dress. A piece of her dress." She waved in the direction of the bar again. "Journalists—they stirred up the trouble," she said, pointing with her eyes at her two friends. She'd ask them to uncover some of the unwritten details for her. She wanted to know as much as possible and couldn't think about anything else. How was that possible? "The whisperings of friends and relatives snuck like mice in the moldy corners of the basement. Like shadows, vague and frightening. They were hiding something dark and ominous. I knew that, but I couldn't imagine what it was all about. They were obviously talking about my mother. They mentioned Margi, who was decaying at the cemetery, and they told stories about her life and raised their eyebrows in surprise. I ought to have ignored all that. But the stories died down and soon everything was as it should have been. Until, yes, until I bought this dress and put on exactly what I'd been fleeing from," she said. The music built up, and while I tried once more to distinguish the last line on the fabric, Ana kept talking and asking, "Is that right? Do you believe it? It would be shocking if your father . . . if he . . . if it's the truth . . . How horrible. I thought he adored her . . . that he loved Margi immeasurably. That's how it seemed," she said. But I no longer heard anything. Her left leg just above the ankle showed purple sores from jabs of a needle. She sensed I was looking and crossed her legs to conceal the signs. A man came up to our table without asking, stroked Ana on the shoulder, and whispered in her ear. She waved dismissively as if he was a bothersome mosquito and paid him no more attention—she seemed to have become quite used to this. She got up and told me she had to go to the bathroom. "I won't wait," I said. It had been enough for one day. We'd meet again when she'd sorted herself out and recovered. She managed to put together a few mangled sentences. "I have to . . . something more that's important. Let's talk . . . Don't . . . Wait. As you like . . . but . . . ," she murmured quietly. But it wasn't emotions that perplexed and shook her. It was the tremble of veins yearning for another dose of yellow solution. She got up and took me by the hand. "After the dress of text . . . After the dress of text . . . ," she muttered, and fell silent. I asked her to go on and said I was listening. But Ana waved and moved off toward the nether room to the rhythm of the music. The flab on her buttocks and thighs swayed. She was getting fat. I only recognized a few bygone fragments of elegance and style. Today she'd put on a completely white dress. *After the dress of text*, I thought on the way out. *After the dress of text*, I repeated aloud, watching as she scarcely managed to keep her balance. She reeled and staggered, and then vanished in the red twilight. Little Ana Ostojić, after the dress of text.

# A Head Full of Joy

HE SAID: TRY to imagine a scene, an action, or a situation. Do you understand? Try to think of something that will calm you. Devote a few minutes to that vision and do your best to keep it in your mind.

I said: And?

He explained: Whenever you feel the way you've just described you should close your eyes and think back to something you imagined in the past—something you attached feelings of pleasantness, calm, or indifference to. Yes, even indifference, why not? Do you understand now?

He looked at the tip of his cigarette, blew on it several times, then held up the lighter and sucked in the small flame.

I said: Do you really think things like that help? And what should I imagine? Wild goslings among flowering water lilies? Innocent little creatures with their quack, quack, quack, and soft down that I'm supposed to associate with warmth and protection? Well, you know what? The very next moment I imagined going up to the little things, lifting my leg, and taking aim with my foot. I squashed them one by one, and their tender bones crunched. So much for pleasantness and calm. Your method doesn't work, not for me.

He said: Quack, quack, quack. Could you please try to be serious. You're not the first, and you won't be the last person to visit this "surgery," as some call it. I actually prefer to avoid strictly medical terminology. A room. This is first and foremost a room. Comfortable, aired, and well lit.

He stubbed out his cigarette and shook the ash off his shirt, then he got up and opened the large double window wide. A breath of cold air entered the space. He went on: As far as methods go . . . I prefer only to use treatments that are tried and tested. So please try to concentrate. Repel those bad thoughts, close your eyes, breathe deeply, and imagine a scene, an action, or a situation that will make you feel calm, at least for a moment. And don't worry. Many take an attitude similar to yours at the beginning, but later, after a few weeks, they admit there's an effect. I'm not asking you to believe me, but it would be useful if you could at least accept everything that takes place in this room as one of the possibilities—one of the ways to make your life better.

He put his head out the window and surveyed the street, then raised his eyes to the milky sky. A car honked its horn loudly, followed by an explosion of expletives from an irritated driver.

I said: Could you shut the window?

He glanced at me: I'll close the window and leave you for several minutes. You need to loosen up and try. If you'd like a cigarette, help yourself.

He put a pack and lighter down on his desk. He smiled and pointed to the door and then went out on his tiptoes as if he was leaving a room where children were sleeping. I pulled up another cushion behind my back and rested my shoes on the armrest of the couch. The cushions smelled of other people. Traces of perfume mingled, making a sweet cloud of indistinct smells. The windowpane started to fog up, and the horn out on the street wailed a few more times. The housing of the computer whirred at high frequencies that I picked up with my right ear. The pale glare of the screensaver illuminated the bare wall. The walls of my skull were filled with *emptiness*, so after a brief thought about emptiness I immediately shut my eyes tight and tried to reflect on exactly this state being one that was supposed to produce feelings of pleasantness, calm, or, ultimately, indifference. The absence of images, sounds, smells, and taste, the absence of light, darkness, or any sensory associations that could summon real images or predictions interned in the labyrinth of thoughts consumed long ago—all that was a magnificent but at the same time aborted idea, a stillborn brainchild, after which I abruptly opened my eyes and quietly swore several times, thinking about the doctor, his room, and the fifty euros I'd be leaving there when I cordially shook hands with the cur. I also thought about the remaining twenty, with which I'd have to order malodorous draft beer instead of whiskey. It crossed my mind that I should get up and leave straightaway; I'd run down the stairs without looking back at my decisions; but the couch was just too comfortable, and the cold outside unbearable. The conformism of the moment prevailed convincingly over anything vaguely like decisions, so I just snuggled even tighter into the large cushions and randomly chose one of the books that lay scattered on the low table by the armrest. It was a pocket miniature, a hardcover with thick pages: *The World's Most Beautiful Mountains*. The snow-covered cap of distant Kilimanjaro graced the title page, and after that the mountains were listed in alphabetical order, through to exotic $X$, $Y$, and $Z$, dotted across the equatorial belt, Transcaucasia, and the northeastern regions of China. The horn outside sounded several more times in a nervous, organized rhythm. The fog on the pane gradually evaporated. The cigarettes were far away. I browsed slowly, page by page, and stopped at the letter $N$. Snowy slopes and conical outlines of extinct volcanoes, then something resembling the head of an emaciated cat, followed by green slopes, lakes in the foothills, various glacial formations, thermal springs, and vast expanses of coniferous forests. I forgot about the cigarettes. My right thigh went slightly numb: a pleasant tingling ran all the way down to my knees, my heartbeat slowed, and my rib cage rose and fell evenly to the rhythm of the screensaver in the shape of a big soap bubble. For the first time I thought the space I was in—that high-ceilinged room outfitted with a minimum of furniture, but solid and expensive, in a large, fourth-floor apartment facing onto the street, with apricot walls—really did have the effect of linden tea or some other soothing beverage. I felt better than I had the previous day: my arms rested alongside my body with outstretched fingers, my feet stopped feeling cold, and the blood flowed evenly in my arteries. Nor did the doctor's broad face seem as wide and ugly as before. The horn out on the street wailed four more times, and I was now ready to satisfy the ridiculous request of the practical psychologist who asked me to close my eyes and imagine beauty garnished with artificial peace. I stretched my lower legs and breathed in deeply, and then exhaled while looking at the gentle shadow of the philo-dendron climbing up the wall. I closed my eyes. My eyelids slowly drooped. The soft, rosy darkness set the scene on which the settings of a new, therapeutic world would grow.

The door opened at almost the same instant. The doctor mut-tered something like uh-huh and sat down in the high-backed leather chair. Then came the rasp of the lighter and the scarcely audible crackling of tobacco. His fingers pressed several keys on the keyboard, and the horn out on the street sounded in inter-mittent sequences of varied length and equal intensity.

I turned the palms of my hands toward the ceiling and pro-nounced most quietly: A Japanese village.

The doctor sat up straight in his chair. The leather creaked, and he said: Yes? Once again please. You said . . .

I: I said, *a Japanese village.*

He: Yes, yes, yes . . . Do go on.

I: In a small Japanese village the first snow is falling.

New beads of perspiration gathered on my hot palms. I wanted to open my eyes and make abrupt movements to break the silence. By accepting the rules of the game I felt seduced, defeated, cheated. It seemed my gray cells were drowning in stupidity and the normally distinct shapes of brain tissue were being deadened, but I kept pressing my eyelids shut as broad roofs of wooden houses and the outlines of a mist-shrouded mountain could now gradually be glimpsed amidst the nebulae of that rosy infinity.

I expected the doctor to speak first and that several mock-in-quisitive little questions would crush those inceptions of a futile landscape, but apart from the sound of the horn that filled the street only the hum of the overheated hard disc could be heard, together with the blowing of smoke that accumulated high up near the ceiling.

I said: In a small Japanese village the first snow is falling. Great swirls of thick mist are flowing down the slopes of Mount Nantai. The houses are crowded close together along the winding stone road that leads to the springs at the end, no, at the beginning of the village. It doesn't matter. It depends whether you're coming down the mountain or going uphill. The windows are tinged by the yellowish light of petroleum lamps. No one is on the street. Neither is it a street—more of a narrow path paved with red slabs worn smooth by the feet of people and animals. It's twilight. Pale and wintery. Inhabited by silence. A vast silence. The kind you can only hear, of course, in a small Japanese village when the first snow is falling.

There was a rustling. I assumed the doctor crossed his legs and reclined even deeper in his chair. The glass ashtray rocked. His hand stubbed out his cigarette, he cleared his throat softly, and then asked: You're not cold, are you? Would you like me to turn up the heating?

I shook my head, and he said: Go on. Please do go on.

I: Night is falling with the sounds of snowflakes. They are large and sway like feathers as they fall through the thick air. Bare fields, hilltops, and the crowns of tall cedars are covered in a gentle white. There's no wind. The chimneys are hot, and bands of white rise high to merge with the clouds. A few children put their heads up to the glass and try to look at the lovely change. They'll sleep peacefully beneath heavy woolen blankets, waiting for morning.

I turned my forehead toward the ceiling and took a deep breath. The doctor asked: Do you have children?

I shook my index finger, and he said: Please go on.

Just then I really had the whole picture before my eyes. I didn't want to open them anymore and was so excited by the constancy of the landscape taking shape all by itself with every passing moment.

I breathed slowly, without my usual smoker's cough, and my alveoli seemed to take in more oxygen than usual. Soon came the babble of a stream, several large birds flew over the roofs, and the peak of Mount Nantai shimmered briefly in the afterglow of the sun's last rays captured high in the stratosphere.

I waited for the horn out on the street to end its cacophonic crescendo, and then I said: The lights slowly fade. People go to bed. The horses in the stables sleep standing up and the goats lie on thick layers of straw. Half an hour later, only two windows are still illuminated. One at the foot of the village, the other at the end of the stone path.

Doctor: Do you like the countryside? You should spend as much time as possible in the countryside.

He lit another cigarette and emptied the ashtray into the bin under his desk. The stale ash began to smell. I almost opened my eyes and reached for a cigarette. Nicotine addiction tickled my palate. My nostrils flared, trying to inhale as much as possible of the smoke.

I said: I don't like the countryside.

I told him I didn't like the countryside although I do occasionally enjoy cycling by the river. The old road is untended, cars are rare, and the countryside almost untouched. Decrepit cemeteries near crumbling villages, big frogs and bold hedgehogs, sluggish green bugs plodding through shriveled leaves. In some places the water is a turquoise blue and I view it from the shade of the fig trees. Swallows swoop down low to catch little flies above the rippling veins of water, red flowers bob, and tall rocks radiate the heat. My years of fervent addiction to tobacco meant that all scenic places provided a good opportunity for a smoke. An old bridge or the chilly stairway of a cemetery chapel, a spring encircled by rocky outcrops of limestone origin, a shady sandbank near the foot of cliffs full of birds' nests—the aesthetics of all those places were condensed in the short-lived flame of my lighter, accompanied by the crackle of the dry crumbs of tobacco at the tip of the cigarette. Then vigorous, boundless inhalation followed by exhalation. In different circumstances, thinking of those rituals, I'd certainly have said, *I love the countryside*, but the first snow was still falling in the small Japanese village on the slopes of Mount Nantai. It covered the roofs and the narrow dirt paths that wound between the houses. Night fell with all its weight, torpid, like a slumbering black animal of titanic size. And the two illuminated windows, one at the foot of the village and the other at its far end, became the sole mise-en-scène, showered with flurries of large snowflakes.

The doctor crossed his legs again, and I said: Thirty-eight-year-old Masaso Ibaraki is sitting by one window, and there's no one sitting by the other, at the end of the stone path.

I went on: Masaso works at the shore of a lake. A fish farm was opened last summer and Hideo Maeda, a forty-five-year-old teacher of French from Osaka, breeds three species of carp there. Thermal springs ensure that the surface of the water is free of ice even in winter, so despite the high cost of transporting the fish to the nearest road, Maeda's business can be considered successful. Carp grow fast and gluttonously devour the feed that Masaso Ibaraki shovels in for them from large linen sacks. He is tall and strong, as well as being a responsible and dedicated worker, whom Hideo Maeda chose from three candidates after just seven days' probation. The dexterity Masaso demonstrated when binding the heavy metal cages and immersing them in the cold water of the lake without words or pulling a face, as well as his reserve and his understanding of the system for raising large carp, made Hideo Maeda even more firmly convinced that leaving his job as a high-school teacher in Osaka and coming to live in the village was what would change his life in the right way and finally allow him to devote himself to writing. The raising of carp would occupy the body, and writing, the mind. Masaso Ibaraki's twenty-nine-year-old wife, Kazuko Ibaraki, would be the sole obstacle to the attainment of those goals.

The doctor cleared his throat, but this time it was more a stammered warning than a typical smoker's creak.

He said: Yes, it's getting interesting, though perhaps you've painted too broad a picture. But please go on if it satisfies you. That's the purpose of the therapy, and it seems I can already declare our meeting a success. Have you been to Japan?

I said: When he first came to the village, Hideo Maeda was received with polite restraint and moderate hospitality. People came out of their houses to have a look at him and say hello, but no one dared to be the first to invite him in for some tea. He briefly inspected the house, nodding with satisfaction, and returned to the village seven days later with a roll of paper tied with a red ribbon, a large rusty key, and an overnight bag. The purchase contract had been signed the day before, and his home furnishings were already on their way. The two strong horses and the cart that would haul his books, the dining-room table, and several shelves up the muddy path to the village belonged to Masaso Ibaraki. During the three hours of that very bumpy ride over winding pastures he'd become acquainted in detail with the plans for the construction of the fish farm. Once they'd unloaded things together and he'd touched the *Large Encyclopedia of Japan* for the first time, which until then he'd only ever seen on the shelves above the head of the local prefect and considered it the greatest treasure, Masaso Ibaraki generously invited Mr. Maeda home for dinner. It was then that the French teacher from Osaka first set eyes on Kazuko Ibaraki, Masaso Ibaraki's twenty-nine-year-old wife, whose large and firm breasts visibly rocked beneath the single layer of linen fabric.

I turned toward the doctor with my eyes shut, expecting him to interrupt me or at least try to cut my narrative short with one of his usual comments, but for the first time a deep silence came from the direction of the desk. A car's horn blew a few more raucous octaves, an unintelligible voice yelled out on the street, but I nestled even more comfortably between the large cushions and said: A small correction. Her breasts were not exceptionally large. Not of the sort that sway uncontrollably, in different directions. They were firm and beautifully rounded, pointed and symmetrical. Actually, it would be enough to say they were perfect, but each of us has different parameters of perfection. That's why it's sometimes good to clarify things.

And her shirt . . . the material . . . It couldn't possibly be coarse linen. You wouldn't be able to make out the subtle curves of her white skin beneath it that smelled . . . that smelled . . . Yes, that smelled of wild carnation oil. Mr. Maeda was surprised that Mrs. Ibaraki insisted on a modern cardigan and didn't wear a traditional kimono, which all the other village women appeared in. And when he spotted a dozen neatly stacked books on the shelves, next to a few ceramic jars with dried flowers, he realized he'd met two people who would make his life in the remote village on the slopes of Mount Nantai more bearable. Even at that first dinner together their conversation turned into a calm exchange of useful information seasoned with humor and bonhomie, further boosted by sake. Mr. Maeda tried hard not to look directly at Mrs. Ibaraki's curves, which especially stood out when she got up from the floor, elegantly balancing armfuls of crockery.

I rubbed my eyes and asked: Are you following this?

The world beneath the thin rosy skin had expanded, and at that moment I could hardly remember the doctor's broad face and the contents of his *room*.

I heard a gentle rap on the desk. I assumed he'd put down his glasses. He settled in his chair again, blew out some smoke, and then said: Yes, yes, yes. Do go on.

I continued: The equipment for the fish farm arrived seven days after their first meal together. In the meantime, Masaso Ibaraki and Hideo Maeda toured and examined several miles of the lake shore in search of the most suitable spot. And when they'd completed that task, another dinner was organized, this time at Mr. Maeda's. Washed down with a bottle of French pinot noir and sweetened with dark chocolates wrapped in red foil, that meal made Masaso and Kazuko once again unfurl their dreams about a city life before going to sleep—a life free of the smell of goat droppings and sticky mud. They both agreed that life in the village would be considerably more interesting now that Mr. Maeda had arrived, but there was one thought that Masaso Ibaraki didn't reveal as he pressed himself up against the nude, moist body of his aroused wife.

Because when Mr. Maeda had recounted events from his school years in an outer suburb of Osaka and drew an invisible

map of the courtyard to help describe the appearance and position of the stairs that the fat headmaster tumbled down, Mrs.
Ibaraki's gaze had been glued to the face and eyes of their new
neighbor. Besides, Masaso noticed that the laughter from her
throat had never been louder and at the same time more sincere.
It was clear to him that Kazuko's heart warmed in the presence
of that man and that his charm, reinforced by an abundance of
experience unknown to them, entertained her in a completely
new way. He took a sip of pinot and disgustedly rejected such
thoughts that could sow the worm of distrust and allow it to
gnaw at their newly developed friendship with the teeth of
unfounded jealousy. He raised his glass high and wished for
the carp to spawn and for their meat to be red and rich. Their
three glasses met with the clear ring of hand-carved crystal, and
months later Masaso Ibaraki would identify that moment as the
point when unexpected happiness began to give way to unexpected misfortune.

I creased my forehead and covered my mouth with my hand,
trying to remember an appropriate place in the narrative to continue the story. Then the phone rang on the doctor's desk. He
lifted the receiver, muttered something like, *No, I haven't forgotten. Everything's as we agreed,* and lit another cigarette.

He said: Would you like to go on? If not, keep the story
for the next meeting. We've begun just as I hoped. Very nicely.
Exceptionally well. Clear pictures and correct sentences. You
ought to write it down and carry it with you at all times.

I said: The fish farm was opened one month later with a small
ceremony, which was also attended by residents of the nearby
villages.

He said: Good. Go on about the fish farm.

A car's horn blared from the street several more times, and I
continued: Fish fry was tipped into small cages close to the shore,
while the breeding males and big red-tailed females were put in
cages and submerged twenty yards farther out. The red ribbon was
cut by the local prefect, who expressed the hope that Mr. Maeda's
fish farm would be the cornerstone of sensitive industrialization

of the whole mountain region. Everyone nodded together in approval, and Mrs. Ibaraki cast a handful of rice over the now-tranquil water and laid her hand on Mr. Maeda's shoulder.

A hut of untreated cedarwood, with a single-sloped roof and two small windows, a desk, a bed, and several shelves, would be where Masaso Ibaraki would spend progressively more and more time. A pedantically detailed schedule of feeding the fish and graphic depictions of the cultivated species with their basic characteristics were nailed above his desk. A small cast-iron stove was put in one of the corners and, regardless of the limited size of the space, Mr. Maeda attached a total of six petroleum lamps to its board walls. Do you think the description of the hut and the fish farm is excessive?

Doctor: Pardon?

I: Do you think it's excessive to describe the situation at the lake, doctor?

Doctor: At the lake . . . Yes . . . I don't know. You decide.

I: You're not listening to me.

Doctor: I'm listening carefully, I assure you! Feel free to go on if you want. We don't have much time left, but do go on. It's important.

I: Important?

Doctor: It's important for you. Try to focus and go on. It's important for me too. You are the measure of my usefulness in this regard. I'm committed to helping you. I want you to feel better. And please don't call me *doctor*. It puts unnecessary distance between us. The fish farm, the lake, petroleum lamps . . . I want to hear more.

I: The detailed description of the situation at the lake is excessive, I admit. Although it would be nice to mention that Mrs. Ibaraki planted chrysanthemums along the edge of the hut in the spring. Together with two dwarf sycamores, one under each window.

I closed my eyelids tight, imagined large petals in several colors, and then said: It was clear from the beginning of operations that the fish farm demanded round-the-clock supervision. Nothing was to be left to chance. The north wind that blew down from the icy peaks of Mount Nantai at the beginning of February could easily overturn the buoys that the cages were attached to. Hideo Maeda therefore offered to triple Mr. Ibaraki's salary if he'd work a twenty-four-hour shift every second day. That was an amount one simply couldn't refuse, and it prompted the Ibarakis to give up the arduous raising of goats without much hesitation. Feeding the fish four times a day, skimming off leaves and dead fry with a net, and monitoring the number of breeding specimens was essentially all that Masaso Ibaraki had to do. The bed was comfortable and the space well heated. Kazuko brought him his main meal at two in the afternoon, and Mr. Maeda would drop by in the early evenings for a half-hour chat and a glass of sake. The new routine of life connected the three of them and created an almost flawless mechanism consisting of work, orderliness, polite communication, and financial stability. And things were like that for a while until Mr. Ibaraki was getting ready for bed one night in April and, searching for the itemized account of the last delivery of food pellets he'd intended to go through at home after dinner, he discovered a French textbook and a half-used wad of notepaper, on which he recognized his wife's handwriting. The clumsily written lines of Latin letters were crossed out here and there in red ink and tiny comments had been added, evidently in Mr. Maeda's writing. Masaso carefully reassembled the pile of paper and returned it to its place, under an earthenware dish full of walnuts, and then without a word lay down next to his wife, who had dozed off. But he got no sleep that night. He thought of the long winter hours Kazuko spent in Mr. Maeda's house sipping French wines. The pale-purple flecks on one of the pages bore witness to that, and they made Masaso think of his wife giggling at her poor pronunciation of some word; there was bound to be a deal of tongue twisting involved. He drew away to the edge of the bed and nervously hugged the pillow, looking at the reflections in the black hair that spilled down her naked back, and then he imagined another man's hands on that back and shut his eyes tight, immediately trying to free himself of the picture that had formed in his mind.

The door of the office abruptly opened. The philodendron leaves rustled, and a woman's whisper murmured two or three addled sentences, which the doctor, I assumed, replied to with a nod. I fell silent and turned toward the door, like a blind man. The door closed, and several more drawn-out howls of a car's horn crept up from the street.

The doctor tapped four times on the glass surface of the desk and said: You know, we're exactly twelve minutes over time. Perhaps it would be best for you to remember where you stopped, and then we can continue next time. Even tomorrow, for example. I'm not insisting, but I have an elderly patient who I've been seeing for over two years. A very complicated and interesting case. If you can round off the story in the next ten minutes or so I'd be happy to listen. The whole narrative is maybe too broad to serve as a therapeutic accessory later. You seem to have embellished the story with too much detail but ultimately, I must emphasize, I'm very satisfied with our first session.

The doctor's businesslike tone unsettled me slightly. The story was not burdened with excessive detail. Besides, in recounting *a scene, an action, or a situation* that would soothe me I'd skipped a whole chapter on Mr. Maeda and his life in Osaka that would have made the presumption of an intimate relationship between him and twenty-nine-year-old Kazuko much more evident.

I: You don't understand. I'm narrating all this so we can go back to that night when the first snow is falling on the small Japanese village.

Doctor: Of course I understand. You express yourself with great precision. Have you ever tried to write a short story, a novel, or anything like that? If you haven't yet, you should. It can also have very effective therapeutic implications.

I: The next day Masaso Ibaraki was silent at breakfast. He had the afternoon shift ahead of him and just two feedings of the fish. He'd spend his remaining hours of spare time developing a scenario to explain how, in his absence, Mrs. Ibaraki regularly went to Mr. Maeda's and shared much more with him than just tepid sips of French wines. He thought of them getting undressed, and then he imagined them naked, on the table, on the bed, on the floor, leaning up against the wall, rapt in passions that, Masaso Ibaraki believed, were ignited that day when pinot noir first splashed in the crystal glasses adorned with the glints of petroleum lamps.

The carp soon disproved the myth about their libido. They mated boisterously at night, flinging themselves out of the water beneath the full moon.

Masaso had observed that spectacle with delight up until the day he found the French textbook under the earthenware dish, and afterward the images flowed together by themselves, every day and without order, against his will and in spite of the rational defenses he prepared in his attempts to calm down. Every scratch on Mr. Maeda's forearm was made by his wife's nicely manicured nails, although rusty wires protruded from the corners of the fish cages like cat claws. The scarcely visible bruise on her neck became the result of a lovebite by the French teacher from Osaka, although he, Masaso, had enjoyed that long neck himself the previous night. And the looks of his fellow villagers seemed to have changed: each time he returned from the fish farm carrying a cloth bag with the crockery from his last meal he believed they gave the obligatory little wave and then traded spiteful comments about his wife's frequent visits to Mr. Maeda's house. From week to week and month to month, the reciprocal invitations to meals became more seldom until they ceased completely. The wad of French vocabulary sheets grew thicker, and instead of the frequent crossings-out on the first pages, the later ones were ornamented with ticks of affirmation for work well done. Am I speaking too fast?

Doctor: No, please go on. Five minutes more.

He seemed to have become nervous. He rapped his glasses on the desk, and the fine crunching sounds led me to conclude that my practical psychologist was chewing his nails. I was reconciled and almost grateful. I breathed deeply without any need for a cigarette. The morning pandemonium of my thoughts had been erased by the story about the small Japanese village, and a warmth coursed through my body that condensed in the soft cushions stuffed with eiderdown.

I said: Now we come back to the night when the first snow is falling on the small Japanese village.

I gave a portentous cough and continued, trying once more to summon the large snowflakes that sink through the silence: Where was I . . . Masaso Ibaraki spent that cold fall night at the fish farm. Mr. Maeda's evening visits had ceased several months previously, so he gulped down his sake quickly and in silence. He killed time by thoroughly sharpening the small fishknives or sleeping a forgetful sleep that would take him away, at least for a short time, from the painful suspicions regarding his wife's relationship with the French teacher. Several glasses more before midnight, together with an accidental cut down the side of his thumb while whetting one of the knives, were all it took for his mood to finally plummet into the abyss he'd been digging for months. He slid the blade deep under his leather belt, and after just a few agile steps he stuck his thumb under his tongue and sucked the metallic tastes of hot blood. He walked, jumping over muddy puddles and rocks, whose positions he knew off by heart. As he went, he periodically looked up at the sky and the clouds that had merged into one gigantic, crumpled mass. The remnants of the large moon illuminated the far edges of that meteorological inevitability, and Masaso Ibaraki came closer to his own house, ready to finally confront the doubts that had been consuming his thoughts and his substance for months. The large courtyard window was lit up by the mellow light of a petroleum lamp. He hurried along the stone path, ascended the six wooden steps, and tore open the door. He was met by a warmth infused with the sweet smells of the spices Kazuko had used earlier that day when cooking the main meal. The French notebook and textbook weren't in their usual place. He did a quick tour of the lounge room, went through the kitchen and the bedroom, and uttered his wife's name several times, which for the first time struck him as harsh, even ugly. He stood and drank a few mouthfuls of sake, and then he began to undress.

He threw his things around carelessly, wanting to free himself as soon as possible of the heat that pervaded him from within, spreading like a tide and filling even the most hidden nooks of his powerful body. When he was down to just his coarse fisherman's trousers, Mr. Masaso Ibaraki crossed his legs and sat down by the large window, through which his gaze extended down the winding stone path, all the way to the end of the village. One other window was lit up, but no one could be seen in it. He wiped the sweat from his face and grabbed the haft of the knife that pressed against his bare belly. He thrust the blade hard into the wooden floor. Several large snowflakes clung to the warm windowpane and then vanished. Watching Mr. Maeda's distant window, Masaso Ibaraki could only hear the sound of his own breathing, which slowed as it followed the rhythm of the white down descending from the sky in ever-thicker flurries. And so, Doctor . . . the story's over.

I clapped my hands and abruptly opened my eyes. The outlines of the village's low houses shimmered on the bare walls; or at least I wanted something like that to happen. I expected the doctor to immediately get up and try to push me out the door as soon as possible, but he just crossed his legs and stared at me strangely askance, holding a cigarette between his fingers with a drooping tail of ash about to fall off.

I sat up on the couch, stretched my back and asked: What?

The doctor said: Are you sure that's right? Is that the end? Masake is sitting . . .

I: Masaso.

Doctor: Masaso is sitting by the window, resigned to his destiny.

I: No, he's sitting by the window, watching the first snow and breathing calmly because he's now decided what he's going to do.

Doctor: And what is he going to do?

I: How should I know?

Doctor: What do you mean *How should I know*? You said yourself that he'd already decided.

I: I did. That's what I said. But it wasn't me who decided. Masaso Ibaraki did.

The ash dropped off and ended up on the doctor's white shirt. He brushed it away carelessly and looked outside.

He said: But if you created that person, you ought to know what Masaso has decided and what he's going to do. You are his father and his god.

I said: I *created* him?! Doctor, for heaven's sake . . . I only created, and I quote, *a scene, an action, or a situation*, something that would soothe me and to which I'd be able to attach feelings of pleasantness, calm, or even indifference. I did just what you suggested.

He got up abruptly and opened the window. He moved aside as if Kazuko, Mr. Masaso, and the French teacher Hideo Maeda, together with the whole village, the fish farm, the lake, and Mount Nantai, were about to fly out and climb up into the sky. In the distance, two birds cut across the large window frame to the sounds of a car's implacable horn. The doctor nervously crushed out his cigarette butt in the ashtray and then said: Yes, you're right. You really did make a good effort. I think our sessions will be even more effective in the future.

He went to his desk and let out something like a sigh of relief, but his forlorn expression, his hands that absently fumbled the buttons of his shirt, and his partially raised eyebrows revealed embarrassment.

He came up to the couch and said: Well, whenever you feel like you described at the beginning, you should return to that picture. I think your Far Eastern excursion will be able to swiftly redirect your thoughts.

He headed for the door, and I got up and laid fifty euros next to the ashtray.

I said: It was worth every cent, Doctor. I really feel much better than I did at the beginning of the session.

I wanted a cigarette. I'd left mine down in my car, by the gearshift, so I took one from his pack and immediately lit up. He opened the door and waited for me to go out. An expression of embarrassment still covered his face. I enjoyed the generous doses of smoke and thought for the first time that my mother was probably right when she encouraged me years ago to seek *expert* assistance. I think my life would have been different: fewer disappointments, less depressive states, less aggression. The doctor escorted me to the front door: See you in a week then, at the same time?

I strode over the threshold: Of course, Doctor. And in the meanwhile . . . I'll try to follow your advice. Whenever I feel like I described at the beginning . . .

Doctor: Exactly. Whenever you feel bad, return to the picture you described. Goodbye.

He smiled and slammed the door. I wanted to exchange a few more words, but I really couldn't complain. I'd lolled around on the couch more than twenty minutes past the end of my appointment while the other client had to wait. I took a long puff and started down the staircase, which reminded me that it was very cold outside, and at the same time I remembered the cold on the slopes of Mount Nantai. That made me laugh, and so I imagined I was already enjoying the first benefits of a successful therapy. As I went down the marble steps I thought how lovely it would be if I could also be humming a Japanese folk song about the unhappy love of—what a coincidence—Mr. Maeda and Mrs. Ibaraki. But before that I ought to learn Japanese and find out a bit more about the country than just the fact that Mount Nantai is on page fifty-two of *The World's Most Beautiful Mountains*.

I politely greeted a middle-aged couple on the third floor. Both of them eyed my cigarette sternly, and I said with absolute servility and understanding: Rest assured, good people, the butt will end up in the trash can. I haven't seen such a neat stairway since my childhood.

They saw me off with wry looks that seemed to say: *We've lived in this house for two thousand years, and you are an intruder—a barbarian with a cigarette.*

I kept my calm. Like the stones in a Japanese garden. In normal circumstances I think I would at least have spat with relish on one of the polished tiles, out of dread of straitlaced, petty philistines, but every next step took me closer to the conviction that I really did feel different.

When I reached the first floor, the cold made me jam the cigarette between my teeth, and I pushed my fingers as deep as I could into the pockets of my trousers. My car was parked to the right, toward the intersection. I prepared the keys on the way, hoping the lock wouldn't torment me too much. I took out the whole bunch and immediately noticed that all the key rings and appendages were at rest; my fingers too, although in ordinary circumstances they'd have been trembling badly. I approached the lock like a jouster with a downsized lance and instantly bull's-eyed the tiny opening that I'd needed several minutes for that same morning and rained a dozen juicy swear words on. Then the air began to quiver to the unpleasant, raucous notes of a car's horn that penetrated my eardrum and skull from the left, transfixing my body with hysterical disharmony, after which, when the horn fell silent, there came an equally nasty woman's voice, followed by her body.

She got out of the car next to mine, panting in an obese rage that made her double chin inflate even more, and the wisps of her greasy hair spilled down her sweat-beaded forehead and clung to her fat cheeks. She started to rant: "You bastard! You swine! So you're the road hog! I've been blowing the horn like a maniac for an hour and a half! Don't you see that I can't budge because of your rattletrap?! They waited for me, but they're not waiting anymore. That's it! You son of a stupid bitch!"

She stormed toward me and stopped just a few feet from my nose: "You assface! Who do you think you are? You heap of shit! You think there's no one else in the world except for you and your jalopy, huh?"

When she finished her last vowel, my face was struck by a cloud of warm molecules combining the unbearable odors of caries, rotten food between her teeth, and the stench of her throat, a cloaca of cheap beer and mayonnaise. I also smelled her sour sweat, whose vapors rose from the collar of her woolen coat. The image of thickets of greasy black hair in her armpits imposed itself on me along with several other bodily landscapes that caused disgust. She continued her barking: "Why don't you say something, you cunt of a man? Come on. Do you know how pathetic you look, huddled like a shivering puppy? Serves you right. You've ruined my chance of a lifetime, you rat!"

When she brought her face a few inches closer, I made out four hairs on her bulbous nose. My fingers started to shake again, and my temples pounded to the rhythm of my maddened heart and rapid breathing. I don't remember what she said next, but after the very first syllables some slimy chunklets of food showered my face. I moved back a step or two and then lashed out. I wanted to give her a slap, but my fist clenched all by itself and struck the fat creature at the side, somewhere behind the ear. She staggered backward, all the time blathering utter crap. She tried to lean against the wall, but a protrusion in the sidewalk was all it took for her fat body to go sprawling over the concrete with all its weight. And when she raised her head and swore, mentioning my dear mother again, I leaped like a rabid orangutan and pinned that torso down with my knees. I punched hard, taking my time, aiming for the soft tissue of her shocked face. Her right browridge split and she lost a good cupful of blood. I kept on hitting her with the sharp knuckle above my little finger, accurately striking her front teeth, which broke after just a few blows. A tautly tuned drum beat out a rhythm in my skull, and I played to that rhythm with no intention of stopping. A few shouts from windows and balconies of the surrounding buildings couldn't sway me. Only when she coughed and spat out the yellow debris of her front teeth, and when her big head turned loosely to the right and quavered with a hacking cough—only then did I straighten up. I inhaled slowly and deeply. My fingers were at rest again. I glanced around and my gaze stopped at the fourth floor. The window of the office was open. The doctor spread his arms and shook his head, heavy with disbelief. I got up unhurriedly, raised my bloody hands to the sky, and bellowed: "Doctor! Dear Doctor! In a small Japanese village the first snow is falling."

# The Map of the World

## 1.

As I LOOK through the peephole, it seems as if the woman is holding a lance—a long, wooden, non-functional, and sloppily sharpened one such as a galloping knight would use to break against the breast of a similarly galloping opponent. She is clenching it in the middle, balancing the unwieldy object while holding a bag full of black grapes and tomatoes in the other hand.

## 2.

That woman is my mother, and the bell has been out of order for several months already. To draw my attention, she is forced to beat her forehead against the thick wooden door. My hearing is fine. But the dull thumps I heard as I sat in my easy chair doing nothing seemed strange, not quite of this world. One short and hard one, and then three in a row, with her forehead, as it turned out. Because when I held my eye to the door, that forehead took a run-up to gallantly assail the black, lacquered surface once more. I let her hit it and only then opened. It smelled of my mother. Her breath had the aroma of filter cigarettes, and beads of perspiration evaporated with a hiss that I couldn't hear but which spread along the corridor and resonated in the sound receptors of the hidden rodents, large flies, and sparrows sitting in the attic.

## 3.

"The elevator . . ."

"Yes, Mom . . . Lugging all this stuff up to the fifth floor . . ."

"The elevator is out of order . . ."

"It's a wretched nuisance, I know. The grapes go in the fridge. Let me help."

"First wash them and let the water run for a bit. I want some cold water, that's all I want."

"Your wish is my command. And as soon as you sit down, I want to know everything about that lance."

"Rubbish. There's nothing to tell. At school they insisted I take it with me. The projection of sentiment or something . . . They think this object belongs to me and me alone."

"And this object is . . ."

"A glass of water, please."

"Right away. And this object is . . ."

"And put in a wedge of lemon. There's one left in the fridge door."

"This object is . . . Oh, come on . . ."

"The map of the world. Aw, a few seeds have ended up in the glass . . . That stupid map of the world that hung over my head for thirty years. More water, please."

"Which world?"

"Don't be facetious. Besides, I wanted to ask you . . . Go and put it down in the basement, burn it in the courtyard, give it away to hungry and neglected children, because I don't want to have it around. That smell in the house. Never! I've retired, and that's it. I don't want to hear about school anymore."

"The big map of the world from the geography classroom where you spent some of the most memorable moments of your long career as a high-school teacher? This is that map? For heaven's sake, Mom! Burn it? Throw it away? I won't have blood on my hands. Period."

"What hands? What blood? You're all pathos, like your father. I can just imagine the same words coming out of his mouth. I suppose you'd like us to set it in a gilded frame and hang it just here, above the couch?"

"Well, yes, Mom! I'll look after it. Why not? Fine matte glass and an inch-and-a-half frame. It would freshen up the room. The whole world in one place. And then leisurely, with our morning coffee, we'll be able to examine all those seas, the Straits of Gibraltar, America, India, the archipelagoes, remote Pacific islands, and everything else. The world! Our world! Mom."

"Now you're being ironic. Is that irony? Pretty damn impudent in any case."

"No, Mom. Me? How can you say that?"

"Get away from me. Scram, d'you hear? The details give you away. And bring me some more water. Examine the Straits of Gibraltar? As if there were six of them."

"This morning it seems turbid and warmer than usual."

"What?"

"The water, Mom. Look."

"Water is water."

"Yes, what a lovely way of putting it. Water is water."


## 4.


A river divides a city in two. Its name and shape do not exist on the map of the world. This is micronic, unknown geography and a fact about this place that can only be ascertained on the very spot.


## 5.


The dialogue under number three never took place. But everything leading up to the moment my mother banged her forehead against the thick wood of the front door did happen. The polite exchange of correct simplex and complex sentences that takes up a bit more than a page is a pure fabrication. We never talked together in that way. Scarcely distinguishable mumblings, fragments of rage, or just the most basic information about food and bills that needed to be paid—that was us. Number three never happened, but it's very important for the overall story nevertheless. I wanted to use the form of short dialogue to illustrate the lie I've read many times—in various corpses of modern literature—that pretends to represent nothing more or less than life itself. Conversations between mother and son, father and child, an altercation of two brothers, best friends, partners in love, in crime, it's all the same—lines filled with predictable mock bitterness, the rustling of paper and the smell of plastic, the taste of artificial vanilla pudding powder, apocalyptic tones and small apocalypses, unfinished sentences *full to bursting* with synthetic flowers, *filled* with synthetic eyes, synthetic hearts, and synthetic emotions, open endings, closed endings, cocks, and the occasional thumb. Tragedy after tragedy, paradoxes at every turn, the world is a bad place, isn't it, you'll explain it to me, my friend, but first please try living with my mother on the fifth floor of a concrete eight-story block that stretches from north to south. Even that isn't so terrible. I'll only mention it every now and then because my life is no better or worse than the billions of other lives whose hum I sometimes hear in the drops of rain committing suicide as they fall onto the tin porch of the western terrace slanting toward the Adriatic Basin. And I'm only doing all this, of course, so as to explain to myself that this story is meaningless. Whoever manages to find sense in it deserves a fat piece of my shit right between the eyes. If that's you, I congratulate you warmly, right from the bottom of my heart.

6.

I'm a writer and thirty-six. Baldness, signs of impotence, bowel problems, a smoker's cough, deep dark rings under my eyes, back pain: none of those things have happened to my body. I'm a healthy and vigorous individual with a high brow, of average education, attractive to women, and acceptable to men. How I love to write that *I* from whom I expect nothing, from whom no one expects anything, but here it is again, *I*. The lines just keep coming, unsightly little plants sprout beneath the numbers that will eventually entwine like the lower stories of the Amazon rainforest, whose shade I regularly enjoy as I watch the endlessly boring programs on cable television that try to compress the entire enthusiasm of the host and the producer into another painfully empty lie, into one single sentence: Life is a wondrous thing. It makes me feel sick.

## 7.

I open the door and she casts down the heavy lance. She nods her sweaty head and raises her chin: "Retirement time," she says. "Congratulations," I say and light a cigarette. She watches in disgust as the smoke creeps slowly through my nostrils. Literature? It stinks too. Yellowed pieces of cow cheese on the dining-room table. She says: "You could at least . . ." She opens the trash can and scrapes the scraps from the green plate. I say: "Yes."

## 8.

I'm not interested in any settling of accounts. Especially not a duel with myself. But that doesn't prevent me from sometimes looking at my own mother through a long tube—an imaginary rifle scope. I'd aim for her bloated belly, hoping to smithereen the rotten remains of the ovaries that bore me. Not so as to establish the absurdity of my own life and existence through that symbolic act, but just for the sake of it. Large-caliber emptiness into high-fat tissue. Matter against matter. Havoc and death. Thinking in metaphors. Satisfaction on the toilet seat. Brief episodes of lucidity that vanish like large chunks of shit carried away by a gush of cold water. Fragments as the solution. Shit in pieces. Miniatures, scores, and ensembles of dried-up imagination scattered in something I could combine under the title *My Gangrenous Life*. But that can't class as misfortune. And it will never be literature.

## 9.

After she'd shaken the last little pieces of cheese from the plate, my mother started to vomit, kneeling on the little rectangular rug next to the dining-room table. I recognized a few poorly chewed pieces of mandarin. Her ovaries, I thought, and examined the mandarins on the dining-room table. When she'd finished, I helped her get up and wash her face. I never touched that fruit again.

## 10.

Ignacio and Thomas, crew members of a B-52 strategic bomber cutting the sky at 600 mph up in the stratosphere, gazed into the cloudscape above the Pacific, waiting for the ocean to come into view. The cumulative, gray swirls of Cyclone Parsifal became ever thinner, and then all at once, like a faceless deity, there appeared a sky-blue reflection of the sun that could have been eight and a half or even nine miles in diameter. They lowered the tinted visors of their helmets, plugged in their intercom cables, and began to talk.

## 11.

I spent three months in jail for inflicting grievous bodily harm on a minor. I was given this reduced sentence thanks to the expert psychiatric witness, who affirmed in his report that my action couldn't be characterized as attempted murder but as the inarticulate, compulsive act of a mentally ill person. It was like this: I was standing and waiting for the large elevator. I wanted to take it up to the cafe on the third floor of the shopping mall where

I go for coffee from time to time. It isn't an environment that excites me in any way: filtered air, sweet smells, and the chirping of sparrows that live under the metal girders of the roof and fly from one television screen to another down the length of the large hall. Being in the mall guarantees me a degree of anonymity because none of the people I know from the bar of Cafe Berlin as much as set a foot in that neon hell. That gallery of people consists of individuals I could call acquaintances in a broad sense of the word, friends in a few cases, more or less amiable people whose awkward sentences are drowned out by the music from the five-foot-tall speakers. The sparrows in the mall are actually mechanical devices that are supposed to make the aluminum ambience of that consumerist oasis more enticing for mothers and their children. After all, what's good for animals must also be good for people. In a hidden corner of the attic, between the dry plaster walls, is the workshop of a man who takes pains to make the birds do exactly what's expected of them. His name is Ferdinand, Fernando, Sigmund, or in the worst case Esteban. A man-bird, a strictly guarded secret, a precision mechanic and patient analyzer of the frequent breakdowns that occurred due to the cheap materials the workshop was supplied with. Me standing in front of the elevator door in order to go up to the espresso bar had no influence at all on Fernando-Sigmundian reality, so I won't allow myself the pleasure now of telling that man's unique and exceptionally interesting biography.

I shuffled from foot to foot. The wide steel door closed somewhere in the heights of the concrete facades. The box slowly descended. An electronic beep announced its arrival, the door opened, and in the middle of the large elevator stood a five-year-old boy ready to bawl and blubber. He stared me straight in the eyes as if he'd find the nuclear energy there for the hysterical outpourings that were to follow.

He started to scream the moment I strode in with the aim of bringing him out and comforting him. I assumed his mother was roaming the third floor, infected with irrational assumptions about the disappearance of her child, and therefore I just wanted to clasp him in my arms and wait for the woman to appear. But when I gently put my arm around his tiny shoulders and moved my face close to his red cheeks, that small, richly-toothed jaw opened and seized me by the nose. I was amazed by the demonic force of that bite, which made my cartilage creak and tears seasoned with searing pain spring from my eyes. Everything that happened after that was clouded by rage. But the statements of the two witnesses were almost identical. Therefore I have no doubt that I grabbed the boy by the head and flung him some ten yards out of the elevator, toward the lingerie store. I believe I kept my eyes shut tight, and that's another reason why that regrettable action is reduced to auditory impressions. Because as I was listening to the witnesses in the courtroom, my thoughts summoned the impact of the body against the impeccably polished ceramic tiles at exactly the moment when David Bowie screamed *Let's dance* from the speakers along the walkways of the mall. I said all that in front of the judge and the boy's parents, and my lawyer complained that those few sentences ruined his case, and that was the reason I got three months in jail instead of six months' parole. Mom just shook her head sadly.

## 12.

She leaned the big map she'd dragged home from school, together with her pension ruling, against the bedroom wall next to the ironing board. The representation of the world rolled up in the long plastic tube smelled of naphthalene. When I took off the lid for the first time I was struck by that snotty smell that made me think in metaphors and try to define the absurdity of my mother's existence in relation to the outright stupidity of that object. The plastic tube was covered with the signatures of her fellow teachers, among which one somewhat larger expression stood out with an exclamation mark: *Good luck!*

## 13.

The events under number eleven are fictitious. I never had any problems with the law, and in the mall I always take the escalator. Years of literary endeavors have convinced me that my intellectual mechanism consists of several models of imbecilic readers who always expect prose to be about extremes. Those people—if I can call them that—have finally killed the writer in me. Because no one accepts the commonplace misfortunes anymore that are lived out in the rooms of small but perfectly comfortable apartments like this one that my mother and I call home. Things have to be pushed to the extreme in line with the false logic of a literary work. And when I say it's so false as to be a *lie*, that isn't a high-calorie word for the bitter opposite of the truth. No, I mean the blatant *pretenses*, the servile and sordid hiding behind the prettified masks of linguistic reality, whose goal is not the representation of an aesthetic idea in a work of literature but babbles multiplying and amplifying the most banal of tragedies in an attempt to proclaim that our world is a bad place. The *lie* as a state of the mind, not short-term intent. Pandering to the smart and aggravating the simple. Literary awards and a pose of concern about the chaos of the world. Style as inertia. That's why I decided to present the illusions from the mall first: the hint of a dark aesthetic that on the one hand captivates with its narrative prowess and on the other hand gratifies the reader with information worthy of the crime columns in the tabloids. Because a person can only produce high-quality lies when he talks about himself. I want to scratch the eternal declaration of truth off literature, where it shimmers like the little labels on rotten bananas. I want to be somebody else, not what I am now.

## 14.

"Thomas? Can you hear me? Tommy?"

"Yes. I can hear you. And I've asked you before not to call me that when we're on a mission."

"Thomas?"

"Yes, Ignacio?"

"Why are you sore? No one can hear me calling you that now."

"You're shaking with fear. Is that what's up?"

"Meaning you're not afraid? You don't give a damn?"

"Don't lift your visor. You'll ruin your eyes."

"They got rid of your fear on the operation table, but you lost a bit of sense in the process. Brave Tommy. Brave, dumb Tommy."

"Cut it out."

"What are those islands down there? Look."

"We're not allowed to verbally define geographical positions when we're on a mission."

"You're so boring."

"Chicken Ignacio."

"Cut it out."

"Chicken Ignacio flies into the blue."

"Tedious Thomas. Te-di-ous . . . I can split it into syllables. Listen: te-di-ous."

"*Lucy in the sky with diamonds . . . Bam bam bam bam . . . Lucy in the sky with diamonds . . .*"

"*Bam bam bam bam!* And you don't care? Don't you ever think about your role in this world? As cold as ice? Is that what you want to say, Tommy?"

"Don't touch your visor with your hands. It leaves marks."

"I don't give a damn about any marks!"

"You don't give a damn about any marks?! And what if you misread the air-pressure value because of your greasy thumb-print? Or if your pretty blue eyes read YQW/73 instead of XQW/72 and the bomb goes a few hundred miles too far west?!"

"That's not my business."

"Correct. But it'll be your business if anything happens to me. Yes, yes . . . That's right. No need to raise your eyebrows."

"What can happen to you up here, Thomas?"

"Clean the visor from the inside as well."

"I asked, what can happen to you?"

"I don't know, Ignacio. Things simply happen. Blockage of blood vessels in the brain, bursting abdominal arteries, abrupt and inexplicable blindness, kidney failure . . . As long as we wear these bodies, everything's possible."

"Now you're trying to be clever. Plus you want to frighten me. Lift up your visor. I want to see your face."

"Oh, Ignacio . . ."

"There. I knew it. A smile. A dastardly smile. Wait!"

"What?"

"Did you feel that vibration?"

"I didn't feel any vibration."

"There . . . Now . . . That's it again."

"Why are you looking out the window, Ignacio?"

"I don't know."

"Do you expect to see the hand of God shaking the plane?"

"I don't know. Quiet!"

"Yes. It really is shaking. I felt it now too."

"Thomas . . ."

"Ignacio?"

"Thomas . . ."

"What's up, Ignacio? Stop it! If you want to say something, then out with it."

"I forgot our Polaroids. Thomas . . . Tommy."

"You what?"

"I left them under my pillow in Hotel Albion. Under my pillow, Tommy."

"Are you talking about the photos from Mahershalalhashbaz's wedding? Tell me you mean the photos from Mahershalalhashbaz's wedding! Tell me straightaway, Ignacio! Look me in the eyes and tell me you left the photos from the wedding of Edmond Mahershalalhashbaz under your pillow in Hotel Albion!"

"Tommy . . ."

"Ignacio! Fuck!"

"Tommy . . ."

"We're done for."

"Tommy . . ."

"This is what can happen up here, Ignacio. Your stupidity

is happening up here. Your stupidity is making the fuselage of the plane vibrate and the air thicker. How could you forget our photos, *those* photos!"

"Calm down, Tommy. Please calm down."

"What? Me calm down? How? Explain that to me! Has Ignacio the dumbfuck got a solution? You'll call the editors and ask them nicely not to publish the pictures of my ass, your ass, and my cock in your ass. Oh yes . . . Via satellite. It's simple: Dear editor, please do not publish the photographs you paid chambermaid Matilda a few ten thousand bucks for because the two of us are up in a plane that in a few hours' time is going to drop a hydrogen bomb on a densely populated part of West Asia."

"Don't be so gross, Thomas. The bomb is a solution after all."

"Oh God!"

"Thomas! After a few hundred thousand dead, do you think people are going to worry about our asses? Tommy . . . We'll be given a heroes' welcome! Because we are the people who are going to put an end to the insanity once and for all. The fusion of light atomic nuclei—hydrogen and lithium isotopes. Imagine, Thomas. A few moments of intense light and then silence, which puts things in order. We are the Lucifers of a new age, Tommy! Apostles of meaning! History will record our names on the roll of the great! Come on, tell me . . . Who'll want to worry about naked asses then?"

"Oh Darwin!"

"Tommy, you just need to think differently. Major historical events bring with them what we could call 'collateral gain.' Do you see what I'm getting at? Just think how many serious family rows were stopped when it was announced on television that Jupiter's average orbital speed had trebled, and that its Galilean satellites, above all Ganymede and Callisto, had broken off and formed their own orbits. The thinking of the masses suddenly changes. The danger of mass destruction obstructs the acquired models of behavior and we all return to primary instincts. Lovers return to the families they abandoned, conductors allow passengers to ride without tickets, and dog owners forget to feed their pets. Do you really think anyone in that situation will care about your sweaty but admittedly pretty ass? Thomas . . . Tommy . . . Cheer up a bit, for God's sake. Let down your visor and try to calm down. We've finished this story."

## 15.

It seemed the map of the world would diligently gather dust like the objects arranged on the shelves in Mom's bedroom. Whenever I turned the large ceramic vases upside down in search of money, which she always hid in standard sorts of places, the tips of my fingers would get covered in a fine, black powder. The dead sediment of a billion seconds smelled of dried figs. I had to wash my hands twice to completely get off that putridity. But when I took the lid off that tall cylinder for the first time, hoping that the hole concealed a somewhat more significant amount, I noticed that the whole surface had been painstakingly polished and several of her fellow teachers' signatures had been thoroughly shaved off the plastic surface. Clearly, she often returned to that object that had hung over her head for decades. The deleted signatures obviously suggested a settling of scores with unpleasant memories, perhaps unhappy love affairs, or was it just that she missed the good sex on one of the school trips? Of course, Mom also got rid of the *Good luck!* The scrape marks here were considerably deeper and not so accurate.

## 16.

Thomas sat up straight in his seat, raised his head, and stared at the tangle of cables on the aluminum ceiling. Ignacio, after convincing himself that his copilot wasn't going to talk anymore, moved up to the small window and rested his helmet against the Plexiglas. A large formation of cumulonimbi reared up in the southern sky. He looked at them from above and discovered the shapes of animals, exotic plants, and musical instruments in them. Most of all he liked the titanic baobab that rose up crook-edly, toward the west. The clouds soon vanished. His view was filled again by the mighty blue of the Indian Ocean. Ignacio gave three big yawns and continued to gaze at the bright red numbers on the digital clock that counted away the hours, minutes, seconds, and milliseconds until the great explosion. Ignacio looked serene, breathed calmly, and reflected on the nature of transience.

## 17.

Rudolf Baumgardt, *Ferdinand Magellan: The History of the First Circumnavigation of the Globe*: "Kings wish us to thank them for their benevolence especially loudly when the expressions of their favor begin to fade. In Magellan's name, Haro sends King Charles a colored map of the world with a gilded pair of compasses: His Majesty may choose to use them to mark all the meridians his subject will cross for him."

## 18.

Six times in my life I started writing a novel, and only recently did I give up for the last time. The quiet morning of the decision was more pleasant than all the past euphoric moments put together. My mother was spending her seven days at a hotel for pensioners at the coast, and I awoke in silence, naked, wrapped in a thin sheet. The early-June summer was still graced with after-noon showers. I'd lie around in bed until it became too hot. After that: a cold shower and coffee that I drank while reading one of the unfinished texts, determined to continue writing. Usually I'd put on Miles Davis's *Sketches of Spain* nice and loud, light a cigarette, and for a few moments I was Hemingway, Faulkner, and Fante in the same mind and body. But whenever the tip of the expensive Parker rollerball pen came close to the paper, all those spirits of great minds would disappear, leaving behind an

unearthly husk of the desire to write, in which talent figured like
a pair of sickly and balding pigeons that flew to and fro, without plan or purpose. That morning, that important morning,
I had to become a writer again, just like every other morning.
Without my mother in the apartment, without that lumbering
silhouette that snuck from the dining room to the kitchen, bur-
dening her body with unnecessary, tiny movements and remarks,
that morning in the silence of Miles's Spanish trumpet I calmly
lowered the tip of the pen to the paper, expecting a word, any
word, even a wretched conjunction halfway through a sentence
where I'd broken off the day before, but nothing happened. My
thoughts levitated in the indifference of the moment, the taste of
coffee and cigarette smoke created the perfect blend of pleasure,
and the light divided the room in halves. The ink slowly ran, the
dot spread, the tip of the pen stood in the same spot, and then it
moved in a gradual arc toward the middle of the page, plotting
a spiral that ended in a central spot. I sat up straight, let my
back fit snugly into the easy chair, and put the pen down onto
the armrest. I shut my eyes and turned my head toward the
speakers, which the bronze dust of Miles's chords spilled from,
combined with the absence of any thoughts, intentions, or the
desire to write. The clear line of the spiral appeared against the
background of my closed eyelids. That pure shape, freed of metaphors, was balm for my weary senses. All the unfinished ideas
of my great novels flowed together into one point and vanished
in their insignificance. It became completely clear to me for the
first time that I wouldn't be able to finish even one of the pieces
in which, a few minutes earlier, I'd found serenity and sense. I
sat there calmly with no desire to open my eyes and hoped I was
knocking on the door of the momentous decision that would
eliminate my dysfunctional aspiration to write once and for all.
I longed for the morning I'd awake free of the large prose ulcers
that spread the smell of failure and ruin, but literature wouldn't
be so commended and eminent if it constituted just surficial
wounds of the brain. Because as soon as I opened my eyes, the
illusions I'd nurtured for many years offered a new solution: *The*

*form is the problem! A novel isn't the format that sustains my talent.
Great narration and a multitude of figures are unable to express the
subtle aesthetic principles that I've honed for years like the finest jew-
els. The short story is what will ultimately establish me as a writer, in
my own eyes and those of the world.* The text under number eleven
originated that morning. Miles Davis condensed the traces of billions of photons into several orange rays, and I wiped my damp
forehead with the palm of my hand and contemplated the great
solitude of true genius. I began to write again.

19.

I was right to be afraid of that enormous change, which meant
that my mother would be home much more often. I didn't enter-
tain the illusion that she'd turn her retirement into a senseless
sequence of rituals, visits to the marketplace and the movies, and
mingling with the doddering old women who find refuge on
park benches from the depreciative glances of their children and
grandchildren, with whom they share the same apartment. Forty
years of intensive socializing in a large urban high school and
daily communication with dozens of different people of various
ages wouldn't be quite so easy to find an appropriate substitute
for. Especially because Mom was aware there was no adequate
substitute. Math and foreign-language teachers were at a distinct
advantage: after retiring, they developed prosthetic social mechanisms by coaching weak students almost free of charge, thus pro-
longing their life as educators for years until some serious illness
announced the advent of deep and inexorable old age. But no one
had any use for a classical knowledge of geography. Nor did they
need the map of the world that my mother furtively unrolled on
the sheets of her double bed, where she'd accurately draw in the
borders of the countries that had arisen in the interim.

20.

The first chapter of my unfinished novel entitled *Caw, Caw*. A disaster of a street—plain and rough. A crooked line of oleanders on one side of the road and a procession of field maples on the other. That cancer-tree doesn't belong in these climes. Our hot summers and mild winters produce invalids with rotting branches, which drop dark fragments. The treetops are full of gaps and abnormal excrescences. To work and back along the same street every day: some of that dismalness has to rub off. A feeling of hopelessness drops from the branches onto your shoulders along with a destructive aesthetic gravity that engenders trite metaphors: you compare yourself with the unfortunate trees. My life, doomed to endless wanderings on the hard sidewalks and the inhalation of gases. You become sluggish and unsightly, on the downhill slide to death. You are disintegrating slowly and thoroughly. Like the large Madagascar turtles. Alive or dead, there's no difference. For years you keep tabs on your breath ever more often, comparing the quantity of stench. You shift the threshold of tolerance. In the end, no toothpaste can help. The decay comes up from below. It spreads through your entire body, rending your bowels, liver, and lungs. You fear you'll go mad before your brain turns to mash. It's hard to write about this—a state of madness whose clinical definitions are as useless as saints. (The magic of the psyche masked with language!) A thousand thoughts in a tenth of a second. Colors splash in all directions. Words are even faster. A thousand of them in blue, and on top of everything there are vocal cords, an organ that makes you feel helpless. Because the words you speak seem incoherent. The neon lights make five thousand flashes per second, and the flashes merge into a constant. My brain produces fifty thousand words per second, but my vocal cords pronounce only five randomly chosen ones! A big problem. You go mad in the blink of an eye. Your wife is crying. Your father and mother ask themselves where you went wrong. The job, the car, clean clothes, a comfortable bed, Marlboro Lights, Jack Daniel's— everything vanishes in a moment. The job as an editor at a daily paper, the career as an aspiring young writer, the daily flirt with the eyes and breasts of women—everything turns to memory. You find yourself in a bush next to a bronze monument that dim-wittedly watches and, if you're lucky, doesn't speak. Flashes of lightning split the sky. Rain starts to fall. It's hard to count all the drops. You're not wet but soaked with sparks. A feeling you don't know. You feel every particle of water differently. Your body changes. Is it worth investing effort? Putting up your defenses? Halting the changes? Sending your demons packing and starting from scratch once more until you go mad again? Is that how it works? Is there any going back? A big struggle: laying the figures in an order that makes sense. To eat roast potatoes with veal again and get up every damn morning to write a few lines that give you heart stabs and make everything hurt afterward. That's no phantom pain. It has neither place nor definition. Sometimes it glitters like crushed green glass and spills everywhere in waves. The work of a writer has nothing to do with conditions like this. Writing is, like everything else, just a pretext for death.

I don't really remember when I decided to pee in my pants for the first time. But let's say I was wet to the skin. It's pointless to leave the portico of a railroad station and piss out next to a railroad car—your clothes will get even wetter. Besides, urine is a natural antibiotic and so the wounds on my groin would heal faster. I stood leaning with my back against the wall. My muscles relaxed; warm goose pimples crept down my leg, and the train hysterically announced its departure. I breathed in the smell of ammonia. I pressed out the last yellow drops and watched my reflection in the small puddle that collected around my left trouser-leg. Then I realized something had changed and that it would mark the rest of my life. The whistle of the train, the warm stream running down my skin, and the reflection of my face in the yellow secretion—together they sang a hymn. A majestic hymn devoted to ruins. I felt neither happiness nor sadness. I stood in the bounds of a dark marble slab at the railroad station and closed my eyes. For the first time I didn't feel anything. Or would it be more exact to say: I felt *nothing*? The metal wheels began to clatter, and a black eddy of air remained where the train had just been. To take a step or sit down? To take a deep breath and fall asleep standing up, on the spot? Only the body examines the elementary possibility of choice, not the mind. I wouldn't budge for seven more centuries if the sounds of Mozart's Requiem, the Dies Irae sequence, were to resound beneath the railroad station's portico just now. I have to harmonize my relationship with time as soon as possible. Plans mix because I'm beginning to imagine I can feel eternity in front of me and behind me. And until that's sorted out, I'll have to make a few more important decisions and figure out: Does me writing a story about the history and the genesis of my own madness mean a return to reason through the magnificent chambers of lateral consciousness? Truly: I couldn't give a fuck! Leaving aside the fact that my penis really has been hurting recently and the scabs are slow to heal, the attitude in the prior statement of not caring to fuck is actually a philosophical category employed as an ultimate negation, an irrefutable assertion. I'm not particularly prone to vulgarity, but I've realized that people better remember foul language. And that makes it easier for them to recall the primary sense of a statement. I could have said *I don't care!* or *It doesn't matter!* but I said *I couldn't give a fuck!* in order to clearly establish my deep indifference toward the readers, which includes above all my father, mother, wife, and the child they called Danilo. At the mention of the word *child*, certain regions of the brain instantly begin to secrete substances that the alchemical processes of the organism turn into emotions the very next moment. Yes, I said *child*. You can ask the logical question of parental responsibility, which you have good reason to query, considering the nature of the changes in my life. At the moment I'm writing this, my son is eight years old. But the chemistry of my organism no longer corresponds to the customary model of *Homo sapiens*. I assume that's the core of the problem. My brain is disabled, in a way, and my body has adapted to different conditions. Emotions appear when I find an unopened can of Rio Mare tuna in the dumpster or when I use the money I've picked up off the streets over months to indulge and go and pay for fellatio. A decently remunerated service in the entrance of one of the buildings near the bus station is more of an experiment than satisfaction of my sexual urges because there's something divine and entertaining in occasionally paying a prostitute with money God has gifted you. How many miles do you have to go, with unparalleled straining of your sense of sight, to find ten paltry cents, while a blowjob costs twenty euros? How many? God only knows.

My son, Danilo, has the blond hair and gray eyes of his mother. It would be more exact to say that the son of the man involved in Danilo's conception a few years ago has the blond hair and gray eyes of his mother. Because I no longer feel I'm his father. Anyone who thinks that at some moment there could be a moving encounter of this delirious man and his descendant who yearns for his father is seriously mistaken. Things are considerably more complicated. After all, I'm writing these words after the most significant events and horrors have played out, and I'm unfurling them again now with great effort. My life has changed radically. I'm not talking about simple social actions, divorces, running from different sorts of unbearable relationships, abrupt changes of geographical latitude, and the like. It's far from my mind to reflect on my situation through the prism of a family drama of abandoned people whose lives have become horribly scarred from one moment to the next due to the painful absence of one person. I'm talking about my own madness, the only one I have any practical proof of, a condition that doesn't demand any clinical definition and futile elaborations by a psychiatrist. After several years' break I took up the pen again, and I must admit that now it really hurt, to the core: bad enough to draw blood! I'm talking about loss and gain. I'm telling a story where miracles and tragedies occur, where emotions are depicted as memories of love. In a nutshell, it's a story about a man who at one point in time was largely normal, and at another largely mad. The amazing line connecting those two points, the limbo that opened up between the two worlds so that the change could occur and everything become different—those are the directions I'll try to follow. At the moment I have enough energy for the necessary feeling of amazement, which allows me to expound certain things with a classical literary method. If I'd waited a few more months, even just a few more days, I think this story would have been lost forever in eternal darkness or, again, in the beautiful and blinding light of a condition that *humanity*—why not use that word—knows nothing about. The territory of the *Columbian* new and biblical old world of madness, a region of a planet that's always being rediscovered and forgotten again. The only civilizational constant that remains untouched by new technologies and the flux of ideas and generations. Madness is a state of the mind cocooned like a chrysalis that waits for the right moment to change into a captivating, blue-winged butterfly. Or green? Or is red the artistic equivalent? That's the mystery. It's impossible to write about madness in any particular way. It's impossible to view it from a set perspective. There's no scientific framework that can define it and thus narrow the gap between it and the conventions of language, imagery, or sound. Clearly I have no desire to exaggerate the importance of this text, nor do I intend to attach any diagnostic qualities to it. Because someone flawed by madness is the last person who can be called as a witness of their madness. And what then are all the others? My son, Danilo, and my simpleminded wife? Objectively, they became victims of the simple power and endless ambiguity of a condition they were unable to understand, and were condemned to suffer. After reading these lines they'll understand even less. What happened to the man who for years slept soundly, had hygienic habits, and achieved a few successes in the field of literature? I'm not searching for an answer. There probably is none, nor will there ever be a system of knowledge that could explain what I'm trying to talk about. I advise you not to wait too long, and to read and analyze this text during my lifetime. When I die, my spiderweb will die with me: they will call this testimony a work of literature and then forget it as just one more of the attempts to express the unspeakable. I notice that several of the last passages take on an enigmatic tone. I want to say that this is a mere coincidence and that the only real feeling that pervades me as I'm writing this is fear. I'm afraid of failure. I'm afraid I won't shine forth. I'll use thousands of words, only to come back to the sense of endless sorrow in the end, that state of dampness and expectation that has driven me to where I am today. That pissing around about "endless sorrow" is definitely one possible version of the truth, or just another lie. This is the creation of a madman who speaks in different voices. Madness is a sophisticated state of mental metamorphosis that doesn't disturb the logical order of things but just fashions it to run on a different fuel. This is being written by a man who still doesn't know what has happened to him.

## 21.

If she'd played the trumpet, everything would have been different. But she played the violin, and I discovered some traces of classical sentiment in that at first. We met on the street, and her name was Kristina. I observed her for a month before going up to her. I watched her sitting at the bar and read into her appearance all the things I later wouldn't find. She was a member of the symphony orchestra, never came late to rehearsals, and thought the brash Russian conductor, to whom she entrusted her talent, was excitable Pan-Slavic trash and an impostor here in the musical provinces. She made my mother's acquaintance just seven days after we started dating. We were sitting on the terrace of the cafe across from the theater; and she with her royal bearing, wide hips, and large black handbag plowed a path for herself through the crowd of people facing the winter sun. Back then, with her high brow, she was still reminiscent of Lauren Bacall. She skillfully concealed her age spots by letting the shadow from the rim of her broad hat gracefully part her wide face, which was appropriately adorned with tinted, dark-framed glasses. I got up to say hello, but her gaze was fixed on the violin case.

"Do you play?"

Kristina raised her eyebrows inquiringly. Mom took me gently by the forearm and we both looked at Kristina.

"My mother."

"Yes. I'm his mother. Is that your violin?"

Kristina took a sip of mint tea and nodded, and then absently reached out her hand. Mom didn't take off her glove and responded in kind. They shook hands without looking one another in the eyes, and after that, Kristina quickly lit a cigarette and blew out the smoke to the left, toward me. Mom opened her mouth to ask something more, but I forestalled her by advancing a clutch of pointless information in an attempt to end the awkward situation as soon as possible.

"Kristina is in the symphony orchestra, Mom. She's playing tonight. Shostakovich, Brahms, Prokofiev . . . Now we're having tea. She's trying to concentrate. The concert is in the main hall. First violin in several of the sections. Isn't that right?"

I freed my upper arm from my mother's grip and waited for Kristina's reply.

She clenched her lips and raised her eyebrows as if she was about to say something important.

"So you're Mom. With a capital *M*."

"I beg your pardon?"

"Mammal."

"Pardon?!"

"Minotaur."

"Now just a moment . . ."

"Mandarin."

I had to intervene and start the next sentence with a conciliatory vowel. But I inadvertently said:

"Mom."

That ruined any possibility of pleasant conversation. The letter *M* multiplied as it covered the sidewalk and filled the ashtray heaped full of cigarette butts. It hung from the branches and the large buttons of Mom's coat, and it tightened against reality on all sides, dragging it like an old fishing net. She straightened her lapels and said with a slight bow:

"I'm glad to have made your acquaintance. Goodbye."

As she left, she sent me a glance that Kristina could neither have noticed nor understood: she squinted, her right eyebrow slightly raised and her lips clenched—a sure sign that I'd screwed things up bad and Kristina was crossed out with a double black line, which also meant thoroughly deleted from her life. Mom really was a powerful woman back then. She skillfully concealed the surplus fat on her body with black silk skirts that always smelled of vanilla.

When she was gone, Kristina said:

"Vicious old bird."

She took another sip of tea and drew in her smoke with satisfaction. I was disappointed by the expression on her face—I thought I detected a trace of the stereotypical triumph of the young female over the barren queen. For the rest of the afternoon I was as quiet as a mouse and strove to gauge the frequency of the letter *M* in her speech. I also stared conspicuously at every female creature younger than thirty-five, hoping she'd notice and that it would provoke at least a smidgen of jealousy. She responded staunchly, pretending indifference, and I tried to give myself an erection beneath my pants to at least raise the thin fabric between my spread legs a little. After a few hours on the terraces of the cafes across from the theater, she embraced her instrument and said it was time for the next rehearsal. I waited for her in the same place, drunk, and afterward we made love in the toilet, ignoring the violoncellist who thumped on the door. A weak prostate and beer don't go well together.

We joined the table crowded with musicians and their instruments. Raised chins and fingers that interpreted rhythms, then a series of intrigues and glances at the next table, which was occupied by the wind section, ambiguous sighs mixed with disappointed nodding: all that, Kristina later explained, was the usual postcoital practice after three hours of fucking around in the overheated hall of the national theater.

We drank on, without regard for losses. I gulped down double whiskeys with ice cubes that slid slowly down my throat. She was content with chilled white wine and the occasional sip of my booze, just to feel the fire. It was unquestionable that we'd go back to her studio apartment, just as it was unquestionable that she'd be getting up at seven. That meant I'd have to take my things and leave too. My bad hangover, lungs filled with junk that provoked a cough, and innate laziness turned that into an incident equal to a death sentence. But when I opened my eyes, Kristina was standing over me with a cup of hot coffee. Fragrant, with a silk scarf around her neck, in a light-blue dress, and with the instrument pinned to her left shoulder, she said:

"You can stay if you want to sleep some more."

I nodded without lifting my head from the pillow. She kissed me on the forehead and left, quickening her pace. I assumed she was excited. She had a premonition that my extended sleeping would grow into something more than that, and I knew it. I woke at eleven and smoked four cigarettes with sips of cold coffee. When she unlocked the door and came in, I was sitting at the meal table and leafing through a book of poetry by Paul Celan. I almost started reading "Death Fugue" aloud as a welcome gesture before she spoke, but I swiftly concluded that one must never underestimate the power of poetry. I thought that the stanzas: *Black milk of daybreak we drink it at evening / we drink it at midday and morning we drink it at night / we drink and we drink / we shovel a grave in the air there you won't lie too cramped,* could instantly change the aggregate state of that lovely day, so I just got up and kissed her on the lips, taking care not to exhale the rotten nicotined air from my lungs. I returned to the chair. She took off her shoes and sat down opposite me. We looked at each other in silence for a few minutes, knowing that the conversation to come could change things.

"You can stay tonight too if you want."

"My things are dirty . . . My pants and underwear. I look a mess."

"We'll wash them."

She picked up my clothes scattered around on the floor, then she asked me to get up. She stripped me. I waited for her in bed. The washing machine started to turn its drum. Kristina came and lay next to me. That was the beginning of the four most beautiful weeks of my life.

## 22.

The conversation between Ignacio and Thomas originated when I was sitting in the easy chair for several minutes and pondering my late father's motorcycle helmet. That morning it was out on the dining-room table instead of being shut away deep in the glass showcase. A little earlier, as I'd been tossing and turning in a heavy doze, I heard Mom rummaging around. I inferred that she'd taken out all the crystal wineglasses, the big ceramic bowl with the application of Van Gogh's *Sunflowers*, and the series of twelve glass figures representing the signs of the zodiac. She cleaned them all once a year, but now it had been done seven days early. That's why I couldn't work out why she was rummaging. My father's helmet stood on the shelf with the glasses, right at the back. Protected by the fragile Czech pseudotreasures, it spent its days in peace and dust, covered also by a patina of sentiment after the family tragedy. The cracked visor and the deep gouges on the right-hand side indicated the manner of his death, which I used to retell to friends and classmates with passion and pride in the courtyard and at school, starting after just a few days of mourning. My father, my terrible father, my aerodynamic father bends over his motorcycle, races along with the speed of a nameless subatomic particle and leaves everything behind him, even light. My father, my terrible father, my aerodynamic father follows the cosmic line of destiny, coming closer and ever closer to the place where his life will end. A large rock rolls down from the peak of the mountain. Death always keeps a tally, and my father crashes into that ancient piece of dolomite in the same moment as it reaches the asphalt. A rock of a man versus a rock of a rock. Powerful enemies facing each other. I've forgotten the embellishments I used to further spice up the story. For years I added details and enjoyed telling the story to whoever requested it. Only Mom never asked any questions. Whenever I sat with friends in the lounge room and she was preparing soft drinks and ice cream for us, she'd stay in the kitchen until I'd showed my guests the glazed showcase and pointed to the motorcycle helmet half hidden behind the rows of ceramics and Czech cut glass;

then she knew I had finished. A few drops of alcohol too many at the end-of-year party at school and her catching me asleep in the easy chair with a burned-out cigarette between my fingers at the age of eleven were reason enough for the truth about the death of my supersonic father to come out, and it was a shock at the time. She talked about cigarettes and health and underlined the large letters on the pack several times with the message: *Smokers die young.* When I said my father had died young even without smoking, Mom launched into a tirade, and after a whole array of associations and curses she arrived at the actual fatal accident. I found out that he hadn't had a 1500cc Japanese dragon under his ass, but his lover girl's Chinese scooter. I also learned of his 0.13 blood alcohol level and the lipstick marks on his balls and groin. The injuries he sustained in the fall weren't life-threatening. The ruptured ulcer and copious internal bleeding happened in the ambulance on the way to hospital. The physicians were preoccupied with the possible symptoms of serious concussion and they devoted all their attention to his dizziness and amnesia. He died the same day during a brain scan, and the true cause of death was only discovered at the autopsy.

"The pig drank himself to death. That's the whole truth, my love."

I went to the vitrine and gazed at the helmet. The tinted visor reflected the wineglasses and the inventory of the dining room. I also saw my misshapen face, distorted between the reflections, and then I walked the long walk to my bedroom and covered my head with the pillow. Never again did I tell the story of my father's death, and if anyone asked, the extensive account was now replaced with a resigned wave.

I realized that Mom had a lot more to stew over because she'd found out about the death of her beloved husband and about his *bitch*, as she liked to say, on the same day. After the tenth anniversary of my father's death, after the cemetery and lunch with relatives, still torn between love, confusion, and hatred, she spent the whole summer smoking countless cigarettes in the dining room, whose walls soon turned yellow. I tried to avoid her bad moods, leaving her to bite her lips and filter cigarettes in peace.

The first day of the new school year brought a change. She got her best and most colorful clothes out of the wardrobe. When she appeared in the living room perfumed, fancily dressed, and propped up on high heels, I started to clap, sincerely admiring her strength of character and readiness to overcome problems. The helmet lay in its place, was occasionally dusted, and when I unexpectedly came across it on the dining-room table that morning, outside the usual ritual, I stared long into its dark visor. One consequence of that meditation was the associations with the crew members of a B-52 strategic bomber, in whose hands the fate of humanity rested. Thus originated another of my futile attempts to transform my delirious reflections into literature. Or, in this way the story about my father's death took on perhaps its most fantastic version.

23.

She practiced twice a day, in the morning and in the evening. When that sound woke me for the first time—that grating of horsehair on taut strings like the meowing of a tortured cat, that disharmonious and impudent cracking of sounds devoid of all meaning, followed by silence, and then the protracted *first reading* of the melody—I just laughed and covered my head with the pillow. I found the freshness of a *new life* in everything, a life in which I'd feel different and eventually become a better and different person. I only got up when she'd finished. I made coffee for us both, and we sat down at the meal table and crossed our legs. The violin occupied the next chair, rigid, like a child. Observing those lacquered curves and Kristina's red throat pressing against the chin rest, I allowed my thoughts to wander through several stereotypical assumptions. I stared at the four taut wires like four tendons of a fragile woman's neck, and I imagined sneaking up from behind and severing them with a sharp knife. I thought about the instrument and Kristina as one and the same body full of sticky sounds that covered everything all around, and when

Kristina asked: "What are you brooding about?" I said: "I love you," and looked away toward the ashtray.

## 24.

When an octopus wraps its tentacles around a blue crab and its elastic arms wind around the chitinous armor and pull the body toward its large and lethal beak, which with several powerful blows will end the life of the unfortunate arthropod, that dumb creature tries to use the last atoms of its strength to grab a morsel of food in the agitated sand and gluttonously cram it into its little jaws.

## 25.

The second chapter of my unfinished novel entitled *Caw, Caw*. I followed the tracks and made it a long way, into bygone provinces of childhood and a sequence of life to which I can't attribute feelings of happiness, unhappiness, or any other state. I was a fatuous, spiteful, and lazy child, and on top of that a coward. I hate stories about childhood. Especially when that larval stage is described as a Garden of Eden. Both the male and female raise their young, endeavoring to afford them the customary degree of retardation that will prepare them for similar social models. A 750-square-foot apartment, education, food, warm water, convenient emotions, a bicycle, premeditated wisdom in conversations about life, death, and morality—all those are privileges I didn't miss out on. The androgynous timeline produces the muffled sound of a flute. The instrument slowly fills with the player's saliva until tainted bubbles of that glandular secretion combined with the smell of brass begin to come out instead of a melody. I had such a feeling when I was fifteen. Looking at my already-dense pubic hair, which I combated unsuccessfully by plucking it out with my mother's Solingen tweezers in the hope that the delicate place wouldn't be defiled by stiff bristles—I experienced that thing with the brass, the saliva, and the feeling of transience that unsettled me. But if I try to assess my childhood according to my situation today, I can definitely affirm the existence of several malignant cells that sowed the seed of madness in my head at a very early stage. Of course, these are only justifications. We don't allow ourselves the possibility of some things in our lives coming from nowhere: people call on God, genetics, astrology, and fate for help—the four horsemen of the apocalypse. But facts should be seen from all sides, so I don't want to circumvent even the smallest personal doubts regarding the causes.

My school was at the foot of a stony hill. The last remnants of massacred greenery that had grown up between the stones—self-seeded saplings of Scots pines, cypresses, nettle trees, and hawthorns—were destroyed by a fire, because of which I missed two days of classes. The shantytown at the foot of the hill was threatened by the flames, so the school courtyard was turned into a parking lot for fire engines. The impoverished residents were saved, the fire was filmed by a television crew from a helicopter, and for months afterward the courtyard was a loitering place for abandoned dogs and cats with burned skin and legs scorched to the bone. The children were convinced they had some terrible wasting disease, so the animals often became the targets of dusty stones. I wasn't a monster who would go that far. But I think it was simple cowardice that stopped me, nothing else. I feared I'd dream of a teetering cat with exposed jaws for nights on end if I added to its pain. On the other hand, I didn't let a chance go by to warn the other kids that a crippled creature was creeping through the bushes. Then I'd attentively watch the game of encircling and the ritual of the hunt, which children equipped with that social atavism performed in a state of trance. The virtually immobile creature was left lying there under a pile of trash and stones, and several hours later I'd experience something like postcoital stress accompanied by tears as I lamented the fate of the victim. A wave of remorse would come over me that I genuinely enjoyed. No, there was no evil in me. At least none more than usual. Only children's evil is pure and free from prejudices. It's nude and ready for misdeeds that in the world of children represent much more than all the Auschwitzes and Hiroshimas in the world of adults. I feel I knew that from early childhood. That's why I didn't let anyone get too close to me, but at the same time I enjoyed the energy of the crowd, which I was able to easily manipulate. Danilo goes to the same school. The stony hill is now covered with ugly houses of children and adults ready to destroy the world: paupers condemned to television as a final mercy. The school courtyard has been done up nicely. The playground includes a dozen comfortable benches and miniature wooden houses. The little houses are raised four feet off the ground. They are protected from rot by a thick layer of red paint applied every year. It makes them smell magnificent inside, almost intoxicating. As soon as they were built they became a popular place for sleeping. The entrance faces south, so the north wind just whistles over the roof and gives you a wide berth. At first I couldn't come to terms with the dimensions. Decades of sleeping horizontally meant that even the smallest change caused indescribable pain in the region of the neck. I spent months on those benches exposed to the cold, the bites of stray dogs, and the stones of children. Then answers started coming to many questions. My body successfully transitioned from one world to the other. It became clear to me why homeless people wear thick sweaters and even winter jackets in the most searing summer heat. It has to do with the cold that gets into your bones and the wind that constantly blows down your back and legs, all the way to your feet. But after just a few months the body adapts its rhythm to that uniform thickness of clothing, regardless of the weather. A winter jacket in both summer and winter, or a thick woolen sweater at a hundred degrees—no sweat! For a few moments you feel ethereal, as if you were gliding beyond the borders of society and also those of your own biology. After all, a homeless person doesn't own a wardrobe, bank safe, or nuclear shelter. If you want to survive, you have to carry everything with you. Judge your own possibilities and keep optimum stocks. If you manage to get some new gloves, throw away the old ones even if they could be worn for a few more days. This is essential for survival. Just one extra bottle in your bag will bring on a pain that will gnaw at your back for weeks. A perfect balance between stockpiling and need—that's the gist of the trade. Only lug around things you could earn a few cents with in the near future, or small objects that will save your life like medicines or precious tins of conserved food. Of all the tablets I used to find in dumpsters, I only took the antibiotics. They are actually the rarest. I was surprised by the quantities of Ativan, Artane, Noludar, Lexotan, Ultram, and other trash. When depressive parents believe for a while that they've overcome their depression, they rush to get rid of these colorful pills lest the children lay their hands on them. But just a few hours later they curse their moments of optimism, run downstairs, and stick their head in the dumpster. When you surprise them and go without hesitation to see what's inside, they usually snap, "I threw my keys in by accident," or something like that and leave with their heads bowed. Ones like that will probably give the stairs a miss next time and land on the asphalt at the speed of sound. The majority of urban homeless are heavy barbiturate addicts. An unnatural thinness, sunken eyes, a croaky voice that begs with exertion for handouts—those are clear signs of their downhill slide. They spend their pittance on cheap alcohol in the discount stores in the suburbs, and that's their prescription for a slow and painful death.

I used to come to the school courtyard just after dark. The school operated in two shifts. I'd wait in the bushes near the fence for the final bell and then occupy one of the miniature houses at the playground. Danilo was usually one of the last to come out. He pushed his blond hair to the left. He carried his schoolbag in one hand and with the other nervously brushed away the curls that drooped down over his forehead. His right leg stepped high, and his left swung out to the side ever so slightly. When he'd passed through the gate he'd shift the bag onto his back and start to run. Danilo disappeared around the corner, and I withdrew into the darkness and tried to find a comfortable position. I didn't feel any love for that child, not even the elemental fondness that arises in a person when they encounter a friendly salesperson or post-office clerk. All manner of scenarios burgeoned in my mind with an abundance of pathos-charged solutions. The scene: a child watches a dirty, bearded, and crazy man; it stares at him because an emotion flickers in the line joining their eyes, a powerful emotion with roots beyond the sphere of the rational. The scene: The father then speaks the name of the child. They both begin to cry, and then they are united in an embrace that will bind them forever after. Just like that. Forever after. The final words of many fairy tales. The final phase of life as the universal end of existence for all living things. Because if even the smallest space was left for doubt about the separate lives of the people, children, or animals, the question would unavoidably be asked: Good, so they'll live happily until the end of their lives, but who will die first and thus become the bearer of misfortune? As a boy, I always asked myself why no one had written a fairy tale that began with the very first moment of them *living together happily until the end of their days* and ended with the natural death of one of the characters. I think Danilo is puzzled in a similar way. I don't have any feelings for the boy, but every time I watch him toss his hair and then run like mad—I have the desire to talk with him. We come up to each other, a few feet apart, and begin a conversation such as the spirits might hold. All the answers and questions, all the suspicions and prejudices have no consequences. A weightless state of mind, a little nirvana without goals or the possibility of choice: that's what I long for. The body of my child represents a problem. It unavoidably calls other people to mind, upsetting the innermost mood of black, yet brilliant, madness I'm infected with. I often dreamed of children's hands caressing my forehead. The fingertips would press against my skull, gently enter, and go all the way to my brain. Then, in my dreams, I'd want to see all those fingers severed and neatly piled in a heap. The pain they produced was unbearable, universal, and eternal. It penetrated my mind with the force of a deity!

My dreams about pain were most often caused by one side of the body systematically going numb—the side that pressed against the boards. However many rags were shoved under me, those boards that meant life always found a way to my bones.

After such an unpleasant awakening it was important to change position for better circulation. If parts of the body go numb they are cut off from the blood supply and are therefore susceptible to freezing or gangrene if there are wounds or parasites on your body. When you sleep outdoors, ticks are unavoidable. However much you examine and clean your body, after a day or two you're sure to find a soft pea-sized lump. Over time you get used to ticks and people, loud municipal sanitation trucks, rats the size of small dogs, and early rising. Things become as familiar as home furnishings once were. Spaces spread and take on new meanings. Any serious conversations have to be conducted with yourself because all other communication is reduced to a few practical phrases and nodding when you want something or when you refuse. I crept into the deepest and darkest caves of my secrets. I peeked into every nook of my brain and unearthed a lot of shit that now stinks to high heaven. Sometimes I doubt that my madness is a consequence of those wanderings.

The first signs I remember, and which led me into extreme physical and mental detachment, appeared early, when I was still a boy.

Walking home from school alone or strolling through town in the solicitous company of my parents, my gaze would roam hysterically and peer into the most bizarre and totally futile images of landscapes, which I devoted myself to with a concentration some would apply to probing the farthest expanses of the universe. I stared at the rickety bushes and looked at the untended pieces of ground at the edge of the park or the concrete islands that intersect the boulevard. I thought of silently slipping out of my parents' hands and going to those useless places to fall into a deep sleep from which I couldn't be woken. I was excited by the thought of myself as a sleepyhead who withdrew from the world without a sound, almost invisible, and humbly paced toward his goal, only then to lie down and abandon his mind to the unknown realm of illusions. For years I carried around that image of the sleeper, immune to sounds and external stimuli, the image of a man whose only power consisted of being able to walk off anywhere, at any time, and fall asleep, and no one could wake him until he himself wanted to be woken. For a long time I didn't dare to put that irritating pseudomyth into practice. I dragged it along like a hungry dog on its master's chain and mused about it with a dose of derision, thinking it part of a child's world of irrational wishes and fixations. I wait for green at the crosswalk and look at the stunted oleander growing in the median strip. Its roots are suffocating in the lead-saturated soil. The heavy vapors from the cars' engines thoroughly dust its leaves. The plant absorbs incredible quantities of noxious gases and survives in that hell. The oleander in the city's central square has never felt gentle hands that water and nourish it. I sense intimacy for a moment and want to lie down next to that paltry bush. I want to embrace it and give it warmth. I feel a woman's breath on my neck and a whiff of chewing gum that warns me and impels me to move. The light has turned green. We head across the street, and I keep dreaming that I'm sleeping, comfortably nestled up to the oleander in the city's main square. Like I say, for years I didn't dare to live out that madness until my wife, Marina, got up before me one morning, like every day, made coffee for us both, like every day, and affectionately reached me the cup as we looked out at the pine forest and the orange sun rising, like every day. The coffee was good and hot. Marina's blue nightie plotted her hips and emphasized her breasts. We drank coffee and spoke about the weather and her pregnancy, our child. She said that if it was a girl it would be called Marta, and if it was a boy—Danilo. But she knew for sure it would be a boy. She felt a surplus of male hormones in her body, she told me, but I said that was no sure way of telling the sex of the baby. Marina insisted, citing medical evidence she'd found in a magazine. Magazines were stupid, I said, because they published speculation by medical dilettantes and charlatans. I told her she really shouldn't take claims like that seriously. Besides, the sex of the child wasn't important. Marina placed her hand on her ball-shaped belly and told me I could say whatever I liked, but she was sure she was pregnant with a boy. Anyway, I'd be able to convince myself in three months' time, if the doctors didn't drop a hint in the meantime. I drank my last sip of coffee and fell silent. A murder of crows landed on the tips of the trees in the park opposite. The sun hung between two clouds. The birds screeched at the world: *Caw, caw.* I observed an indefinite point in the sky and again started to imagine my body soothed by sleep, freed of sounds and thoughts. I got up, put on my shoes and thick jacket, and took my lighter and cigarettes. Marina dug into a large tin of biscuits. She nibbled off the chocolate edges and asked with her mouth full where I was going. I told her I was going out for a walk. I looked into her eyes. The palms of my hands were sweating, and a strange shudder went down from my neck to my feet. She nodded and swallowed a small piece of biscuit. I followed the movements of her jaws. It seemed she was chewing unusually slowly. I listened to the harsh noise of the biscuit crunching. It sounded like when feet sink into fine sand. The crows abruptly rose up from the treetops and flew away beyond the window frame. Marina asked why I was still standing there and why I hadn't gone out. I said I didn't know and scratched the top of my head energetically, although nothing itched. She nodded to show her surprise and lack of comprehension. An inarticulate group of children's voices came up from the street, and every few seconds there was a burst of hysterical laughter. "Marina, I'm going," I said. "Just go then," she sneered and put her face up to the pane. I headed for the door. She stood at the window. Something was going on outside, she said. When I opened the door, my breathing sped up. Stepping over the threshold was like jumping into the abyss. I slammed the door behind me and for a few moments inhaled the dank air filled with the smells of the neighbors' apartments. Sweat trickled down my forehead. My head spun. If I didn't move and start running that very moment I'd collapse there on the landing. I'd die if I didn't get going straightaway, I thought, and with a powerful twitch that activated my body I began to run down the stairs. I took several steps with each leap, and every jump gave me new strength. I came flying out onto the sidewalk and stopped breathless in front of a group of children gathered around the black and mangled body of an animal; I almost trod on it. They stared at me, expecting me to ask what had happened to the dog. But when I lightly hopped over the corpse and kept walking, just one word rang out after me from the crowd in a thin, malicious voice: "Lunatic!" I mended my pace and chose a direction. A stone landed and came to rest near my feet. I outwitted the children because I didn't ask the question they'd been expecting. I didn't show any surprise, although I recognized Dr. Junkić's black terrier. Is it possible that the children already detected traces in my eyes of what today fully occupies me? Were they the first to apply the ancient word *lunatic* to my body and mind? All sorts of powers are attributed to the little demons. I walked on without looking back. I crossed the street and entered the park, and my quick steps turned to running. I passed trees and amateur athletes in Adidas tracksuits. I raced along with all the strength I could muster, jumping over bushes and pine saplings. Behind the park stretched a large yellow field—an expression of the city's incompleteness, dotted with plastic bags in a variety of colors. They hung snagged on the tips of bushes like melted road signs. I didn't feel tired at all. I tried to understand what was happening to me. Young fig trees grew out of the wrecks of rusty cars. I'd been running for fifteen minutes already. My breath became thinner. I heard a creaking in my lungs. My heart was thudding and my brain throbbing. The canopy of a large pine came closer. I imagined its fragrant shade. After several languid steps, I slowed and sat down, leaning against the rough bark of the trunk. My body calmed down. To the left, near a fence, two goats were grazing. Now a fear of my own thoughts arose, of my own reflections, of questions I asked myself, and of the possible answers. I lit a cigarette. My head spun. Panic seized me because I had no idea what was going on inside me. Was a struggle of opposing interests ahead? Should I expect defeat? Or perhaps remorse? All the questions that whistled by were just as confused as the answers. I felt a bitterness in my throat and thought it must be my enzymes playing with my senses. I stuck a few pine needles into my mouth. An old lady appeared near the fence. She fondled the goats on their backs and muttered something like words. I tried hard to understand her. She knelt down between the goats and pointed in my direction. The animals trained their eyes on me. My ears hummed from the strain. I raised my arm and waved to the creatures. The old lady started to laugh, revealing the gaps in her teeth. I didn't know why the hideous cow was tittering, but then things became a hint clearer. She untied the goats and took the ends of the rope in her right hand. But before she slowly turned to point her stiff body in the desired direction, she opened her eyes wide and gradually raised her hand, from which a crooked forefinger stood out. I waited for the punch line. The finger tapped three times against her head, but I knew her head wasn't at the center of attention now. The old hag's black dress swayed as she left. The streak of a yellow kerchief hung down her back. The goats spilled dung from their orifices. I realized that I couldn't hear the noise of cars and the voices of people. Everything was enticing me to sleep. Flies gathered on the animals' droppings and buzzed off rock-hard shavings. When I woke up, I couldn't see anything in front of me. There was only the sound of the wind, and it made me tremble.

## 26.

After three weeks of us living together, Kristina said: "I love you too." I blew out a cloud of smoke, stubbed out my cigarette, and played a few inarticulate notes. She waited for my reply, staring at the instrument seated on the chair. Then I gave the finest string a forceful pluck, not sparing my fingernail. She smiled and covered her ears with her hands. I believe I responded with the smirk that always, almost imperceptibly, contorts my face. I lit up again and went out onto the balcony to watch the swaying tips of the cypresses. She banged the door shut. That morning I began to write *Caw, Caw*, and around noon I was already convinced that the blank pages were being filled by a masterpiece of literature of the twenty-first or any other century. I wrote on my lap, on a hardcover copy of *The History of Music*, reeling off page after page. I wrote fast and with ease. Words matched the pace of my thoughts and flowed together in perfect order, forming long and nuanced sentences. The first chapter developed with clear meanings and strong aesthetic ideas that collided, creating new galaxies of sense. I smoked methodically and slowly, drawing the smoke into my deepest alveoli. The sun illuminated the floorboards. A radiance filled the room. I was feeling like a writer, and then Kristina came in and without a word laid her instrument on the table. She ate a banana by the open fridge, set up her music, and with a deep sigh started to play one of those sluggish, slimy, protracted compositions for violin that make you lose faith in life and sound. I put aside *The History of Music* together with a page, on which there shone the first words of a sentence I'd finish a little later: *I'll use thousands of words, only to come back to the sense of endless sorrow in the end, that state of dampness and expectation that has driven me to where I am today.* Kristina convulsively clenched the neck of the violin. I looked in her direction, trying to catch her eyes and in that way hold a mute conversation. I hoped she'd perceive my thoughts and stop playing, but she sawed at the strings ever more vigorously. I lit up a cigarette and decided I had to smoke it before explaining the situation and reacting. Watching her through the fine curtain of smoke, nervousness, and impatience, I noticed two ugly marks below her right ear for the first time. Her jugular veins strained to the rhythm of the harsh tones, and I tried to think about the novel I'd just started. It didn't work. Whether I wanted to admit it or not, I already knew I'd never finish it. A drop of a nameless poison was injected into my veins, between the sentences and the paragraphs, and everything that would happen in the following seven days—work on the second chapter, and several interesting portrayals—was just a desperate attempt to resuscitate a patient doomed to die. Kristina continued to practice the same composition and didn't ask anymore if I loved her. I wrote out of spite for the violin. And when she asked me quite calmly, over coffee and cigarettes, to leave the apartment, I only raised my eyebrows and blew out a plume of smoke toward the ceiling. I went down the staircase carrying my clothes in a plastic bag, and under my arm was a folder in which she'd neatly laid the pages I'd written. I wanted to bin that monstrosity in the first trash can

I came across, but the egotism of the unfulfilled writer mauled my determination, so I lugged the papers home and buried them in the drawer under the television—a cemetery of literary failures. Mom's perfume filled the apartment. She wasn't at home. Some veal-and-vegetable stew sloshed in the pot. I sat down at the dining-room table and took a deep breath of those aromas.

If she'd played the trumpet, I thought, everything would have been different.

## 27.

Our neighbor Junkić, who I smoked a cigarette with on the bench in the courtyard of our block two days before, told me the following story while staring up at the top of a Scotch pine: I never hit my wife. Did I hate her? Perhaps. But I never hit her. More than anything else, I wished that beer bottle would veer from its trajectory, that by some miracle it would disintegrate and burst by itself, swallowed up by a black hole. I watched that ugly bottle as it flew, turning in the air and whistling fiendishly as if it imagined itself a nuclear warhead. Drops of beer rained like yellow tears, and white froth sprayed from the frenzied bottle in all directions. It hit Tatjana right in the forehead. I threw it in a fit of mad rage and imagined a cuckolding red cock humping her. But even as it was airborne, I begged Saint Peter for it to vanish halfway. Miracles occur, so why couldn't an ordinary bottle disappear without a trace just like that, into thin air, and bless these two lost sheep, giving them one last chance? But then it happened. And how. The bottle really smashed. It hit my Tatjana in the forehead. I loved to kiss that forehead. I watched her packing her things and wiping away the blood with her shirt. It left thousands of tiny specks that I scraped off the parquet floor and the furniture with my fingernail for days afterward. I sat and cried. Words were far away. But while I sat like that in the easy chair and drank another beer, while Tatjana was banging around in the bathroom, collecting her perfumes and eyeliners, I thought that she could have ducked the bottle. I mean, she had time to react. Only the wall would have copped it. The quarrel would have died down, and I'd have come running to pick up the pieces. She would have lit a cigarette, taken two or three puffs, and started grumbling again. I would then have blown a fuse, told her she was a stupid old cunt, slammed the door hard, and gone downstairs in my slippers to get more beer; I realized that such behavior was really not fitting for a doctor, a urological specialist. When the bottle smashed against her forehead, Tatjana staggered and sat down briefly on the floor. I stood for just as long and then dropped into the easy chair. Before the blood streamed down my wife's face, I saw a few small embedded pieces of turquoise glass sparkle in her skin as if they'd always been there. She rubbed her forehead with her hand. The blood started to flow. Tatjana finally fell silent, and that had been my only demand since daybreak. Because she'd been going on and on about money—and about us not having the damn stuff—for five days already. She said she was ashamed of me because I got beer from the supermarket on tab; for every bottle they made a thick red stroke that was really a horizontal pillory. Silly bitch. She told me those red slashes would be the only thing left of me in this world. She was right.

## 28.

She left the apartment less and less often, and I kept trying to write my masterpiece with less and less enthusiasm. I'd sit for hours in the easy chair, burning through my cigarettes, while Mom stayed in her room, occupied with the map of the world. When I knocked, first there was a rustling of thick paper, and then an angry call: "No, I don't need anything. The money's on the table. Buy yourself cigarettes and have something to eat." I'd withdraw and think of her puffy face, which aged rapidly in the first few months after her retirement. She went out once a day, sloppily cloaked in her raincoat, and bought only the most basic of food items from the store across the street. Her look changed, too. She'd roam about the house, squeezing between the large living-room table and the red couch, and hardly seemed to notice my presence. She mumbled unintelligible phrases addressed to who knows which ghosts, and I tried hard not to succumb to the sense of revulsion that sometimes came over me when I regarded her derelict body. All attempts at conversation while watching television or during our rare meals together ended in sullen silence, which gave the light in the room hints of green.

## 29.

The text under number twenty-four is a poor attempt at metaphorically defining the nature of a writer's work. The octopus ought to be life itself, in accordance with the voracious time machine that, along with everything else, devours meaning itself. Its prey, the soulless blue crab (*Callinectes sapidus*) is a human (*Homo sapiens*) and the retarded act of taking food while dying represents the act of writing as a brave and futile struggle in the face of transience. That text lay at the bottom of a heap of paper for several weeks. When I read it again, I was genuinely appalled by the banality of the thesis proposed. I then compared myself with the feces of the octopus, a by-product of the whole process, and equated my wish to write with a position of an ameba striving for immortality.

## 30.

The text under number twenty-seven is one of my unsuccessful attempts at settling accounts with the genre of the short story. Junkić does not exist. Junkić exists. Junkić does not exist. Junkić exists. Junkić does not exist. And so on, endlessly, until the end of time.

## 31.

Mom doesn't exist. I am Nikola Kastratović, a retired geography teacher. I live alone. And I haven't met anyone whose life is different.

## 32.

I am Nikola Kastratović, and I do not exist. But that doesn't prevent me from ending the story begun under number one, because when I knocked on the door of her room that December morning to report the lack of coffee, there was no reply. I assumed she was still sleeping, so I made myself some chamomile tea and sweetened it with four spoonfuls of sugar in an attempt to give the yellow liquid some semblance of meaning. I tried to find her large leather bag, which always had a few wayward coins at the bottom, but the bag was neither on the shelf in the hall nor in the cupboard next to it. I thought she must be hiding her pension payment, which had come a little while ago, and swore several times while watching my face in the mirror. I smoked and drank the sugary tea and observed the pigeons out on the balcony pecking their own shit. A pile of my papers lay to the left of the easy chair. When I cast a hasty glance at it, I was at pains not to read any of the previous night's jottings, afraid of disappointment. I kept drinking the tea, and my eyes followed the specks of dust that mingled with the cigarette smoke. But when the cigarettes ran out I knocked again, even louder and more resolutely. Silence. I thought she must still be sleeping, lying on her back with her mouth wide open. I could get through the day without coffee, but the lack of cigarettes was unbearable. A panic that arose somewhere in my stomach and rose up my spine straight to my brain soaked my body in cold sweat. That's why I finally opened the door and peered in from the edge of the cupboard. The map of the world lay spread over the whole bed, the linen neatly folded on the chair next to it, and the pillows standing on end so as to take up as little space as possible.

A bundle of banknotes lay across the Mongolian-Chinese border, and an envelope with *Dokumenta* written on it covered the territory of Sudan, Ethiopia, Uganda, Kenya, and the Democratic Republic of the Congo. I sat down on the edge of the bed and tried to make sense of things. Despite my worry, I couldn't hide a sense of joy at the money tied together with a red rubber band. Along with a few documents proving ownership of the apartment, incidental records, her identity card, and health-insurance booklet, the envelope also contained a small photograph of my mother smiling against the blue background of a photo studio and looking straight into the camera. Most of the notes written on the map with a thick blue felt-tip were to do with basic geographical information concerning countries and territories. That was presumably her way of refreshing her knowledge in the fight against senile dementia, which her own mother had drowned in. A bold addition in red was clearly visible. A river divided a city in two. Its name and shape did not exist on the map of the world. This was micronic, unknown geography and a fact about this place that could only be ascertained on the very spot. That's why Mom meticulously drew in a thick black curve. A short black line designated a bridge, whose name was written at the side. I stuck several banknotes into my pocket and went out, thinking of the images that could be waiting for me in that place. I bought cigarettes, greedily lit up, and quickened my pace. The flashing blue light of a police car could be seen in the distance. A red fire truck maneuvered and parked with all the peace in the world, blocking traffic on the bridge. An inquisitive crowd gathered at one end, but an emergency services man turned the people away, waving with his yellow gloves. I walked along the dirt path on the left bank. The swollen, muddy river carried branches and rotten logs together with plastic bottles. Mom lay crucified on a sharp, cone-shaped crag. I believe she chose exactly that rock when she jumped from the bridge, wishing for certain death. Sitting by the hawthorn bushes on the slope that went down to the small sandy beach, I had a good view of the events that were to unfold. After the police inspection, the body was covered with a white sheet and put in a black bag. Several officials animatedly debated and gesticulated at the sheer rocks that were impossible to climb. The emergency services man pointed up toward the bridge, and after a few more sentences they all exchanged glances and nodded in agreement. The bag was laid on an aluminum stretcher and the cable fastened to strong yellow bands. And the very next moment my mother was swaying in gusts of the north wind. She rose toward the bridge, skyward, from left to right, back and forward, and then in a circle, dancing. I returned home and waited for the police. Mom was identified by an emergency services man, a former student. Formal identification of the body was an official requirement. I gazed briefly at the face decorated with dark bruises and nodded, but later I refused the company of the relatives who gathered in front of the mortuary. I wanted to be alone. At least until the funeral the next day. I took the still life off the lounge-room wall and hung the dead map of the world on the same nail. I lit a cigarette and gazed at that mélange of colors adorned with Mom's notes. And I'd do so every other day, too.

## 33.

The people of the tribes that live hidden deep in the mountains of Papua New Guinea will never sleep alone in the rainforest. Although their way of life has evolved over thousands of years to perfectly fit the sinister luxuriance of the tropical jungle, and although they think nothing of sinking their teeth into a succulent larva or grabbing a snake by the tail, these people will go to any length to avoid spending the night out beneath the tall trees. Because solitude, they believe, is what attracts evil spirits, among them notorious Masalai, who appears to the solitary sleeper first as a gentle whisper that wakes them, and then assumes the features of a person dear to them—their child or mother—and lures them away ever deeper into the green labyrinth, from which they will never return.

OGNJEN SPAHIĆ is a Montenegrin writer who has published two collections of short stories and a novel about the end of reality, entitled *Hansen's Children*, which won the 2005 Meša Selimović Prize. *A Head Full of Joy* was awarded the 2014 European Union Prize for Literature.

WILL FIRTH was born in 1965 in Newcastle, Australia. He studied German and Slavic languages in Canberra, Zagreb, and Moscow. Since 1991 he has been living in Berlin, Germany, where he works as a freelance translator of literature and the humanities. He translates from Russian, Macedonian, and all variants of Serbo-Croat.

MICHAL AJVAZ, *The Golden Age.*
*The Other City.*
PIERRE ALBERT-BIROT, *Grabinoulor.*
YUZ ALESHKOVSKY, *Kangaroo.*
FELIPE ALFAU, *Chromos.*
*Locos.*
JOE AMATO, *Samuel Taylor's Last Night.*
IVAN ÂNGELO, *The Celebration.*
*The Tower of Glass.*
ANTÓNIO LOBO ANTUNES, *Knowledge of Hell.*
*The Splendor of Portugal.*
ALAIN ARIAS-MISSON, *Theatre of Incest.*
JOHN ASHBERY & JAMES SCHUYLER, *A Nest of Ninnies.*
ROBERT ASHLEY, *Perfect Lives.*
GABRIELA AVIGUR-ROTEM, *Heatwave and Crazy Birds.*
DJUNA BARNES, *Ladies Almanack.*
*Ryder.*
JOHN BARTH, *Letters.*
*Sabbatical.*
DONALD BARTHELME, *The King.*
*Paradise.*
SVETISLAV BASARA, *Chinese Letter.*
MIQUEL BAUÇÀ, *The Siege in the Room.*
RENÉ BELLETTO, *Dying.*
MAREK BIENCZYK, *Transparency.*
ANDREI BITOV, *Pushkin House.*
ANDREJ BLATNIK, *You Do Understand.*
*Law of Desire.*
LOUIS PAUL BOON, *Chapel Road.*
*My Little War.*
*Summer in Termuren.*
ROGER BOYLAN, *Killoyle.*
IGNÁCIO DE LOYOLA BRANDÃO, *Anonymous Celebrity.*
*Zero.*
BONNIE BREMSER, *Troia: Mexican Memoirs.*
CHRISTINE BROOKE-ROSE, *Amalgamemnon.*
BRIGID BROPHY, *In Transit.*
*The Prancing Novelist.*

GERALD L. BRUNS, *Modern Poetry and the Idea of Language.*
GABRIELLE BURTON, *Heartbreak Hotel.*
MICHEL BUTOR, *Degrees.*
*Mobile.*
G. CABRERA INFANTE, *Infante's Inferno.*
*Three Trapped Tigers.*
JULIETA CAMPOS, *The Fear of Losing Eurydice.*
ANNE CARSON, *Eros the Bittersweet.*
ORLY CASTEL-BLOOM, *Dolly City.*
LOUIS-FERDINAND CÉLINE, *North.*
*Conversations with Professor Y.*
*London Bridge.*
MARIE CHAIX, *The Laurels of Lake Constance.*
HUGO CHARTERIS, *The Tide Is Right.*
ERIC CHEVILLARD, *Demolishing Nisard.*
*The Author and Me.*
MARC CHOLODENKO, *Mordechai Schamz.*
JOSHUA COHEN, *Witz.*
EMILY HOLMES COLEMAN, *The Shutter of Snow.*
ERIC CHEVILLARD, *The Author and Me.*
ROBERT COOVER, *A Night at the Movies.*
STANLEY CRAWFORD, *Log of the S.S. The Mrs Unguentine.*
*Some Instructions to My Wife.*
RENÉ CREVEL, *Putting My Foot in It.*
RALPH CUSACK, *Cadenza.*
NICHOLAS DELBANCO, *Sherbrookes.*
*The Count of Concord.*
NIGEL DENNIS, *Cards of Identity.*
PETER DIMOCK, *A Short Rhetoric for Leaving the Family.*
ARIEL DORFMAN, *Konfidenz.*
COLEMAN DOWELL, *Island People.*
*Too Much Flesh and Jabez.*
ARKADII DRAGOMOSHCHENKO, *Dust.*
RIKKI DUCORNET, *Phosphor in Dreamland.*
*The Complete Butcher's Tales.*

RIKKI DUCORNET (cont.), *The Jade Cabinet.*

*The Fountains of Neptune.*

WILLIAM EASTLAKE, *The Bamboo Bed.*

*Castle Keep.*

*Lyric of the Circle Heart.*

JEAN ECHENOZ, *Chopin's Move.*

STANLEY ELKIN, *A Bad Man.*

*Criers and Kibitzers, Kibitzers and Criers.*

*The Dick Gibson Show.*

*The Franchiser.*

*The Living End.*

*Mrs. Ted Bliss.*

FRANÇOIS EMMANUEL, *Invitation to a Voyage.*

PAUL EMOND, *The Dance of a Sham.*

SALVADOR ESPRIU, *Ariadne in the Grotesque Labyrinth.*

LESLIE A. FIEDLER, *Love and Death in the American Novel.*

JUAN FILLOY, *Op Oloop.*

ANDY FITCH, *Pop Poetics.*

GUSTAVE FLAUBERT, *Bouvard and Pécuchet.*

KASS FLEISHER, *Talking out of School.*

JON FOSSE, *Aliss at the Fire.*

*Melancholy.*

FORD MADOX FORD, *The March of Literature.*

MAX FRISCH, *I'm Not Stiller.*

*Man in the Holocene.*

CARLOS FUENTES, *Christopher Unborn.*

*Distant Relations.*

*Terra Nostra.*

*Where the Air Is Clear.*

TAKEHIKO FUKUNAGA, *Flowers of Grass.*

WILLIAM GADDIS, JR., *The Recognitions.*

JANICE GALLOWAY, *Foreign Parts.*

*The Trick Is to Keep Breathing.*

WILLIAM H. GASS, *Life Sentences.*

*The Tunnel.*

*The World Within the Word.*

*Willie Masters' Lonesome Wife.*

GÉRARD GAVARRY, *Hoppla! 1 2 3.*

ETIENNE GILSON, *The Arts of the Beautiful.*

*Forms and Substances in the Arts.*

C. S. GISCOMBE, *Giscome Road.*

*Here.*

DOUGLAS GLOVER, *Bad News of the Heart.*

WITOLD GOMBROWICZ, *A Kind of Testament.*

PAULO EMÍLIO SALES GOMES, *P's Three Women.*

GEORGI GOSPODINOV, *Natural Novel.*

JUAN GOYTISOLO, *Count Julian.*

*Juan the Landless.*

*Makbara.*

*Marks of Identity.*

HENRY GREEN, *Blindness.*

*Concluding.*

*Doting.*

*Nothing.*

JACK GREEN, *Fire the Bastards!*

JIŘÍ GRUŠA, *The Questionnaire.*

MELA HARTWIG, *Am I a Redundant Human Being?*

JOHN HAWKES, *The Passion Artist.*

*Whistlejacket.*

ELIZABETH HEIGHWAY, ED., *Contemporary Georgian Fiction.*

AIDAN HIGGINS, *Balcony of Europe.*

*Blind Man's Bluff.*

*Bornholm Night-Ferry.*

*Langrishe, Go Down.*

*Scenes from a Receding Past.*

KEIZO HINO, *Isle of Dreams.*

KAZUSHI HOSAKA, *Plainsong.*

ALDOUS HUXLEY, *Antic Hay.*

*Point Counter Point.*

*Those Barren Leaves.*

*Time Must Have a Stop.*

NAOYUKI II, *The Shadow of a Blue Cat.*

DRAGO JANČAR, *The Tree with No Name.*

MIKHEIL JAVAKHISHVILI, *Kvachi.*

GERT JONKE, *The Distant Sound.*

*Homage to Czerny.*

*The System of Vienna.*

---

JACQUES JOUET, *Mountain R.*
*Savage.*
*Upstaged.*

MIEKO KANAI, *The Word Book.*

YORAM KANIUK, *Life on Sandpaper.*

ZURAB KARUMIDZE, *Dagny.*

JOHN KELLY, *From Out of the City.*

HUGH KENNER, *Flaubert, Joyce
and Beckett: The Stoic Comedians.*
*Joyce's Voices.*

DANILO KIŠ, *The Attic.*
*The Lute and the Scars.*
*Psalm 44.*
*A Tomb for Boris Davidovich.*

ANITA KONKKA, *A Fool's Paradise.*

GEORGE KONRÁD, *The City Builder.*

TADEUSZ KONWICKI, *A Minor
Apocalypse.*
*The Polish Complex.*

ANNA KORDZAIA-SAMADASHVILI,
*Me, Margarita.*

MENIS KOUMANDAREAS, *Koula.*

ELAINE KRAF, *The Princess of 72nd Street.*

JIM KRUSOE, *Iceland.*

AYSE KULIN, *Farewell: A Mansion in
Occupied Istanbul.*

EMILIO LASCANO TEGUI, *On Elegance
While Sleeping.*

ERIC LAURRENT, *Do Not Touch.*

VIOLETTE LEDUC, *La Bâtarde.*

EDOUARD LEVÉ, *Autoportrait.*
*Newspaper.*
*Suicide.*
*Works.*

MARIO LEVI, *Istanbul Was a Fairy Tale.*

DEBORAH LEVY, *Billy and Girl.*

JOSÉ LEZAMA LIMA, *Paradiso.*

ROSA LIKSOM, *Dark Paradise.*

OSMAN LINS, *Avalovara.*
*The Queen of the Prisons of Greece.*

FLORIAN LIPUŠ, *The Errors of Young Tjaž.*

GORDON LISH, *Peru.*

ALF MACLOCHLAINN, *Out of Focus.*
*Past Habitual.*

*The Corpus in the Library.*

RON LOEWINSOHN, *Magnetic Field(s).*

YURI LOTMAN, *Non-Memoirs.*

D. KEITH MANO, *Take Five.*

MINA LOY, *Stories and Essays of Mina Loy.*

MICHELINE AHARONIAN MARCOM,
*A Brief History of Yes.*
*The Mirror in the Well.*

BEN MARCUS, *The Age of Wire and String.*

WALLACE MARKFIELD, *Teitlebaum's
Window.*

DAVID MARKSON, *Reader's Block.*
*Wittgenstein's Mistress.*

CAROLE MASO, *AVA.*

HISAKI MATSUURA, *Triangle.*

LADISLAV MATEJKA & KRYSTYNA
POMORSKA, EDS., *Readings in Russian
Poetics: Formalist & Structuralist Views.*

HARRY MATHEWS, *Cigarettes.*
*The Conversions.*
*The Human Country.*
*The Journalist.*
*My Life in CIA.*
*Singular Pleasures.*
*The Sinking of the Odradek.*
*Stadium.*
*Tlooth.*

HISAKI MATSUURA, *Triangle.*

DONAL MCLAUGHLIN, *beheading the
virgin mary, and other stories.*

JOSEPH MCELROY, *Night Soul and
Other Stories.*

ABDELWAHAB MEDDEB, *Talismano.*

GERHARD MEIER, *Isle of the Dead.*

HERMAN MELVILLE, *The Confidence-
Man.*

AMANDA MICHALOPOULOU, *I'd Like.*

STEVEN MILLHAUSER, *The Barnum
Museum.*
*In the Penny Arcade.*

RALPH J. MILLS, JR., *Essays on Poetry.*

MOMUS, *The Book of Jokes.*

CHRISTINE MONTALBETTI, *The Origin
of Man.*
*Western.*

---

NICHOLAS MOSLEY, *Accident*.
*Assassins*.
*Catastrophe Practice*.
*A Garden of Trees*.
*Hopeful Monsters*.
*Imago Bird*.
*Inventing God*.
*Look at the Dark*.
*Metamorphosis*.
*Natalie Natalia*.
*Serpent*.
WARREN MOTTE, *Fables of the Novel: French Fiction since 1990*.
*Fiction Now: The French Novel in the 21st Century*.
*Mirror Gazing*.
*Oulipo: A Primer of Potential Literature*.
GERALD MURNANE, *Barley Patch*.
*Inland*.
YVES NAVARRE, *Our Share of Time*.
*Sweet Tooth*.
DOROTHY NELSON, *In Night's City*.
*Tar and Feathers*.
ESHKOL NEVO, *Homesick*.
WILFRIDO D. NOLLEDO, *But for the Lovers*.
BORIS A. NOVAK, *The Master of Insomnia*.
FLANN O'BRIEN, *At Swim-Two-Birds*.
*The Best of Myles*.
*The Dalkey Archive*.
*The Hard Life*.
*The Poor Mouth*.
*The Third Policeman*.
CLAUDE OLLIER, *The Mise-en-Scène*.
*Wert and the Life Without End*.
PATRIK OUŘEDNÍK, *Europeana*.
*The Opportune Moment, 1855*.
BORIS PAHOR, *Necropolis*.
FERNANDO DEL PASO, *News from the Empire*.
*Palinuro of Mexico*.
ROBERT PINGET, *The Inquisitory*.
*Mahu or The Material*.
*Trio*.
MANUEL PUIG, *Betrayed by Rita Hayworth*.

*The Buenos Aires Affair*.
*Heartbreak Tango*.
RAYMOND QUENEAU, *The Last Days*.
*Odile*.
*Pierrot Mon Ami*.
*Saint Glinglin*.
ANN QUIN, *Berg*.
*Passages*.
*Three*.
*Tripticks*.
ISHMAEL REED, *The Free-Lance Pallbearers*.
*The Last Days of Louisiana Red*.
*Ishmael Reed: The Plays*.
*Juice!*
*The Terrible Threes*.
*The Terrible Twos*.
*Yellow Back Radio Broke-Down*.
JASIA REICHARDT, *15 Journeys Warsaw to London*.
JOÃO UBALDO RIBEIRO, *House of the Fortunate Buddhas*.
JEAN RICARDOU, *Place Names*.
RAINER MARIA RILKE, *The Notebooks of Malte Laurids Brigge*.
JULIÁN RÍOS, *The House of Ulysses*.
*Larva: A Midsummer Night's Babel*.
*Poundemonium*.
ALAIN ROBBE-GRILLET, *Project for a Revolution in New York*.
*A Sentimental Novel*.
AUGUSTO ROA BASTOS, *I the Supreme*.
DANIËL ROBBERECHTS, *Arriving in Avignon*.
JEAN ROLIN, *The Explosion of the Radiator Hose*.
OLIVIER ROLIN, *Hotel Crystal*.
ALIX CLEO ROUBAUD, *Alix's Journal*.
JACQUES ROUBAUD, *The Form of a City Changes Faster, Alas, Than the Human Heart*.
*The Great Fire of London*.
*Hortense in Exile*.
*Hortense Is Abducted*.
*Mathematics: The Plurality of Worlds of Lewis*.
*Some Thing Black*.

RAYMOND ROUSSEL, *Impressions of Africa.*

VEDRANA RUDAN, *Night.*

PABLO M. RUIZ, *Four Cold Chapters on the Possibility of Literature.*

GERMAN SADULAEV, *The Maya Pill.*

TOMAŽ ŠALAMUN, *Soy Realidad.*

LYDIE SALVAYRE, *The Company of Ghosts.*
*The Lecture.*
*The Power of Flies.*

LUIS RAFAEL SÁNCHEZ, *Macho Camacho's Beat.*

SEVERO SARDUY, *Cobra & Maitreya.*

NATHALIE SARRAUTE, *Do You Hear Them?*
*Martereau.*
*The Planetarium.*

STIG SÆTERBAKKEN, *Siamese.*
*Self-Control.*
*Through the Night.*

ARNO SCHMIDT, *Collected Novellas.*
*Collected Stories.*
*Nobodaddy's Children.*
*Two Novels.*

ASAF SCHURR, *Motti.*

GAIL SCOTT, *My Paris.*

DAMION SEARLS, *What We Were Doing and Where We Were Going.*

JUNE AKERS SEESE,
*Is This What Other Women Feel Too?*

BERNARD SHARE, *Inish.*
*Transit.*

VIKTOR SHKLOVSKY, *Bowstring.*
*Literature and Cinematography.*
*Theory of Prose.*
*Third Factory.*
*Zoo, or Letters Not about Love.*

PIERRE SINIAC, *The Collaborators.*

KJERSTI A. SKOMSVOLD,
*The Faster I Walk, the Smaller I Am.*

JOSEF ŠKVORECKÝ, *The Engineer of Human Souls.*

GILBERT SORRENTINO, *Aberration of Starlight.*
*Blue Pastoral.*
*Crystal Vision.*

*Imaginative Qualities of Actual Things.*
*Mulligan Stew. Red the Fiend.*
*Steelwork.*
*Under the Shadow.*

MARKO SOSIČ, *Ballerina, Ballerina.*

ANDRZEJ STASIUK, *Dukla.*
*Fado.*

GERTRUDE STEIN, *The Making of Americans.*
*A Novel of Thank You.*

LARS SVENDSEN, *A Philosophy of Evil.*

PIOTR SZEWC, *Annihilation.*

GONÇALO M. TAVARES, *A Man: Klaus Klump.*
*Jerusalem.*
*Learning to Pray in the Age of Technique.*

LUCIAN DAN TEODOROVICI,
*Our Circus Presents . . .*

NIKANOR TERATOLOGEN, *Assisted Living.*

STEFAN THEMERSON, *Hobson's Island.*
*The Mystery of the Sardine.*
*Tom Harris.*

TAEKO TOMIOKA, *Building Waves.*

JOHN TOOMEY, *Sleepwalker.*

DUMITRU TSEPENEAG, *Hotel Europa.*
*The Necessary Marriage.*
*Pigeon Post.*
*Vain Art of the Fugue.*

ESTHER TUSQUETS, *Stranded.*

DUBRAVKA UGRESIC, *Lend Me Your Character.*
*Thank You for Not Reading.*

TOR ULVEN, *Replacement.*

MATI UNT, *Brecht at Night.*
*Diary of a Blood Donor.*
*Things in the Night.*

ÁLVARO URIBE & OLIVIA SEARS, EDS.,
*Best of Contemporary Mexican Fiction.*

ELOY URROZ, *Friction.*
*The Obstacles.*

LUISA VALENZUELA, *Dark Desires and the Others.*
*He Who Searches.*

PAUL VERHAEGHEN, *Omega Minor.*

BORIS VIAN, *Heartsnatcher.*

**FOR A FULL LIST OF PUBLICATIONS, VISIT:** www.dalkeyarchive.com